Books by Judy Jarvie

Sassy With Sir

Scoring With Sir
Spying With Sir

Spying With Sir

ISBN # 978-1-78686-051-4

©Copyright Judy Jarvie 2016

Cover Art by Posh Gosh ©Copyright 2016

Interior text design by Claire Siemaszkiewicz

Totally Bound Publishing

Published in 2016 by Totally Bound Publishing, Newland House, The Point, Weaver Road, Lincoln, LN6 3QN, United Kingdom.

Sassy With Sir

SPYING WITH SIR

JUDY JARVIE

Dedication

In loving memory of my dear amigo Elaine D.
Sadly missed.

Prologue

I open the front door and a packet skates across the floor, grabbing my attention.

I'm not expecting mail, plus I'm a TV news reporter with colleagues who've had fan porn by post. I've long occupied the junction between Suspicious Street and Cautious Close, but I eagerly tear the wrapper, while prying off my gym trainers and abandoning my work bag in a heap.

So I'm disappointed when it's just a book with a mysterious, shadowy cover. But a note reveals it's from Izzy, who I haven't seen in way too long.

How are you, Princess Kate? Doing okay?

I finally wrote my book — I figured since you were the one who encouraged my writing I'd send you a copy (bestseller, crazy huh?) It's probably not your thing — twenty chapters of smut, swearing and full-on sweaty sex. Sex toys and bondage too. Don't feel you have to read it. I hope you might, as you inspired some of the wildest bits.

I want to take you to dinner as thanks. We'll go out after and have a riot with Sambucas. Know how mad you get on those — clear the dance floor for badass dancing.

My hero inspiration is my fiancé — Will's a policeman (Scotland Yard) and ex-Spurs striker. Think you'll like him, despite his job and dodgy football origins. I'm Head of English now, too. Life's busy.

So what's new with you — still top telly totty burning the candle at both ends? I'm crossing fingers you haven't seen Bastard? I also need an update on how things went with the Biker Sex Beast. Still his sex slave on the side? Thanks for giving me the writing push and please get in touch soon. Much Love, Izzy. Happier than ever before.

I smile because I'm stoked for Izzy, truly — she deserves great breaks. I breathe deep as my eyes linger on *what's new*.

Izzy's raunchy book resonates with recent issues. When I finally embrace my secret bedroom cravings, the guy I want turns cold. And guilty secrets are stacking up here. A girl can have too many shocks in her attic, surely? To think I'd made it through a day without thinking once about how stupid I've been. Until now.

My stomach rolls as I head upstairs to shower. But nothing can wipe my mistakes clean. Because when you get past my buttoned-up cover, I'm Kate, the girl with too many censored secrets. Dark surprises are my specialty — followed by let-downs and a pulverized heart.

Chapter One

Kate

This is how a maestro must feel — the tap of a baton will herald true magic. Only in this case, it's my finger on my iPod's high-energy track.

There's humming anticipation in the meeting room that serves as our basement gym. Participants for my lunchtime *Manic Mambo* class are eager as busy beavers at a wood-chewing convention. I'm just as keen to get started.

"Are you ready to work it?"

An approving chorus greets me. Shaking their bodies to the music in the new Human Resources initiative to get workers active during lunch breaks has brought a following of diehard fans. Diehard, as in crazy.

"We're ready to shake, shake, shake it!" Cleaning lady Janice Cleary makes a tropical bird call while sporting rainbow fitness gear and flashing sweatbands.

She makes my regular ensemble of gunmetal Capris, black vest and chestnut ponytailed hair look tame. I'm serious about my endorphin-seeking sessions and draw the line at fairground workout attire.

"Thanks, Jan. We're going to work hard, but I want smiles, energy. If holding squats feels too much, don't push. I don't fancy paramedics joining us — as much as I love a man in uniform."

There are whoops just as the door swings back. A hush descends as a newcomer arrives and a sexy spotlight's flipped on — it's the Big Boss.

And this one has youth and looks as security. Plus a

bankable portfolio of hotness bonds.

Dan Draven surveys the room like a proud, Arab stallion in an arena of jostling seaside donkeys. Heralding him as the channel's Adonis, the female staff have been on estrogen overdrive since his recent arrival.

As yet, he's an unknown quantity at Your News Today Channel, though the gossip mill's spilled that he's tasked with streamlining.

"Good afternoon." My newly flown-in, New Yorker new boss watches me. With serious, glittering gray eyes.

My heartbeat goes crazy, and why exactly are my palms damp?

"Good afternoon, come in. I'm Kate, I teach the class," I say, inviting him in. Though a gremlin in my head yells at him to get lost and never return.

Over six feet tall and clearly primed by fitness, he's wearing black combat shorts that display well-honed legs. His silky-smooth running shirt hugs a gladiator's body. But the real killer is his ability to breeze in with alpha attitude.

Right now I'm reeling at the realization that, as an intro to the company, he intends to shimmy and shake.

"Sorry I'm late. My meeting ran over. I like to support valuable initiatives." Even his outfit oozes whispered roar. As do muscles in second-skin fabric.

"Great. We're just about to start."

I summon calm. He needn't know my pulse is playing maracas to a mariachi tune. I'm a seasoned TV reporter. I've done mambo and salsa instruction for fun for years. So why does the thought of Latino dancing for the new boss in my tightest clothes faze me like a schoolgirl before a big exam? Little wonder when Dan Draven is sexier than one-hundred percent proof bottled sin.

He smiles. "I didn't want to miss out."

"Don't worry if you can't keep up. Everyone finds it challenging the first time they try to follow routines."

"I couldn't walk for four days, and almost fainted," says Janice to hoots of laughter. "I still get dizzy when she does double high kicks to Katy Perry, and the Bruno Mars number is a complete no go."

"I've done Zumba," Draven answers softly. The admission warrants a wolf whistle from the crowd. "I like to mix up my workouts. Helps with cardio."

"Maybe you should be up here?" I challenge.

Dan's eyebrow lifts. "Maybe you'd rather I don't stay?"

"Stay!" begs Janice. "As long as I can appreciate that view. Better than *Magic Mike* in 3D!" The awkwardness is dispelled as my group members giggle.

There's more to this guy than spreadsheets, redundancy worries, and parents who own polo teams and racecourses.

But I put my hands on my hips and raise my chin. "Everyone ready?" I hit play. The music lifts me into the workout zone. I let the euphoric beats feed my energy. Soon, I'm wired and ready to let it go. I'll push this class, since this is my chance to target hot, handsome rich boys with too much power and slick moves.

I quicken the salsa march then turn it into fast-paced squats.

"Gimme all you've got — bring on the awesome."

* * * *

"Kate! You haven't listened to a word. You're in a distant galaxy, far away... Come in, Spock!"

I peer over the top of my mug. I've been pretending to read my newspaper. But my brain wasn't tuning in, not even when Mel incorrectly meshed fantasy worlds.

Blame low blood sugar. Blame a man's taut muscles that matched my moves all the way through the hardest routine of the month. So I've been replaying a hot body. The guy who mastered *merengue* as easily as he'd trumped me with his street-style body slides.

Bastard.

He'd moved as if he'd read the instructor crib sheets for classes. Now Dan Draven's borrowed the newsroom's conference room opposite my desk. Refurbishments to the rooftop floor suite are ongoing. I've resisted glances through the glass wall during his smart-board cabaret, but it's taken work.

Has he been sent to fry my patience?

Drooling on the desk isn't good protocol. This guy even has Mel Scott, my News Editor, running scared.

"Sorry. Miles away," I confess to Mel. "Tell me again." I press my temples, trying to press-gang my brain.

"You and the rest of the female contingent." Mel nods toward the meeting room. "Scrambles a girl's transmission, doesn't he?"

I shrug away the lapse. "I'm in need of a sugar fix."

"Show me candy better than *his* and I'll buy boxes." Mel tiger-growls and flexes her fingernails. She's just had three babies in quick succession, and privately confided that her cute, devoted husband Gav was hinting at number four. It's only a matter of time before she's eating Edam and raisin sandwiches again.

I hide my grin. "Don't let Gav catch you coveting the boss. He'll ravish you before you're ready for another belly bump."

Mel answers, "If Draven is going to cause this much inattention, I'll insist he camps in the basement with a bag on his head. I've a news show to air — I need staff attentive. Ready to take details? Your next job's foreign travel — lucky you!"

"Really, how come? Where?"

"Santorini, Greece, tonight. There's an ex-London couple who've an online dating service gone global. Their boutique honeymoon hotel is a sensation — a fun filler piece. Rich Redman is an ex-marine whose actress wife made millions with her online dating club." Mel smiles slowly at me — like a python sliding my way, intending to encircle, then crush and overcome.

I stare at her, then blink twice. Mel may be a good friend outside work, but it doesn't mean I can't tell when there's skullduggery in her back pocket. "Why are you sending me on a whimsy story? I'm your urban commando reporter. I never do fluff—you'd never stoop to sending me on fluff. So why is there more damned fluff on this story than a stair carpet at the mad cat lady's house party?"

I know my protests won't make a stuff of difference. On this, I'm fucked. She has that look.

Mel's blue gaze glitters. "It's not down to me. There are higher forces involved. Draven wants in at ground level. He's your job buddy."

I stare in a combo of shock and horror. "Big Boss? He's getting his own way already? You have to be kidding me."

"He cut his teeth with a camera, Kate. He's assigned you to cover a special interview with the local crime boss. The kind that's a serious scoop—he has connections via his dad. So less of the fluff and more 'thank you for giving me a news gong'. You fly tonight. Go get organized."

I feel something inside quiver and it doesn't promise fun. Mostly because I really don't want to go to Greece with the big guy and his annoying 'hormones on high alert' effect on me as my hand baggage.

This isn't a story, it's a set up.

Being partnered with a privileged playboy whose father holds the shares is a new league of challenge. I don't do rich boys who pull strings—call it an old wound gone septic.

"Do I have any wiggle room, Mel? It's really bad timing— personal stuff."

Mel shakes her head and doesn't answer, just as Dan glances up through the glass and his gaze spears mine.

Shit. Something shimmies inside me. Why does my body experience a frisson of awareness? Just because he has shares in personal shades of hotness does not mean my lady parts can have a party without permission. Right now they're shaking their thang in my thong.

Dan still stares right at me. There is knowledge and enquiry in his gaze.

Double shit. And a litter of mismatched effing kittens to take away.

I maintain steady eye contact with Draven, not daring to even hint at weakness.

"So why did he ask for me specifically?" I say, seeing clearly there is zilch escape hatch on the plan no matter how many fake engagements I conjure up.

"He wants you and you are the best on my team. If you can't stand the heat — keep out of Capri pants in your classes!"

Cornered reluctance is rising like a horror tsunami inside me. I have many reasons why Greece — especially this particular island — is a no-go. Santorini would be my least favorite destination. Me and that island share history and it isn't pretty. With a nightmare travelling companion bonus it becomes hell squared.

"You can demonstrate why Your News Today Show is our flagship. And that we're solid and don't need cuts," Mel elaborates.

"You're sure he's up to taking lead with a camera?"

"Want to see his CV and show reel? He's brilliant." Mel rummages in her drawer. Immediately a box of baby ibuprofen and two packets of baby biscuits jump out of the Mardi Gras of mess.

Mel slams it shut, looking frazzled. I sense the chink in her armor has appeared. "Kate, please don't give me grief. Sophie's teething and I was up half the night. Raising nightwalker babies and keeping a stressful job is living hell. My life's like a *Game of Thrones* cast with merciless toddlers. Add a sex-crazed husband king who's intent on us raising a tribe...my life's no picnic. In fact, I come to work to rest."

I sigh. How can I compete with that pity plea deluge? "We should be sending the boss to hard news. Not Santorini dating."

"Only one thing matters, get Dan on-side."

I shift in my seat to avoid staring at the man who's managed an estrogen impact through glass, and who's put me over a barrel of horse manure. Does Mel realize he turns my knees weak? Or that I'm off men. Totally — signed up Spinster-for-Life Subscription, printed and framed by the side of my bed. Plus I'm a crap judge. I denounce men. Forever. So all the signs are saying — don't sodding go!

"I get that you have needs. But I'd rather fall on my sword than accept," I offer as my out.

Mel, who might appear slender, blonde, fragile and gamine, but who is tough as a commando's boots, spits me factoid bullets. "Half the women in the office would kill for this. Greece with a hot guy. Your News Today is not the team where an axe should be falling. I have a big mortgage and a loan for the extension we built for little Archie's bedroom. We can't be carved up. It's only five days. You're lead reporter. Deal."

Discomfort trickles through me and mallet-smashes my confidence.

Then Mel winks. "He praised your hip wiggling. He's single. You're going to a honeymoon island, how hard can it ruddy be?"

What is she thinking? Is it helpful to slap her hard?

Five days on a hot Greek island might turn my abilities to crumbled feta.

I grab my pad and pen, my iPad and iPhone. I won't argue more.

Dan breezes toward the conference room's glass door, looking arresting in an expensive suit — tie loosened and shirt widened at the neck like sexy on the loose. He stalks to my desk.

"Kate. Can we talk?"

I rise from my seat and follow his well-tailored rear to the 'meet and greet' area of our newsroom. He motions for me to sit and I obey.

"Mel has briefed you?"

I nod. Then, recognizing he might think it's churlish, I employ my voice. "Yes, Sir. Santorini."

"Call me Dan." He smiles lightly. "The travel piece is an entertainment item. The biggie is the Alex Katsaros

13

interview. You know him, don't you?"

Of course I know him. Everyone does, unless they've lived up the moon's bum hole, evading crime news. A big crime boss con-man and rumored bank robber who's slipped in and out of police clutches like a pickpocket in an eel outfit. He's harder to pin something on than a greased dartboard smeared in KY Jelly.

"He's living in Santorini in luxury. He's agreed to talk about the jewel heist from the nineties. This interview will get us noticed." Dan confides, "I've taken the liberty of ordering you clothes."

As if by magic — or perhaps telekinetic summoning — Lara, the PA from the penthouse suite, wheels a large titanium-esque case towards me. "Lara can change or add anything you require. There's a little time to make alterations if needed."

Wow. It's a *Pretty Woman* moment. He clicks his fingers and a personal shopper gets to it! A part of me is hurt that I don't have the wardrobe to suit his high-end needs — come to think of it, he's right, and Pret A Primark is way more my style street, but I'm still entitled to pique.

And all I need now is for him to present me with a diamond necklace and for him to snap the box lid on my fingers to become the purist's Richard Gere clone. I flip the catches on the case and check out folded neutrals that smack of cool in terms of fashion and price tag. I finger the items on top, and their gossamer-wing softness smacks of expensive. We're talking personal shopper splurge supreme.

"All in your sizes. Lara took care to check and the store staff were very exacting," he tells me.

I'd wondered why the recent HR questionnaire I'd filled in featured questions on my size and measurements info. Now I'm not sure whether to feel my privacy's been invaded, or be impressed. "Thanks. I'm sure they'll be fine. Can you arrange to get them to the airport?"

"Of course. Any other personal requests? I'm happy to give you whatever you need to feel assured in this important role."

Except permission to pass.

I stare at him and Dan watches me hard. His eyes are a mesmerizing mix of smoky grays.

He inhales deeply. "Look, Katie, I sense that you have reservations. All I can do is ask you to bear with me and trust this is a big story for your career. I'm talking major league." His US tones glide over me like warmed caramel.

Inside I'm raging, but I nod. It's a *fait accompli.*

"I'd be grateful for one more thing," I venture.

"Name it." His gaze is so intense I swear my skin is searing like I'm being roasted in *piri piri* drizzle.

I stare him down. "Don't call me Katie. It's Kate."

He nods. Then he raises an eyebrow. *Touché.* "Acknowledged—and call me Dan. I'll see you at the airport. That workout—surprisingly taxing." He nods and strides off.

I survey the staring office girls. Their dreamy expressions foretell he is more edible than chocolate ganache on nibble-sized biscuits. If you like high-risk, integrity-deficient, ruthless men as a snack between meals.

I return to my desk.

"Imagine that oiled up in swim shorts," says Mel.

"You need to up your meds. Been drinking too much from the crazy lake?"

But Mel's bubble cannot be pricked. "Make sure your bikinis are skimpy over standard. It's a honeymoon island — we don't want his attention roving. Put it out there." She winks.

But Mel doesn't know I have a secret—that means bits of me stay hidden. I'll be taking clothes that ensure the bits that matter are well covered, most especially when it comes to swimwear. I have to be ultra-careful about the swimsuits I choose.

She adds, "I wish I could be a fly on the wall on this assignment."

Yeah. Not likely.

Yep. Super picnic. Put out the bunting, pimp my body and mount the boss on assignment.

As long as the show's saved, nobody cares if I add Shag Tart to my résumé. Because when it comes to scruples, nobody gives a Santorini drizzled fig about the impact of any of this on *me*.

Chapter Two

Dan

Thirty minutes later than scheduled, Kate Joseph stalks though the Heathrow entrance door we'd arranged to meet near, like a riled wildcat with a grudge.

I've every right to be pissed at her delay, and hadn't pegged her as that sloppy, but her concourse strut and curve-hugging pants suit nix the gripes. Is that heartburn, or maybe my lungs have seized?

If Lara picked this outfit, she needs a warning that she's missed the work dress code by miles. Then I remember I checked the case — so the suit is Kate's. Holy shit on a couture stick. My bar buddies back home would need winches to pull their tongues off the floor.

Her outfit causes stares from guys and girls alike. Right now, I'm commanding my dick to ignore the show Kate's spray-on ladies wear advertises. These next five days will be the hardest assignment of my career. *Hard* being the operative word.

"Hey, Kate," I say, surprised my voice still works.

"Hi there." She draws her mini case to a skidding stop.

"Thought you'd stood me up. You always leave guys waiting?" I meant to tease, but my voice sounds rough.

Her forest-green gaze spears mine. "Transport hell — Heathrow gridlock. My cab bill racked up waiting and I would've called but I must've taken your number wrong. Sorry."

There's attitude bristling, and I feel the toxic waves. "You're here now. Don't sweat it."

She scans me briefly—I figure she's doing that chick thing about clothes. Trying to figure out if she picked the right outfit. But she makes me feel like something the cat wouldn't sniff if it were starving.

If they were here, my bar buds would laugh until they choke. I'd watch 'em with my arms crossed and no intention of undertaking Heimlichs to help 'em.

"I don't like looking bad in front of the boss," she tells me flatly. "The one I'm here to impress so much my manager almost get a hoodie made, saying Dance to Mr. Draven's Tune or You're Fired."

Shit. Unexpected. But total honesty rocks. A very good sign.

"Not that I'd wear a hoodie. I'd rather get my P45, frankly. So we're clear."

I stall. She's primed—and I'm falling for her ballsy 'tude.

"You can't control everything." My smile hits her wall. She's clearly ready for a smackdown. Mine.

"I don't usually do late," she adds. "I also don't do flimsy stories. I sincerely hope the Katsaros interview is fulfilled, Mr. Draven."

"Dan, remember? We should adapt our assignment persona. Come on, let's hit the check-in line. Oh, and trust me. I've got this handled."

My gut tells me this might be a trickier assignment than I've banked on. I'd figured I could handle a hot chick. This perpetrator, however, is more sweet and sour toward me than a Chinatown street food stand.

I pick up gear and shoulder the bagged camera—I've undergone a crash course in camera ops that could fool any pro. Kate's eyes are on me and I feel my jaw tick as if she's rumbled me already. But I had to get her here, didn't I?

My fingers twitch to hold her steady, make her take some breaths and quit trying to piss me off. Why does she make me react?

Gotta be my thing for brunettes. Okay, this one's more mocha caramel, but the dark roots entice. I have a preference for dark, only my girls usually come from the wrong side of the tracks—and their work doesn't involve straying far from their specialist boudoirs. If you catch my drift.

Princess Kate—yes, I've already heard her nickname—couldn't be further from my type. I yank my thoughts back. I need my head on straight or I'll screw up.

"So, let's go fly to Santorini and nail this show."

I was sure I had my dick under control until Kate placed her hand luggage on her case. Her ass speared my attention, giving my cock a lift. Shit. I'll need more than one cold shower over the next five days.

Fortunately, the line moves as fast as my pulse rate. We check in and make our way through security to departures.

I kinda wish I hadn't seen her in action at the Mambo class. While other airport passengers preen and pose, Kate is oblivious while turning male heads.

What the fuck are you thinking here, bro? Get your mind on the job.

So not easy.

Figures I'd balls up my undercover assignment before we're even airborne.

* * * *

Kate disappeared into the Glam Diva boutique in Departures. God knew what she was buying, but I make my own needs plain on her return. "My throat's dry as desert roadkill, Katie. Too long without java."

A female agent would have enjoyed my road kill comment. Kate acts as if I've just passed gas. After Mexican food.

The distasteful grimace on her face gives me a kick, until I realize that I'm blowing my Manhattan tycoon cover. I can hear my former NYPD partner telling me to engage my brain.

"We can take a pit stop if we must."

"I'll dock your wages later for the shopping spree." I feign checking my watch.

She scowls as she pushes her purchases into her bag. "I wasn't expecting Greece to drop into my lap."

I pause. "You need to take a trip to the light side, Katie."

"It's Kate. If you don't mind."

"Sorry. I have a friend called Katie—force of habit." One of my girls—petite and perky. Though Kate here doesn't need to know. Or that NYC Katie may be great as a stress reliever but her goose laugh gives me the jeebs.

"Can it, Danny Boy." She's even faking my accent badly. At least she has a humor chip—bonus. Kinda.

"Perhaps recall I pay the wages. The last person to get big ended up in a cast."

Shit. Had to stop myself. I'd nearly said 'cuffs'.

"I'm not going to dance around you to keep your ego straight. I'm surprised you're so keen to get your nails dirty on this job."

"Can the cute, sweetheart. Sucking up to me won't cut any ice. You always grovel this much with your superiors?" I say, just to rile her. I high-five myself that it works and she shuts up.

But hello, Mr. Boner—you're still listening. I'm watching her every move like a tongue-glued wuss.

"I'm man enough to get back to basics when the stakes demand it," I answer.

"So what makes this trip high stakes? Sounded pretty dreary dull to me."

My mouth dries. For a sassy sourpuss she ably sidelines in the ballsy factor. I sense I'm a primary target for it too.

"Exclusive news. The thing that keeps you in work."

We stop at the info boards as a public address system voice interrupts. My attention is hijacked by the announcement that Flight 752 to Athens is delayed, departure time estimated two hours later.

"The late thing's catching," she says, knitting her eyebrows.

It gives me another window on Kate Joseph, who so far I've only known on paper. Vetted fully, I've seen the clearance reports, she's clean as a very shiny whistle. With credentials that gleam. Perfect. For a civilian to intrude on this classified mission, she'd have to be. She's our hope of luring the guy we want to capture. Making Kate a key player. All will be revealed on her arrival in Oia.

Her body, no, her total presence continues causing male heads to swivel, clocking her as she glides. My inner caveman glowers at the gaze-groper men I feel a strong need to arrest. All over a woman who doesn't like me, and that's before she knows I'm a cop. One who is tasked expressly with nailing the bastards at the heart of the Operation Mountain Goat fraud ring. To bring them to justice, secure convictions and make them pay.

Yet I can't help a certain frisson of thrill that, on this, I know more than her. Because I sense she's a woman who'd hate it. Sometimes being an undercover cop has private *Yay* moments — this is one o' mine.

Yay me. Yay Santorini crackdown. Yay hot woman with an ass that drives guys crazy.

Yay how ya like me now, sucker all the frickin' way.

* * * *

After reaching the coffee lounge, I snag a table, then motion to the vacant seat opposite. Kate's eyes are on mine briefly, then her mouth twist reads pissed, but she slides in without a quibble.

"Time for a drink, and I'm buying."

"Hot water please. I have herbal teas with me."

She's hot water for me. Rolling boil and dangerous. I sense it from every pore.

"They'll let you pay for water if you ask nicely so nobody gets in a bunch."

"Cheap date," I answer. Then I grin.

"In your dreams, Draven," she answers. Then says, "Dan."

The female barista has snapped to attention, waiting for

my order. The NYC charm is not without benefits. Kate rolls her eyes as if I asked for it.

"Not every day I travel with the heir to a broadcasting dynasty as my elbow buddy. You always get this VIP attention?"

And suddenly I get to the root of her vibes. She's pegged me as Big Bucks Golden Spoon Jackass. Has a thing against money and might. She's opposed to catching something I carry. And I don't mean my filming equipment — more like tycoon's typhoid.

Yet, Dad disinherited me from the family hotel empire. Fortunately, these days Dad's resolved his issues — enough to allow me to use his name and faked media mogul chairmanship for our mission and take pride in my work.

I shake my head. "So we're clear, I asked you to be sent on this job because it needs special handling. I think you're best for the assignment, and before you think all the worst things about my position with the company, my aim is to focus the channel's efforts for best value. My presence is about accountability and I'm not squeezing operations dry. I won't tell you I'm not the bad guy — I'll make a point of proving it."

Though why I care what Kate thinks bothers me almost as much as her misplaced disregard.

"And, FYI, I'm an economy class guy at heart," I say spearing the point.

She stares me down. "Don't think so."

Crap. I just keep slipping in my own web of lies.

I probe her depths at this point. "You do a neat line in forcing people away, I notice. Do you realize you do that? Why are you so scared of being human?"

"Surely you can take a little horseplay?" she answers, but I see her lip twitch.

"You're still doing it now." I shake my head. "Yeah, Kate. You have me so worked out. Why would there really be more to me than shafting the company and you in the bargain? That guy worked you over so bad it's worthy of a psychiatric dissertation."

"What guy?"

"The one who made you shifty about guys." It's a pure cop move to sniff out the perp's reaction. I give the pause hang time and know from the look in her eyes I've poked her wildcat with a very sharp stick. "We should just get this job done. Your hang-ups are your own affair."

She glares at me as if she wants a machete to use on my limbs. "Keep your assumptions to yourself." Her voice is so soft I almost miss it. "It's nothing you need to know about."

In the Traveler's Lounge, Kate bites the edge of her lip and checks her phone. But after she's finished, her eyes meet mine and cause strange sensations to zap through my veins. Is it lightning? Or just regret at having sounded off enough to now feel like a dick?

But she swiftly puts my sympathy vote on hold with a fast-track interrogation. "So what do you really think of your UK operation? I want an honest answer. Why are you here? I know it's not this story. Call it gut instinct."

Her answer triggers my auto-response but the unimpressed distaste in her eyes has me getting pissed at her smarts. Damn, but she's got a built-in bullshit detector. "To undertake a fact-finding exercise and to report back to New York. There's no reason to think UK operations will have to change"

"Seems a crazy way to get the full view of the company. Santorini with me? I'm not convinced. Back to your views on our chances of surviving? Mel, my editor, wants assurances. Can I give them to her?"

"Your show will do okay. The staff is welcoming." I raise an eyebrow in challenge, ignoring that our drinks are being served. "Most want to please. Some need work, not naming individuals..." I hide behind the rim of my cup feeling smug at the slice.

Her eyes widen and there's a glimmer of 'gotcha' glee behind those green eyes. "I imagine most of them just want to date you. Or earn a pay rise."

Now isn't the time to reveal I haven't had a date in years. How can it be fair to hate me this much when my only mission is to serve and protect?

Her eyes drill into mine. Oh, how I'd love to have my mouth open hers. To bite down her gasp of shock. I sense she'd blow us both away, if she'd let me lean in, to bite her lip and press her back, to do her against the wall...or tied at the ankles and wrists and blindfolded, waiting for my touch...

As if reading my X-rated mind, Kate's just taken out her lip gloss. The tube glides along her lips and I clench my jaw tightly to keep my tongue in my mouth. Shit, my semi-erection is replacing my good sense.

I handcuff the betraying thoughts. When this job's over I need to get laid more. A week of women on a conveyor belt of recreational sex is long overdue. Brunettes who know my preferences. My favorite type — seasoned, submissive — and unopposed to active and therapeutic kink. Plus, not opposed to turning the tables on me either...

She intrudes on my thoughts with more questioning. "So how did you get the assurance of a Katsaros interview?"

"Rich Redman — we go way back. I used connections for Katsaros. I think you'll make this story great."

"I'm not in the habit of failing, Dan."

"Me either. Finally we agree."

I retreat from memories of past epic fails just as a plate smashes on the other side of the restaurant. I'm on my feet in seconds, reaching inside my jacket.

"Hell, Dan. What's got into you?"

I'm standing. My hand on my breast pocket feeling for the gun that isn't there. People all around us — Kate included — are staring.

The sound of a gunshot replays for the hundredth time in my head.

"It's just a clumsy barista."

I rub my temple and sit, trying not to care that half the lounge is staring. Or that I'm breathing fast and I can feel the heat rising over my face. Will I ever recover from past mistakes?

I'm here as the FBI's top blackmail ring cracker and the Oia scam will be the success of my career, but I'm already screwing up, having a coffee in downtime. I feel naked without a weapon and I won't get that back until our driver at Oia airport discreetly obliges.

"We're a team, so you're just gonna have to get over it and try for more professional!" I say finally, but my voice is rusty and rough.

Kate won't meet my gaze.

Will you let her down too?

I've counted the cost of my best friend's death every day since it happened.

And now I'm going to Santorini for a faultless capture of bad guys who have it coming.

The display flashes revised timings for flights, confirming boarding for Athens will begin in an hour. We won't miss our Santorini connection. The faster we get there, the faster we'll get this over with.

I raise the cup, then fake a smile. I've so much going on under the surface it's enough to fry neurons. "Next stop, a read from the best-seller list. You in?"

"I'm impressed you can read," she answers.

"Whateva, whateva. Sassy-assed as well as belligerent— who knew?"

As she rises from her seat I see her belly stud, visible through the gap at the edges of her shirt. I'd clocked it at fitness class. Only now she sees me watching.

Busted. Rookie error.

"Good view?" she asks softly. "Sloppy for a daddy's boy."

"Let's get outta here."

She's a Toxic Temptress with barbed wire deflection tactics. She's also been 'volunteered' for a mission no civilian should be involved with. But she's the only one who can get us close to our target. This op sucks tits.

Thinking Kate can stay in the dark 'til some suit gives

the okay might be a mistake. When it comes to work she's smart—she could be Kryptonite. She may spell disaster for this mission's success.

Chapter Three

This job is going to be trickier than navigating quicksand in spiked heels. I'm scanning the row numbers for our plane seats. Dan's back with the air stewardess detailing camera storage requirements. He's likely causing her lust surges — if her earlier rapture was any indicator.

Why the hell would Mel think I should be cozying up to him? The freak out stunt in the lounge — is he for real? Yes. I clocked he was belly-stud staring — he watched me as if he's ready for a hot meat meal against a wall. As if he's been subsisting on salad in small portions.

Big newsflash — my roadside cantina's permanently closed. Santorini is not a route to takeout temptation. No matter what Dan and Mel try.

I sigh, watching from a distance and pretending I'm not noticing that the combat trousers showcase thighs built for sport, and the beaten-up leather jacket clinches the sex god title. Mr. Draven's been taking dress-down lessons from some rocker stylist — my radar stalls on the sprinkling of chest hair through his unbuttoned T-shirt... I'm not a chest hair girl, but it could redefine my preference parameters.

I squash the thoughts, slip into my seat and remove my jacket. "Over here," I say when he approaches.

"You don't want the aisle seat?" So he thinks he can be gallant after the ego ritual with the scarlet-lipped blonde for the last ten minutes?

"Fine here. I don't think you'd fit somehow."

"Never know 'til you try." He grins. My walk right into

double entendre territory dings my patience. But legs as worked-out as his are going to fit in the middle seat about as well as a nun could run a strip club.

He removes his beaten leather, then gets into his seat. *Angels from the highest realms, there are muscles wearing tattoos!* His tribal artwork tatts band each biceps like a sinful barcode. Tatts are my nemesis. They smack of past crazy risks I took for a well-inked man. One who made me fall so hard I'm still not quite healed.

"Let me stow your bags?" Dan offers, after I'm through trying to wrestle it beneath the seat. Our hands touch and his gaze slides over mine.

"Thanks."

"My pleasure."

"You need to get out more."

"I'm being polite, Katie."

"Call me Katie one more time and I won't be."

Am I being too spitfire? There's an inner doubts elf tapping its foot at my snark. But he brings out my hyper-sensitivities, and I auto-react.

I had a fiancé styled and wired like him back when I believed in happy endings. Before he hurt me and cheated, then took me for a fool. So my bad luck with men is still my heart's Trojan pop-up, and these days I have inner defenses to keep intruders out.

"C'mon," says Dan. "Let's play nice."

He smiles as if he's been given the big boy's medal for bravest of the brave conduct, just for stowing bags. His dimple is the work of the devil on a very devious day.

I flip the force field switch to high in my head. The one marked *Past Mistakes No Go Zone.* Dan Draven undoubtedly wouldn't like *his women* with big, bad tattoos on their bodies like mine. My skin ink overshadows his completely. Safe to say he'd be shocked to hell and back.

"You okay?" Dan asks.

"Yes." I focus on the seat in front.

Then he shakes his head. "You got a problem with me? I

can talk to the flight attendant to move?"

I click the belt and force a smile, tight as a shrunken wool sweater. "Only if you just want to schmooze her again?"

His bulky form is clearly cramped, so he moves his hips to find a comfy spot and my mouth dries.

"Kate, I'm worried we're getting off on the wrong foot. When you get to know me I'm really not that awful, I hope. Think of me as just another colleague and aim for a good working relationship."

"We can try."

"Want anything else stowed?" he asks. "With our gripes?" He smiles. Wow. The women must usually fall for it too — it's a pin-up poster special.

"Damn...I forgot to get my book out," I rise, but so does he and we bump. Arms touch and chests too near for extra-awkwardness. We jostle to escape the buzz, and he takes over book retrieval, and I find my attention drawn to a beautiful girl and her partner taking seats nearby. Despite her Helen of Troy similarities Dan doesn't notice. He's occupied with finding my bag, and when he hands it to me and I rummage for my paperback, I'm still waiting for him to notice Ms. McGorgeous. Yet, his attention isn't nailed. His gaze roves on by without clocking.

I'm surprised. Seb's actions would have been so different. He's the reason I always had cause to check — fiancé with a wandering eye brings back a forgotten neurosis that was hell to bear. I realize I'd never admitted that to myself. Seb was a player but I plastered the cracks. But I had tailed all the signs like a stalker.

Hurtful in too many ways. God, I'd forgotten that.

Dan restores the bag, and the view of his crotch in his combats is too close. "Here's a magazine too," Dan thrusts the inflight tourism thumb-through at me.

"Thanks." But flicking through proves the mistake of my day. When I open the pages, I'm hit with the one thing I've kept firmly distant.

Bride Special — Honeymoon Paradise Fairy Tale Perfection.

I grind the urge to cry tightly. They're not sad tears, they're fueled by anger, and I find that particularly tricky to rein in. How dare they betray me.

I use my finger to blot the moisture in my eyes that's come without a visa. I'm so over Seb it's laughable. But the woman in the double page spread wears a dress uncannily like the one I sold at a bargain on eBay — the one I never had a single photo in, despite the photographer being booked a year ahead. She's posed against a backdrop of the exact kind I'd dreamed about having before the bastard left me with only bills.

Even though I hate Seb and am so happy I didn't pursue the marriage from hell, I've been hijacked into staring at my unfulfilled dream. These tears aren't over the tragic Greek wedding disaster — they're because I'm not over losing Slash, the guy I really wanted.

"Katie? You okay?" Dan says softly. Shit, now he thinks I'm loopy. "Here." He hands me a handkerchief. A proper silk one. He may be dressed down, but his tycoon class still shows in the soft, black silk. I try to ensure my eye make-up isn't Kiss Convention face wreck.

His fingers slide to take my hand to squeeze. I breathe deeper. Then he nods and 'shhhs' me. "Whatever it is — you're going to be okay."

Why do I only now discover I have a thing for New Yorkers with gravel tones?

"Hey, we'll nail this. Don't sweat it," he adds.

There's a ping, and the stewardess is with us in a moment, responding to Dan's smile more than any alarm caller button summons. I'm embarrassed at my crying face in the presence of Barbie made real.

"May we have some brandy? My friend has travel nerves."

"Certainly," the flight attendant agrees. "Sir — your camera is stowed — please let me assist when you disembark." She's glowing with the estrogen rush. But he still has my hand.

Dan lets my fingers go, then flicks his attention to the book he bought. The title reads *Dark Engagement*. I sense

I've strained our embryonic working relationship way past its flex limits.

I've noted glances at Dan from passengers and staff. They've labelled Dan handsome cargo. To underline it a woman in the aisle throws him a smile he ignores. The stewardess bears my brandy. I sip – and I do relax.

Dan leans his head to the side. "Fear of flying?"

I go for broke – since he thinks I'm nutso anyway. "Santorini aversion. Honeymoon destination that nose-dived." His gaze comes back to meet mine and our faces are close. "He jilted me at the crucial moment. Not at the church, but just before I was due to leave. So yes – he did a number. Apologies the pity party landed without clearance." I'm left feeling somewhat tired by the outburst.

"Katie, sorry. I'd no idea. You're permitted emotions – sounds like a big deal to me."

"It's okay. Saved me marrying a jerk. I'm pretty pissed off at getting it off my chest now, of all times."

His kindness doesn't help. I feel panic climb inside my lungs. Hyperventilating is not a good move. I'd die of self-induced suffocation before I'd permit a panic attack, so I regulate breath by breath. When I regain equilibrium, there is Dan watching sagely.

"For me Santorini's the honeymoon I paid for but never went on. Nobody at work knows this – except, now, you. He used to call me Katie. It's why I hate it."

His large warm fingers thread through mine again. Startling me. "I'm sorry. If you don't mind me saying, your fiancé was a low jerk."

"Rat bastard mini-prick." I do a good act, but the sympathetic look in his eyes slices inside like a paper cut to my heart. "And lately, a guy I thought was the one proved he wasn't either."

"Want me to field a replacement for the job? Couple of calls…" He offers. I'm touched. We're sitting on the flight – he's way more considerate than Mel would be.

"Dan – I'm here at Mel's behest to vouch we've earned

our place. To argue we don't need cuts. She'd go nuts."

He nods. "Does Mel appreciate what she's asked you to endure?" He stares at me so hard I find myself wondering where this nice, caring, considerate side of him hides as a day job. I never condone weakness, but in the gourmet kitchen of soothing reassurance his approach is better than double helpings of choc fondant

"You act tough but you've a melting center."

"You act tough as a shield yourself, Kate Joseph."

"You're more right than you know," I answer.

"Keep the faith. You'll find a guy who'll make dickwad a distant memory."

I feign Dan's accent. "Maybe I attract dickwads?"

"Is that why you figured I was one back in the lounge?"

I bite my lip. "That touchy?"

He stares hard. "Kinda." He takes in a deep breath. "I've had my share of problems. I can tell when things go deep." He's stiffened. I sense there's a chilled elephant on the plane. And I've no idea why. "Maybe I'm not the bastard you think I am?"

And why does that cause a quiver deep in my womb that makes my clitoris twitch to say *yes please*? Hell almighty. Reminder to self — this man is barred. Dangerous Dan. Boss pedigree means big no-no.

"Maybe we've both judged one another without due credit."

Dan says, softly. "Things can always be worse. It takes someone who's been there to know." His jaw flexes and he turns back to his book.

I still don't speak. I glance at him. I wonder what tough breaks he's faced? So I put the tears behind me. He could have been a stuffed shirt jerk — instead he's deactivated the situation.

Dan watches me. "I'm told viewer ratings for your show are up. You don't have to do Mel's bidding and suck up. Far from it."

"You and Mel — let's have a showdown when we get back

and see who wins?" I tease. "I think it could just be her."

We smile as our eyes meet and Dan grins. A swift resurgence of the melting feeling returns. But we'll get through this job. We're going to Santorini with a truce agreed, and all I need is to make a bad story brilliant—just as I did before with Seb. Like I've done with Slash. When it comes to cover ups I'm a World Class pro. I concentrate on my book—Izzy's blockbuster. Instantly, we both stare because it's in my lap and what I thought was a cringe response with the tears was nothing. The blurred cover is suddenly easy to discern. What I thought was a shadow is a nipple and a rubber dildo. Loud and clear.

I gasp as my toes curl.

Dan's staring and I'm watching his shock.

Why haven't I noticed before? But it was abstract and now it's startling. The nipple is erect, shining and moistened. The dildo is a big, black pleasure truncheon with no apology. Or mistaking it.

"Hard-core reading," says Dan.

I can't reply. I'm mute with mortification. My cheeks sting they're so hot.

"I know the author," I stammer.

Dan chuckles. A low sexy rumble that's hard to ignore. The flight attendants step forward for the safety guidelines, but we're laughing.

"Should keep you up," he observes. "Interesting taste in friends."

"She's a teacher."

"Bet she is." It's just getting worse.

Dan watches me, then nods as if he's read my mind, complete with subtitles and a take-home pamphlet. His jaw twitches, but I can't hold his gaze because I'm too busy flushing like a menopausal women's club on a hen night in a sauna. But bluster beats defeat.

Izzy Tennant. Thanks. Just thanks.

"Ruddy priceless," I mutter.

Team awesome.

* * * *

We finally arrive in Santorini under a climbing moon that causes magical shards to sparkle on an inky sea. The island's charms are evident, even by night, and a cab is waiting to take us onwards to a villa that's been booked, Dan tells me. So much for my usual slumming it in economy-rate hotels.

This is Greek paradise found — with postcard views. From sea vistas to quaint village-scapes — no sold out commercialism, but a cocooning sanctuary.

"In daylight Oia will be show-stopping," I tell Dan, who's standing nearby, looking broody before a view that should be blowing him away.

"Should be. Though we're not here for sightseeing."

"A little won't hurt."

"Ready to get in the car?" I sense he's disinclined to linger. But this is the first breath of fresh sea air I've had in a long time, so I'm reluctant to speed away. I motion to the cab and waiting driver.

"Sorry — is he charging by the minute? Wow. Your PA really is prepared — that's what I call an executive chauffeur. I'm not used to this treatment," I observe the driver in shades and a suit. He snaps to attention and helps with the luggage as if we're visiting dignitaries. Though why Dan is helping store luggage in the boot seems odd. After all, this guy would shine his shoes if asked. Why have a pooch and bark yourself?

The driver had handed Dan two cases at the airport, come to think of it. Titanium, fit for a movie prop room. Maybe it's Dan's bespoke toiletry case? I smile, imagining him with a Harrods high-spec shaving kit preference.

"Tavi has been assigned as our driver for the trip," Dan confides. "Time to leave."

I nod. Mostly because I don't know what else I can say. I've never had my own driver. In fact, I've sometimes taken public transport on jobs. This is a new league of special. He must sense my mixed feelings.

"Pays to have things covered," Dan tells me, then cups my elbow when he slides inside the car. The touch sears me. *Yowk.* Which is mad because he's just doing what he does best. He's a hot, wealthy toxic blow to my sanity. With wrecking ball potential.

And my reactions are most likely because I've spent the flight reading a full-on erotica novel that's singed my privates in its intensity. I'd've stopped, but I had no other reading matter, bar the Greek Brides Special. I'm impressed at Izzy's writing, though. At one point I could feel the sweat run between my breasts — as Dan sat unaware beside me while I worked to resist creaming like a rampant chick starved of personal attention.

Dan stares at me now. How does he manage to make my thoughts feel inspected and found lacking? As if he is head boy and I'm errant rebel pupil?

"We do need to go," he says again. Why the rush and fuss?

"You probably come to places like this all the time," I say, as the driver takes us in our cream leather-lined limousine along a dusty dark road off the main Santorini drag. "Being the corporate tiger. Jet set life. Villas and yachts all over the world? You probably always stay in the exclusive joints?"

"One desk is pretty much like another. I don't get out as much as you think."

"Shame we're not staying in Oia," I tell him. "It's so pretty. I'd hoped to explore and buy some souvenirs."

"I don't think you'll have any complaints when you see where we're staying," he answers. Call me psychic, but I detect a frisson of unease. Call it the tic in his left jaw and the corded muscles in his neck. Then he sees me watching, and it's gone like a magician's illusion.

"We're going to get fantastic footage," he says, but I confirm in his tone that he is far from relaxed.

"You okay?" What's up with him?

"Fine." But I know he's not. He's watch-checking. He points into the distance. "That's where we're staying, Villa

Missori."

I whistle between my teeth. Wowzer. Visible as a white dot on the landscape, but I'm in no doubt that when we get there it'll be a Greek castle with all the modern shinies thrown in.

"That's what I call assignment pay-off," Dan tells me next to my ear. His gravel tones are a sensual caress. Unfortunately my womb is listening and kinda partial, and a bit hungry for tuck-in time. "Like it any better now?"

Don't speak to me that way when my pussy is craning and listening.

I can smell him. Citrus, musk, spice. I recognize cedar notes, and it makes my nipples peak. I'm turned on from just a whisper, a sniff and a touch — how easy am I?

I blame Izzy's book — on return she's *so* gonna pay.

I pull myself together. Yeah, right. Get a grip. I move out of his allure zone. Our ultra-swank accommodation looms ahead. It hangs starkly upon a clifftop to hijack the best views on the island and show off its majestic charms. The road is clear and the scenery is less like the Oia I know from tourist photos, but even better for the stark solitude.

"So far out?"

"This is no ordinary assignment," Dan answers.

"Meaning?"

"You'll be fully briefed in due course."

"Dan?"

His gray eyes meet mine. My mind is too caught up in helter-skelter thoughts about what he's not saying to fully focus on the questions I should be asking.

"Are you telling me that I don't know the full story here?"

Dan's lips become a thin line. "Things will be clearer shortly. As for this place, it belongs to a friend of my father's. The best sea views. We'll have our own car and driver. Excellent security, which is paramount in this situation."

"So no wandering the alleyways of Santorini in downtime..." I remark. "I think you need to start telling me what this is all about. Is this because of the Katsaros interview? Are we in danger? Tell me properly what's going on."

He doesn't answer. I can see in his taut expression he doesn't intend to. Instead he stares at the house, concentrating on that as he ably ignores me. "Tavi is at your disposal if you wish to explore. Yes—we are taking precautions because of the nature of this interview. You gotta remember this is no ordinary assignment. All will become clear in due course."

But then this must be how tycoon heir billionaires do their thing. Inside, I'm longing to explore the biggest villa I'll ever have the privilege to visit in my life. But right now I want to know the full script on exactly what he's talking about. I'm already mentally planning a Jacuzzi selfie for posterity.

But first I want my answers.

With perfect timing we drive right up to our palatial villa—a Greek modern architect's mansion that could throw a party for a hundred without breaking sweat.

"You can hardly complain about this," Dan says.

"Let's wait and see what's ahead first, shall we?" I answer.

I take the hand he offers to help me from the back of the car as the driver goes ahead to open up. This must be what executive drivers do for jet setters. He's using a security keypad rather than a plain old set of keys. But I'm hardly out of the car when a shot rings out and we both instinctively crouch.

The shot is so loud I flinch—every cell pretzels inside me with the shock of a real-life gunshot fired so close to my flesh and bone.

"Fuck!"

"Tavi!" Dan shouts.

I glance across to see Tavi lying flat across the threshold of our villa, slumped, oozing dark blood. The villa door is ajar. Who knows where the shot came from, though it sounds as if the rocks to the left of the villa grounds would be first bet. It's too dark to properly tell.

But I'm not thinking. My heart's hammering. I'm on auto-react. Getting into as crouched a ball as I can and trying to get out of the damn way.

"Holy shit."

"Down. Stay down," Dan orders, and I can't even see his face. I'm so contorted as Dan drags me behind the car at speed. Lord knows how he does it, except I'm glad of it when I hear and feel bullets hit the road where we were moments before. More shots. Big, live, rattling fired metal that can maim and kill. Somebody is out to do just that. To us.

But my brain is too occupied with fixating on the fact that our driver has just been shot. I've gone into a spasm of shaking and I feel as if I've fallen into some crazy, macabre Shitty Wonderland dream. But it's real—my knees and hands are scratched to hell. One ankle aches but compared to losing your blood? Your life in a single, stalled moment of time?

"What the hell just happened? Aren't you going to go see if he's okay?"

"He's not okay. Things just hit a new league of serious," Dan answers. He's close. His face is ashen and sculpted with the gravity of the situation.

"What does that mean?" I lie there, shaking and watching Dan take a gun from his jacket. A gun! Big, scary. I'm so shocked I can't compute.

"What the hell, Dan?"

"Don't waste your energy talking." His tone is low. More shots are fired, and these ones hit the car, making me clench up in a tight ball of fear. The sound is unbearable. Stark. Ominous. As serious as it gets.

"Stay here. Keep your head down. Don't move." Dan pulls back the top of his serious and scary-looking gun, slotting ammo, I guess. He places his finger over the trigger, ready for God only knows what.

"You've done this before," I whisper.

"Shit, babe. Wish it weren't true. But trust that I'm also

damn good with it. Knew we should've told you sooner," he whispers on a rough breath. "Knew it every step of the fucking way," he says, looking as grim as I feel. "Do not move an inch. I'll be back for you—trust me." He opens the car door and motions for me to crawl inside. "Get in. Stay down. I'm coming back. On no account leave here."

We're in Santorini under a full moon. But it's not paradise—it's a living nightmare. And I'm here alone without a roadmap or any answers. Having Dan with me suddenly counts most.

This Santorini assignment has just dealt a full-on kick in concrete boots.

Chapter Four

Dan

My gun's in my hand, and it's a shitfest. Leaving Kate, I edge around the car. I fire twice at the rocks to the east of the villa during a pause in gun fire, but it's too dark for good sights. My shots hit boulders, but more thunder back.

Fuckers. Doesn't help the car's in a lamp-lit drive. It's one sniper, maybe two. But it's having Kate in the mix that's frying my brain, though I blank it. Taking out assholes with guns is one thing — a civilian woman cargo on my conscience, is a new league of crap.

I ease out again and aim a pristine shot that's full on the mark. The shot fires. Bang. No answer.

My jaw grinds. "C'mon you bastards, what're you made of? Too easy."

No answer but my staccato heartbeat.

Tavi lies flat out and hasn't moved. Not a flicker, and he took four shots in the chest so worst-case scenarios are sprinting through my mind.

I'm dialing Max at HQ Control seconds later. It rings as a volley of bullets hit. One flying right past my ear.

"Draven? What?" Max. Riled but not rattled.

"Party's started. Tavi shot. Get your asses here pronto, pal. Get word to Rich."

"Tavi dead?"

"Enforcements ASAP. Send Havana for Tavi — must be dead. Saw the shots."

I pocket the phone, scuttle round the car to the front for a fresh sight. I'm stoked to see the sniper's buddy clear as I'm gonna get in this light. I aim with calm, detached precision—big flesh-seeking boom.

The body slumps, though I'd aimed for torso.

I'm hoping hard Max gets the cavalry pronto—and, as I think it, I retrieve the phone.

"It's Redman." Shit got real? Now our Troika base big boss himself is on the line.

I fill him in as briefly as I can. "One down. One or more to go."

Rich orders, "Get out now. To the cave base—stay there. Two miles, coastal trail. I'll text directions. Your job is keeping her safe."

A fresh volley spurts jagged stone chunks from a nearby planter. My head is white heat with a wet forehead, but I fire back shot for shot. No time for Band-Aids. Cuz this so ain't gonna stop me.

I stand and launch three quick-fire bullets in a row at sniper one. These ones are for Tavi. But three shots spit dust in a line inches from my leg that yells time to fly. I hunker and creep round the car. There's another intensive firing assault as I throw the door open and myself inside. Tavi's keys dangle in the ignition and cause me to me swallow. He's saved our balls.

"Tavi. Gonna nail the bastards in your name."

I pull my body to drive position, turn the ignition, find gear and slam my foot on the gas.

"Outta here. Hold tight, honey. Hold damn well tight."

A bullet might shatter the windscreen anytime and black my tomorrows, but I zoom away, trusting in karma—door semi-open, first gear screaming banshee's revenge.

"Keep low. Don't get up yet," I command.

But Kate hasn't surfaced or replied. She doesn't know we're headed for an underground cave base, over savage ground, in the dead of night. With no equipment and depleted ammo.

We're out. Shaken, and going by the muffled wails of the crying woman on the floor of the car, scared to fuck and back.

"Gunna be okay, Kate. Gunna be fine."

But I sense this assignment may never be okay for her again.

* * * *

I take the car into the dense woodland as far as possible. I know these caves, have been there by boat. But on foot with a civilian, in pitch blackness, will be tougher. I spot a clearing ahead, the trail path bathed in moonlight like a promise. I'm thanking the Almighty for that blessing as I get out and round the car to find Kate shaking on its floor.

"We've left those guys behind now, honey. C'mon." I touch her back, prepared to hug and soothe if she'll let me. But she shakes me off as if she's feral and stick-poked.

She's working an intense mix of anger and tears like the Trevi fountain with a toxic leak. The sight spears my gut because she won't look at me. Likely blames me as the worst bastard she's ever had the bad luck to breathe near. She's probably right. It's thanks to me she's just woken up in shooter-shitola.

"Damn, Kate. We really gotta get outta here, for both our sakes. Those guys are gonna come after us if my team don't stop them in time — so we gotta move fast."

Kate finally meets my gaze, then squeals. "My God. You're bleeding. Your head!"

I can't be hurt because it doesn't compute. I'd barely registered the sweat I've been wiping from my eyes wasn't sweat at all but blood. I fear it'll send her into freak zone and I'm charged with keeping her tight and safe.

I touch the spot gently. "It's a scratch."

But she shoves my handkerchief at me — the one she used on the plane. "It's bad. You'll need it attended to."

"Don't sweat it — we have a medic at base. As long as it doesn't spoil my good looks, hey. You okay now, bud?"

"Base? What base?" She doesn't keep eye contact. "How

can you joke at a time like this? *We? Base?* We've left our driver lying dead! When were you planning to tell me you carry a gun, buddy?" she adds dryly, but her eyes are saucer bowls of doom that don't blink. "Tell me what is bloody going on, Dan."

"We'll talk this through like rational adults when I get you to safety. That's the priority before debrief."

"You have some effing nerve." Her face says 'yeah not likely'. "Unless I get answers, I go nowhere."

I palm my hair. "I'm no dynasty heir, Kate — turned my back on Dad's boardroom years ago. Cop dreams branded my heart from boyhood and I took 'em all the way through NYPD to the FBI. But you weren't supposed to know any of this 'til you were briefed in Oia. By the top guys in my team — Interpol's finest. I'm temporarily assigned to Interpol. This is a mission, not a story."

"And when the hell does asking my permission to participate come into it?"

She gapes at me. Her eyes are wild with fire but she stares silently. Then she goes to land me a smack in the chops, but I catch her hand. "Can we save this delight for later and go now? You have to just trust me here — you *will* get answers — just not this minute. I need to get you somewhere safe, as tasked. Trust me — this is a top-secret, high-priority mission, and I'm charged with keeping you alive."

Her usually full lips are a thin hard line. "Hard to trust someone who's got me into all this via lies. One thing's clear — somebody really mustn't like you."

"Don't think I like them either."

"There's no way you can even guess how bad I think you are right now."

"Actually, think I can."

And it has nothing on the bad thoughts racing through my mind. Was Tavi tailed? Has Andreas' identity as a plant in the Katsaros lair been sprung, or what? Are we about to be ambushed again?

Earlier, I was counting down to debrief — to shaking off

43

Kate's questions, thinking she'd have enough on her mind when she was inducted into the mission proper. Now Tavi's dead, the mission's blown and Kate is *my* problem.

I knew this mission was off — felt it like a premonition read from a seer's old tome of prophecy. Knew it when I nicknamed her Kryptonite Katie. But now, I just have to wear the hero suit and tights, and act like the shit's not hit the fucked-up fan for both of us.

I screw up an eye as I dab my head, thankful the wound isn't full gush — I'm seizing the positives popsicle and sucking the damn thing dry. It's all I've got when faced with getting a woman with the shakes, in stilettos, who hates my guts, to comply and get to safety over a blacked-out assault course.

"I can guess how much of a shithead I am to you right now. Listen, honey…"

"Don't dare honey me!" She spits pure fury, then the tears start afresh.

I hold out a hand and gently grasp her wrist. "Please understand it was above my jurisdiction to brief you. Only, the bad guys improvised with an all-action demo, to set the scene without permission."

Sensing she's either gonna cry again, hit me or verbally abuse me more, and knowing time's the thing that's hemorrhaging here, I leave her and go to the driver's seat to study the sat nav. Looks like we're as close as we can get to the trail. The caves link underground to Villa Missori by labyrinth tunnels, but they're accessible via woodland paths — they offer a storage base facility and an emergency billet for personnel.

I see the mistrust in her eyes but proceed anyway. "You've a right to be pissed. But we still need to go — to hide out in the caves. It's night, it's gonna be a task. Boss orders us to wait for help — so save discussions 'til we regroup. Two miles on winding wooded track in the dark ahead."

"Two miles? In heels? Do I have time to grab a change?"

Typical woman, typical civilian. I'm pissed enough to

want to point out my colleague and buddy Tavi is dead until she adds, "I have a scarf for your head bandage and water. Running shoes too. We'll need them."

Inside, I warm up and curse my nasty-ass assumptions. She's not a mall bitch — her head's on straight. The fact that she had my mind doing somersaults earlier, thinking about her when I shoulda been focused on taking out the bad boys, almost makes some sense now.

Kinda. On Planet DoucheBrain. Where the crapola cops hang. Fuck.

"Good thinkin'," I answer. I re-load and replace weapons pre-expedition and grab as much spare ammo as I can fit in a rucksack along with scant supplies we may need — maps, more water, a spare shirt and blanket from the car.

"Wanna get moving quick. They mean business. I'd rather we were farther out of harm's way than this."

My mind's occupied with thinking, what if they're lying in wait at the cave? What if they know we have this island rigged with covert bases and surveillance hideouts in our arsenal? They're fighting back 'cause some fuck's snitched and they're wise. If they're waiting *we* could be next.

Kate's stopped crying, but her face is ashen and she shakes like a cold turkey junkie. Guess that's natural for a gunfire virgin. Sadly, I'm way past first times.

I feel for the kid, but a voice in my head is pissed — worst job ever. Civilian bodyguard and a head wound. Feelin' like a beat cop — demotion all the pissing way.

Then I can my dickassed complaints. Remembering the Mexican blow-up, I count my blessings. The jettisoned job that caused everyone to question if I'm worthy to wear the badge. A shot nails my heart at the mind-blast of losing my partner Nathan on my fucking watch. I was captured, Nathan shot dead.

I nix the recriminations. Kate's non-stop shaking is freaking me out enough to want to move pronto. I pull on a black-ops sweater, hand her a spare and shove my leather jacket at her.

"C'mon, wear it. Nix the chills with layers. Times up. Let's go."

* * * *

It takes two hours to travel the two miles to our cavern sanctuary. Two freakin' miles. We have multiple twig scratches, foliage abrasions and Kate has jarred ankles, even in sneakers. Kate also took a lash in the moosh from a tree branch and yelped in pain. Kinda figure it was payback for the crap she's dealt me for too long.

And the fact I was treated to a reporter gone wild question-fest en route.

"So you're not our company chairman? It was all lies and a smokescreen."

"Nope to being chairman. Not so much smokescreen as mission rules."

"And…"

"And I'm not here to get a story. I'm here to catch a bad guy."

"So you're police?"

"FBI. Interpol. I said already. Can we can the questions?"

"What does that mean? Are you going to keep giving me minimal answers?"

"Yup."

"Very funny, Dan. I deserve way better than that."

"Hardy friggin' har. That's me. Comic genius as well as Interpol stud and patience-sapped police pro."

"Just let me in on some of it, can't you? This is way too big to cover up and deal with later."

I sigh and my chest's tight, opening this worm can up for full inspection. "Interpol Sex Crimes Protection Division. Let's just can the interrogation 'til later. We're not just alerting any following snipers to our presence, we may as well have a frickin' marching parade band and a pony mascot, for shit's sake."

"God. You are so self-centered."

She huffed half the way, but we hung in and found the cave mouth—hidden so cleverly we could've missed it. The red crosses on trees every ten paces and pebble bed markers helped. The cascade of steps to the pool-filled caverns was a welcome sight and the 'spa scene' is a mirage, because taking center-stage are three vast, state-of-the-art speedboats and a mini-control room built into rock.

I don't put on the lights. Figure we don't want to advertise our arrival. I take her to the back of the caves, and we find a spot at the darkest point.

"Time to sit it out, Katie."

"Sit? And wait? That's it?"

"We made it. Let's just sit and regroup. Get strength back in case we need to move fast again."

"Some place," said Kate. "Think we could sleep on the boats?"

"If you think you could. Sleeping, I mean." I add the last bit in case she thinks I'm talking about bunking with her and seeing where it leads. Perish that thought. "After what you've been through, sleep may be hard to nail for a while. Kind of a perk of the job."

I'll wager that for the foreseeable she'll be reliving the Tavi thing on a nightly basis. I know—been there and worn the wardrobe of insomniac side-effects. I've probably just summoned a fresh mental portrait of Tavi lying bleeding for her right this minute—nice work, Draven. Top of the dip-shit class. I'm so playing this like a second grader.

"I'm so cold, that's why I thought of the boat, for heat," she replies, and her teeth are chattering in sync with every word.

"Come here." I press the blanket I've brought in my rucksack into her shaking hands. "Want me to wrap you in it?" She's still in my leather. Which makes her look sexy, badass and childlike all at once. Bad news for my anti-Lolita ethics and my anti-boner defenses.

"I can manage. So. Get to it, you were about to tell me all. Now we're here and there's no excuse not to," Kate

47

prompts.

I take in a sigh to sustain me. "So I'm not the CEO of Your News Today. But my dad does own companies—hotels actually. On that much I wasn't lying. Useful cover."

"Okay. And the rest."

"Katsaros and his henchmen are nasty-ass bastards. We need you on this case because you're the double of someone who may just have the power to be the Achilles Heel of the big guy. They're way worse bastards than you even realize."

"Nice. Shame nobody thought to let me choose." She nods. But when I don't say more, she probes me with a gaze that drills like an oil rig. "The whole story. Surely I deserve more than scraps from your fit-up table. Full explanations are the very least I deserve."

I'm chastened by her directness. I realize I continue to underestimate her.

Slam dunk to Kate.

"He's not only a fraud and a thief—he's big-time nasty pimp. A fully-fledged scum of the earth human trafficker of the worst kind. Young girls—for porn rings and massage parlors. Kids in their teens from poor families, taken from their homes, sometimes in broad daylight or lured with fake promises and never seen again."

"Shit."

"And that's a nice word for him. They farm them out to his client base of perv bastards and serial rapists. Oh yeah, this one's a real peach."

I figure I've gone from weak frothy cappuccino not enough information to a dozen shots of pure Columbian espresso, too strong, with tequila on the side. Sex trafficking is one of the worst kinda plagues to humankind.

Her face reads pure Shut-the-Front-Door snapshot.

And maybe ready to shock-vomit or faint right about now.

"You okay?"

I jump forward to grab her arm in case she passes out. I

have to keep reminding myself that Kate's no agent. She's not hardened to this murky underbelly world. She's a stranger to the scummiest sides of the worst kind of lowlifes ever to pass themselves off as humans.

Is it too late to retrace steps and ask her to summon her 'happy place'?

"Sorry. Too much, too soon. Shoulda censored that."

"No. I want the truth. No point in evading when I've just seen a man die. So why do they want us dead?"

"Honey. I don't actually know all the answers yet. But I'll damn well work to make sure they don't achieve it, and I'll get to the bottom of why things have turned, too. Count on it."

She goes to rise and move away, but she slips, almost, over-balancing, and she could have nearly fallen into the water, which is only a step or so away. I catch her with a firm hand. Steady her and don't let go. She's still shaking as if she's been hugging ice.

"You need warming up. Want a hug? A purely platonic, professionally initiated hug for warming purposes alone? Ain't got no heat pads." Who am I kidding? There's a part of me that's heated up just fine at her scent and her proximity. But I try with self-deluding lies.

She shakes her head, still driven by her thoughts. I can hardly blame her. "Why me?"

"My superiors will explain and show you photographs. You're a double for a key contact. You were hand-picked." This is all I've been told to pass on.

"Isn't impersonating somebody a stretch too far?"

"Not for what we had planned."

She searches my face. "But didn't I deserve the right to sign my consent first?"

She has a point. I'm flailing on how to answer, but I'm so damn travel-jaded my brain's seized and Kate's weary from events too, so I can't do either of us justice.

"That's for my bosses to justify. I'm following orders to get you here for debrief — 'til the guns got in first. I give you my solemn oath you'll be protected every step. These are my orders."

"Wow. Big thank you on that, Dan. Doffing my cap. So not worthy." Her irony makes me feel like a cock and a half. With no balls or idea of how to salvage her respect.

We sit in the cave listening to the solemn echo of water dripping steadily, and neither of us have further words, beyond what's going on in our heads. If this water stuff continues we're both gonna need to pee, and that could be awkward.

"You need to bathe your wound," she tells me, and turns to the task with perfunctory calm, removing my bandage with only slightly shaky fingers. Surprising me with her leap into the mundane.

"Leave it. It's cool."

"Let me clean it at least. You're the one who's made all the calls so far."

"Okay. If it makes you ease up." I move closer as she inspects my head.

"A nasty gash on your forehead — left side, but you'll live. Bled quite a bit but it's stopped. I'll fetch clean water."

I hear her ramped breathing and pretend it doesn't give me a semi-erect dick. What's up with this? No idea. Never had a boner from a Florence Nightingale offer before. Shit. Though I kinda blame the book she read on the plane for starting things. Hadn't pegged her as an erotica chick — was that Mummy Porn? The cover caused my dick to press against my pants fly uncomfortably, and it hasn't accepted the 'go to sleep you're not welcome' edict yet. I'm even summoning images of my female ancestors looking pissed off in historical garb to tame it.

A cold shower would be next on my agenda, but isn't possible. We're in a cave. Together and alone 'til hell knows when, and no chance of dick control without a scene. Though, when I get the passcodes for the adjoining bunk rooms built into this place, at least we'll have a wash-room and privacy.

My erection is all the more poignant, as for two years I've battled dick issues—a by-product of the messed-up Mexican job. Being tortured by a drugs cartel and having your career and life blown apart with the consequences can do that to a guy. Mexico left scars, and not just the ones on my body. So I've had to be creative in terms of sex. A lot of strict madam action with candle wax and whip play with a series of mistress whores has done the trick, where vanilla has failed.

So having a wild hard-on pushing its presence now isn't just damn inconvenient, it's a big freakin' surprise. Trust my dick to come back to work with shit timing. Kate could file for harassment if I get a boner whenever she's near.

She slides away to the water below us. I watch her graceful, quiet moves. I like that she gets on and does things without flap or fuss. On that, we're aligned.

She returns, then hunches down and gently dabs my forehead—her breathing close, her scent subtly discernible.

"There, better already," she tells me.

"Am I decent?"

"After the lies you told, you'll never be that. So—we're staying how long?"

I shrug. "They're coming for us. Guesstimate they'll handle the villa situation and reassess our men at Katsaros' place."

"So we stay put. You're my bodyguard now?"

"Don't make me sound such a bad room buddy." I watch as she moistens her lips. "I don't snore. I'll keep watch for as long as I'm guarding you. Go lie down now. I won't encroach on your personal space if I can help it—well, not unless you want me to."

She doesn't move to go. Her gaze lingers on mine. "Thanks for what you did in the car. I may be pissed off at the situation. But you saved my life. If you hadn't been there to fire at them and keep me safe, I'd be with the driver too."

I gulp when her gaze travels over me. It feels positively

needy, and it blows me away because I really did not expect that from this woman. But it's hero complex. Nothing more. Drill that into your brain, buddy.

But my swelling dick ain't listening and it's making me horny. This close contact, sensing chemistry, feeling her need is the cause. The passion that's under the surface and could go boom with the merest spark is volatile. It's causing me untold heat and sparks jive around my body like thrill-seeking missiles.

"Shit, Katie. I don't know if I'm getting things wrong, but I think I need to back off and you need to have some space." I have to moisten my mouth by sipping from my water bottle because my brain isn't functioning on thoughts beyond sex.

"You're frightened of being around me?"

"You affect me. In ways I find hard to control."

And I just admitted that out loud. Fuck.

Sweet Jesus — happy place where are ya?

She stands up — she's demure, yet a sumptuous, sexy feast all at once. I realize that from up there she's gonna get a prime view of me sitting here with a growing dick.

And that's with three layers of clothes on.

I stand up. "Go. Get some rest. Do you good."

I'd do her good.

But she's not listening. "Why do I scare you, Dan?"

I move closer and cup her face in my hand. The other slides over her ass. Her peachy ass curve makes my dick cry out in exquisite torture.

"Because I want to kiss you. And fuck you. But I'm only here to do my job. But I'm a big boy. Trust me — I can restrain my urges. In case you hadn't noticed, we're not in an ideal situation for getting it on. Anyway — thought you hated my guts. What's changed?"

I remove my hand. As difficult as that move is, I have to.

Her eyes say she's not quite ready to quit yet.

"Maybe realizing life can be more fleeting than you know alters things." Her eyebrows draw together as my pulse fires into the crazy palpitation mode that happens when you're near to something hot and lethal, and it's a scary place called attraction. I know it and can feel it in my bones. But it's exciting scary. Especially when she looks as if she's challenging me to grab her and cease the talk, via the best human use of tongues.

Her hands creep over my chest and my boner's in full-on party mode.

"Would a kiss and a hug be out of the question?" she asks.

"You really know how to make an impact," I whisper.

She slowly brushes her thumb over my cheek. Her hand drifts over my face. Not touching the wound, but gently stroking around it. The merest of touches. But wow, the spot zings. My cock is now fully ready for intervention. "Why are you doing that, Kate?" My dick screams at me not to interfere. It's willing me to let it be soothed by her attentions. Let it go with the moment. Traitor dick needs its license revoked.

"Please let me kiss you," she asks, and pushes so boldly against my chest her tits autograph me with a sensual promise. "Why not?"

"Can't—job. It's how I roll. Protect and serve. Focus to the max."

Almost can't believe I'm resisting this. She's über hot. I must be crazy.

But I'm lying here because I'm already under her spell. Inside my head, as her lips meet mine, I'm yelling, *see — you were right to be nervous of this. Of her. This attraction should not be let loose. You'll regret it and you clearly can't trust yourself with this magnetizing minx.*

Her hands are on my shoulders and her lips travel to mine like warmed, honeyed wine. Her tongue opens my lips, and I welcome her in without a search warrant—or complaint. I'm frisking her fully with my crazy energized mouth as soon as she's inside. Wow, if this is kissing, then any previous attempts with other women have failed by a mile.

And that makes me need to investigate further. The detective info-seeking urge goes deep.

I kiss her with a ferocity that nearly lands us both on our asses. Kissing hard and fast, and my hands are all over that tight, sweet, warm body. Her breasts are divine. Hot and tight. The memory of that body at mambo and in the airport fires me further.

"You're in the danger zone, honey. You're sucking me in too."

"Maybe it feels safer than anywhere else," she whispers, while creating alchemy, involving lips and entwined bodies. Her hands steal around my shoulders and her blanket slips. It's probably in the water, but neither of us care. I ease off the leather and she blows my brain cells inside out when she starts unbuttoning her shirt. Then the jacket is tossed.

"Kate...take a moment." My buddies would not believe this resistance ethic — nor condone it.

But she doesn't answer or halt her strategic strip tease. Even the lightness of her breathing and gentle moans as we kiss have me craving more. So much for back-off orders. Am I really this easy? More to the point, is she? What's this about?

I kiss her with fervor, touching her peaking nipples through fabric, and moments later, I've a handful of her breast, encased in white lace bra. Can't see her nipples through the peekaboo 'cause it's too dark, but hell — getting a holy smoke reaction without further details. I simply don't want this kissing to stop. I want her areolas in my mouth. My dick inside her.

It's hot, she's so warm and welcoming, with a body made for sin, and I haven't even had a chance to fully ogle that perfect, gym-work honed chassis. She's too addictive to resist. My dick is on fire for the first time since Mexico, and it wants to take the lucky ticket home and celebrate.

She's the sex candy piñata. My stick's up for damage.

But something makes me tense. In fact this feeling has the power to negate the action — raw instinct. I heard something outside. A crack and a click. Two simple sounds and I'm primed.

"Stop." I halt her mid-kiss, with hands on each side of her head. "Wait!"

I stare at Kate as I process what's wrong here and she stares at me, prone. She knows something's amiss and we're in sync. But this has the acrid stench of not-right on the air.

My gun in is my hand in a heartbeat.

"What is it...?" Kate whispers, but I shush her with my finger on her lips. The need for silence is paramount. I keep the finger pressed there, and her eyes widen more.

I mouth, "Trust me," against her cheek.

She backs up as if in a trance. The best sexual promise of my life is on hold now. That raw electric charge moment passed as swiftly as it began, and she's shaking. Kate stoops for her jacket, shirt and blanket as I grip her arm and push her to the nearest boat. She's half-dressed by the time I watch her jump on the boat, then follow her on board. In a few fast moves I push her face-down inside the hull, then shake the blanket to cover her head to toe. Squeezing her arm in a silent promise, I jump out and creep, ninja silent and hugging the wall, to the steps.

My semi-automatic is ready to be fired when a brittle crack sounds starkly — a branch underfoot. An interloper's found our hideout. We're headed for a stand-off — could it be a gang? I suck in a breath, summon energy. We've unwelcome company and the party's about to be crashed.

Chapter Five

Kate

Dark, creeping fear chills my bones with foreboding and leaves me both tight as a high wire and spent with exhaustion. I hate it – but I hate Santorini more.

Dan's left me here alone, in the dark, under a blanket on the bare hull of a boat that is cold and hard. While he takes on a gang single-handed, gets killed and God only knows what.

It's not so easy to stay quiet as the grave when your teeth chatter from fear like wind-up joke shop toy teeth. I force mine together so hard my jaws ache. All is silent for an eternity.

There's no sound to suggest a gun-fight. The only things I'm aware of are my discomfort, my beating heart and my growing need to indulge in a long, misery-sating pee. We went so fast from crazy kissing – *was I mad, am I still in shock?* – to action movie antics resumed. It's exhausting for my fried nerves.

"So. You guys. What took ya?" I hear the words distinctly. Everything slows as I crane to hear.

I move slightly to alleviate my beach-ball bladder plight when I hear talking. Male voices. I stiffen and can't decipher more of what's said. I discern the men are close by. I want to scream full tilt. Or run for my life – and the jumping up and running thing is attractive while I'm lying here so vulnerable and soon to be in a pool of my own urine.

I count down in my head. One minute and I'll run. A slow counted minute. If they get nearer I'll spring and go. But then I hear a voice that's definitely Dan. It doesn't sound like a siege.

"You didn't think to warn us of this rescue? Where's the boat, I didn't hear it? Coulda called."

"Boat's nearby, came the last part on foot. Erred on the side of caution. You guys mighta been captive. Or dead. Where's our thanks for the rescue, Sir?"

They called him 'sir'. Is Dan top brass in this? Am I again at the foot of the facts stairs?

And with that nice, rousing, cheery thought, I begin to breathe fast under my blanket. Hyperventilating, I think it's called. Relief? Panic? Desperation? Confusion. Not sure.

My orb of a bladder is so buoyed at the thought of being rescued instead of perforated with bullets I almost let go. Dr. Kegels would so not be proud of my muscle control.

Dan's voice says. "Glad you're here, bud. Situation back at the villa controlled?" Then a pause and I feel the boat rock as somebody climbs aboard.

I also hear the words, "Tavi is dead. Killed outright, man."

"Hey, Kate. Come out, the rescue squad's here for showtime," Dan commands from above and whips away the blanket edge.

I'm greeted by bright light. Our previously dark cave is filled to spectacular effect and has me blinking and squinting. Like waking up in Narnia. I'm slightly confused but embracing that the threat's gone. My hairdo likely looks like it was styled in a bog village by the blind hairdresser everyone avoids.

"We're rescued?" I test my voice. It's croaky.

"Yup. Meet the team. Operation Mountain Goat Interpol Sex Crimes Agents, to be exact."

"S'okay. I can wait for proper introductions when my eyes can re-focus. I feel like I've just had laser surgery." I'm squinting as my eyes adjust, but there are four blurred figures distinguishable now. Four black-clothed, gunned-up, movie set typecast figures. Two Tom Cruise clones, an Italian Stallion and Angelina Jolie with more muscles. Each as gung-hoaction primed and cool as the next. Plus Dan.

They must be agents. They look like agents. They're more agent-ish than *CSI* meets *Hawaii Five-0* investigating a spy play and solving it in five seconds flat like a junior word search. But I'm still in a state of shock. So I sit there shaking and don't get up. I think the shock has immobilized me.

They must know one another, because I'm not even introduced. Bastards. To say I loathe this situation, like a leech with leprosy that's had a swim in a reeking cesspit of spew, is putting it mildly.

I've had the crap scared out of me too often in too few hours, and this lot waltz in all movie-set fresh and start water cooler banter while I'm a shivering wreck.

Then Dan spies me over his shoulder and approaches, hunkers down and re-wraps me in the blanket. Rubs my back. It seems he did the 'civilian pacification' module of his crime cracker course.

"Okay?"

I nod.

"Let me talk to the guys, then we're outta here soon as, 'kay?" He gives me a weak smile, then returns to his colleagues.

"So what's Redman's take?" Dan asks.

"Full debrief on return. We're not yet sure it's related to Katsaros. Might be a rogue coincidence? There's been a spate of shootings for valuables. Word could have leaked that the girl has connections. There's stuff gone from the villa."

"Didn't feel like a jewel or tech raid to me," says Dan. "Big gun for a busted burglary. Big holes in Tavi, for beginners."

I can listen in no more. I'm wishing I wasn't here or tied up in this. I knew my doomed honeymoon should have been a warning sign clue to prep me for shit to follow, and I should've point blank closed down Mel's plan or called in sick. Avoided Santorini and witnessing cold-blooded murder with Crazyhead Crimecracker Draven and his team of arsehole agents.

They're all talking too fast and in such techno jargon I can't keep up. One of them is doing things to a gun that makes me need smelling salts to watch. But a part of me cannot stay silent for longer.

I clear my throat and rise unsteadily. "Hi. Can I go to the bathroom? I think I'm going to either faint, wet myself or be sick."

"Ah, so this is our civilian friend," says the woman in a voice that says she's as happy to see me as an arachnophobic finding the tarantula family at a petting zoo.

The trio of black ops agents turn as a man and look at me as if they've trodden in better quagmires. None utter a word. The woman gawps, horrified, and one guy scuffs his boots as his expression reads 'how low can you go'.

I'm desperate or I wouldn't push. "I haven't had a pee since Athens. I really need to go."

It's as if Dan wakes up from a dream. To a reality where he's stuck with a civilian with a potty mouth and *pathetic wuss* running through the middle of her like Blackpool rock.

"Sure. Gotta code for the bunk room, guys? C'mon, get to it. Lady needs the rest room," Dan chivvies and one of the agents goes to tackle this fresh assignment.

"Baby needs a diaper," the woman adds. She's staring at me like mad, big hungry owls stare at tiny shrews in the corner of a barn—I'm feeling a sense of foreboding that I'm Mama Owl's next rodent taco.

So much for me thinking I might get a girl on my side. This sister's clearly gonna have to do it for herself. For that I'm going to nickname her Aretha. She really should know better and bust out to the Eurythmics when there's only two ladeez in this togetha! Has she learned nothing from Destiny's Child?

But the boys haven't figured out the keypad. I walk up, still wearing my blanket like a shroud. It's slightly galling they can't suss it, as it means I've over-estimated Interpol prowess. Surely if they can handle international crime at the highest level they should manage a few passcode numbers.

"C'mon, Rocco. Man. You got shit for brains — thank fuck we weren't down here needin' real action," says Dan surprising me with his alpha-twatish-ness. But then he is the leader in the mix — once a boss, always a boss.

Rocco does death stare eyes back. "Right man. Big FBI Interpol thing called prick ego always knows better huh?"

"You're a big freakin' shade o' funny ya know that? Plannin' to take me on?" Dan answers.

Shit. Will they fight? Is this what happens when there's no action on an assignment? They just punch shit out of one another instead?

I can wait no longer and if fighting's going to go down I want to just sit it out in the WC. "Effing stop it! Now that you're all nicely reacquainted, can we keep the ruckus for later — is it too much to ask to use a ruddy loo?" I shout. I really am about to embarrass myself.

The male trying to sort the code quips at Dan — he's tall and as Italian-looking as a leaning tower and a square of pizzerias — "Caught yourself a choice one, Bullet Man. Nice and riled. Is she always like this or have you worked her over especially just so she's out of control? Cozy in here just two of you, I'm thinkin', did we break up a private party?"

Dan — he of the handsome chiseled jaw, tight butt, washboard pecs discernible through the T-shirt, fancy police credentials and James Bond moves — just stares. Yes. Him. He doesn't even wise-crack his buddy. Bastard.

"Thanks for sticking up for me," I say.

Only now do I remember that we were almost at intercourse only half an hour before. Almost. I flaming well stripped off ready and willing like a poodle at a primp parlor about to be blow-dried.

And if his kisses and moves hadn't been stellar enough to give me a total wake-up call, I might just be holding it all totally against him. Unfortunately for me, I sense he'll be brilliant at sex crimes. As well as solving them.

"She's always like this, Rocco. Maybe just up a couple of octaves," Dan answers. He flicks me a sassy grin. "That's what happens when girls have to piss. Camels for the most part, then kamikaze when the time comes."

I snark, "He wouldn't know. He doesn't know me. He's a fake and a fraud and he got me here under false pretenses. After I have a pee and get the strength up I'm going to whip his ass. You see if I don't!"

"Woo, Bullet. You've so met your match," says Italiano Rocco. I'd quite like to slap his face too.

I narrow my eyes at Dan. "Is the nickname because you're easily fired? Or lotsa noise and mess but not much conversation?"

"Licensed to kill, babe. Nobody takes me down," Dan answers, but I see his cheek twitch. He'd either like to laugh or kill me. He's definitely pissed I've called him out in front of his hard-ass friends.

Then the woman of the team comes close so she's standing beside me. She fixes me with her cool blue gaze. "I'm Havana. Havana Martinez." I note she doesn't hold out a friendly hand. "Let's get this straight. He may be a dickwad but he's one of my best partners and we're kinda relying on his pulling this mission off. So the next time you dis him you'll have me to deal with. I never play nice. Got that? Civilian or no civilian — we don't dis Sir."

I'm doing so very well today.

"Can't I plead special privileges?"

She grins. Then her jaws snap down like a shark. "Shouldn't'a played hard ball, missy pants."

Now all I need is to lose control of my urine stream and my life's officially in meltdown.

I say nothing in case she beats me up. But I'm huffy as a room of thirteen year olds with full hormones on parade. Normally I'd swear and get lippy but I sense this woman definitely knows martial arts at expert level, and could probably stop me breathing using only one finger such are her *badassery* smarts.

"Nice. Touching. When's the wedding? You having sumo wrestling as a theme? Grenades as a center-piece?"

I do always lose it when I need a wee.

In a matter of seconds something vice-like is around my neck and I'm seeing stars. Havana's eyes are way too close to mine. The squeeze thing gets tighter.

I hear the words, "Easy there, Hav. She's only pushing buttons."

"See how she likes her freakin' buttons being twisted, huh?" says Bananas Havana. Nice that I won't need to call her Aretha — when Bananas Havana is so much better for such a finessed lady. Probably went to finishing school in Switzerland with nunchucks. Followed by High Security Prison executive suite.

Dan takes control. "Havana, put Kate down. Stop it, Kate. You don't know what you're messing with."

"*Robocop* in a bra!" I answer.

I can't reply more because of the breathing thing. I'm hauling in air like a deck-bound dolphin. Not pretty.

"Yey! Knew I'd crack the bastard," says Rocco, and the door to the bunk room springs wide.

I stagger in. Holding my throat and gulping air. Then I start to run for it, knowing that it's going to be a close call if I make it. I bolt the door in case Bananas enters to finish me off.

Five blissful minutes later I have to walk back out to meet the squad with a raging red face and a deflated bladder.

"So let's not wait around here. Get her covered up. Grab the bags."

I don't know who's saying it. But Dan's got me by the arm, and by this time, I'm letting life pass me by as I'm treated like a priority criminal being smuggled out with press waiting.

I'm almost getting my lungs working by the time they bundle me along, two agents carrying me somewhere. Eventually, I'm laid down on my behind. It's in a boat because after my boat-hiding thing I'm now a nautical expert. I can feel the motion — smell the water. I hear the loud, vibrating zoom of a speedboat motor to confirm it. I wonder if I'm going to further mar my day by getting sea-sick in a boat under a blanket.

"Can I take off the cover?" I ask whoever cares to listen.

Dan answers. "Hunker down."

"Might be sick if I don't."

"Realizing you like your body functions, don't ya, Katie?"

I'm still pissed off and raging so I can't stem the retort. "I've even been known to bite men's tongues out. Shame I didn't think of that earlier, you fucking bastard shit." The hiss feels therapeutic.

But I hadn't twigged that Havana was on my other side, and now she's staring at us both as if we just set her favorite lingerie on fire and melted her hair straighteners. I'm sensing our Bananas may have a thing going for Dan the Man.

And I'm going to wind up in a holding cell with her planning how to best torture me. An untimely demise awaits. Maybe I should've kept the blanket on? Or my mouth shut.

I'm certain of only one thing right now. Not where I'm going. Or what I'm going to have to do to get out of this mess. Or even if I'll actually survive. As I said, I'm certain of only one thing — how much I hate Dan Draven and how at some point — if I do live to escape this shit situation — he is going to pay for his bloody treachery in a very painful fashion.

* * * *

When we get to our destination I'm blanket-blindfolded again. Dan says it's for security reasons, but I figure it's because he just likes to piss me off. When I emerge from various walks with twists and turns, the blinkers are removed. I've woken up in an Arctic polar scape. Things are very white. There are no windows.

"Hello. I'll bet you don't know your down from your sunny side up but I'm here to put the perk in your pep," says a voice with a discernible accent. Russian, Czechoslovakian, Ukrainian, Transylvanian? Despite the accent the lingo is definitely Stateside mastered. Via bad TV shows methinks.

I'm not sure, but being here in this no-windowed room, having been dropped off by gun-strapped agents, feels kinda like the stuff of Bond missions. Minus Daniel Craig jumping in with his steely eyed, passionate kisses.

The man with the accent and the strange lines is staring at me. He's no Agent Top Dog. He looks as if he should be on a live demo on the Cookery Channel meets a friendly Hell's Angel Biker Club stalwart. He's wearing a black and white bandana, an apron covered in lipstick print, and the air around us is thick with soy sauce and ginger and something that makes my stomach howl with love—I haven't eaten more than a finger of toast today, give me a break here.

"Woo. Somebody's hungry." The man grins like a circus sideshow host. "Wanna join us for supper? Maybe you'd prefer to eat alone for your first night? They don't do great table manners—could scare a girl off. Choice of noodle surprise or garlic gluttony pasta. Home baked rosemary focaccia on the side or prawn crackers—Bullet Man's favorite. Crème Brulee to follow. Asian, Italian-fusion *God knows what* is my theme for the menu most nights! Afraid we're eating late—one of those days. Happens here—no different from a job in Wal-mart. All hands on deck."

Now this is weird. Weirder than waking up in a Muppet Movie and learning yours is the piggy suit and Kermit's your leading man.

We're near a big white table in a fancy industrial kitchen. I'm sitting with Mr. Fat Cook Smiley Agent, and there's nobody else. Just us. A massive table that's set for dinner with twenty seats and nobody but us crazy clueless chickens at it.

"You should eat first before the mob get here. I'll keep you company. The team aren't very good around ladies. Likely to stare."

"Can somebody please fill me in on what is going the hell

on? Where's Dan now?" I ask. He just marched off with the other Stormtroopers with no explanation, likely in search of galaxy domination. Me caring is stupidity unbridled. I hate him. He's Fucker Numero Uno. So why play elbow buddy with Mr. Set Me Up and care where he's gone? Um...because he's the nearest I have to anything verging on a friend here. Without him I'm burned toast.

"He'll be back. Big debrief...sorry, how rude of me. We haven't been properly introduced. Allow me. I'm Warbuckle but you can call me Warbie. I'm the Fabric Convener — I deal with food, supplies, everything to do with a happy ship in our little Santorini home. You are our latest guest — which means I get to pick out some fancy linen and make you a cozy nest. We even have designer sheets. I'm guessing you might like taupe as a preference? I have a very nice snazzy set. Jewel accents."

"Excuse me?"

"You finding it all a tad tricky to take in?" says Warbuckle. Blinking like *Kung Fu Panda* is wont to do. Warbuckle. Imagine — what a name. Did he make it up? Is he really real? Did he really just offer me bedazzled bedding when I'm in a spy hole?

"This is Santorini Interpol HQ–Troika base. Hidden away from prying eyes underneath the island — a mecca for our mission. A bit like a thirty bed hotel subterra, and we're all persona non grata. We do great parties sometimes though. Shots until you're shot. I mean, even agents get to let down their hair and shake it all out there. For the most part it's all keep tabs on bad guys and plan to catch them unawares. But dinner time's where the action starts — the fights usually break out over dessert. Sometimes there's blood but I'm a qualified First Aider so we're cool. Fun, huh?"

I honestly am gob-fucking-smacked.

"So where are we? Under Oia?"

"Damn straight. Well, not quite beneath the village — we're out toward the forest land to the east. Tunneled below. Main base goes right down, with room for speedboats and submarines storage. There's a helicopter base to consider too. We've other outlying bases all over the island, but this is the daddy. Give you the tour of this place soon enough. Once the others come back from the bollocking from Mr. Big, we'll be free to wander." He holds up a drag queen hand. "Within reason, honey. You do realize you can't leave. You're ours now!" He says it like the pantomime baddie, then pisses himself laughing. "Just a liddle jokette!"

"Can't leave. For how long, exactly?"

"However long it takes. Certainly not until the job's done and we let you go. Waaaaay too dangerous to let you out under current conditions."

"Mr. Big?"

"Rich Redman. Interpol's Ayatollah. He's mightily pissed that his plan to ease you in gently has been badly breached. Suspected leak. Bullet Man Dan won't be able to sit on his behind for weeks. Such a cute ass too—you've probably noticed. Man, is he going to pay for that gaffe. Top tip—be kind to him for a few days. I hear you're quite the shrew when your wind's up."

"Um. It wasn't exactly Dan's fault. We were shot at. He didn't do anything to cause this." I can't quite believe I'm sticking up for him, but there it is. Go figure.

"Oh but it was, honey. He didn't call ahead about the delays at the airport. He failed to accept the second agent in the car—said you'd ask too many questions. Made a big fuss about it when he called in. The agents were a bit too glib about Villa security checks. Havana's tits are on the line. So, somebody has to take the can. May as well be the newest addition to the island—so DanBoy gets a crown of thorns. It's okay, hon. He's a mean motherfucker. He knows how to take it. He's had plenty of experience. Kinda likes the ugly, badass side of the sheets. Anyhoo, but enough of Dan's dirty little proclivities."

That little insight makes my flesh prickle with interest, and something in my abdomen dances the Lambada. Dan likes it badass. I want to know more.

Warbuckle goes over to the steaming wok of food and swishes and tosses with aplomb. I smell the soy. I salivate for the ginger. My stomach has fallen for him in a big way. Wow, those smells are divine. If there's water chestnuts and bamboo shoots I may just love him forever.

"Eat? Come on, peaches. When the others come in there won't be a scrap left. Never is. Rocco would lick the plates clean and rub his ass over the table if we let him."

"Nice. Met him earlier and figures."

"Actually he's bravest of the brave. Trust him with my life. Dan, most of all."

Warbuckle ladles steaming noodles and stir-fried heaven into a wide ceramic bowl and hands it to me, plus fork. "Come to the table — get some nourishment. A girl can't think straight without food. No wonder you've been acting like a loopy loop without a limo. Heard that Havana wants to take your throat out. Nice girl to pick for a sand pit fight. She'll tear you limb from limb." He laughs like a maniac in a psychiatric ward sketch. "Be in no doubt she will win."

"You haven't seen me in action."

"True. Point to you."

I take the bowl and sit, realizing I'm a touch wobbly and weak. Maybe it's just the reminder that Havana wants to kill me. My feet are unsteady just travelling the short distance to the table, and my hand is shaking with the fork.

He notices. "My dear love. Brandy — you need a medicinal snifter."

"What is it with agents and the brandy thing?"

"Basic training protocols. Give the civilian in shock brandy. Or hot tea and a biscuit sometimes works. Failing that, shove them in a blanket or knock them out."

A brandy is duly delivered, and I down it without any quibble, grateful nobody has as yet punched me. I suspect I may now have been inducted into having a brandy habit on the sly. I'm so hungry, I manage to stuff the noodles down. I must look like a tramp eating from trashcans, with soy sauce splashing over my chin. But, such is my shaking and abject hunger, I can't help it. I eat as much as I can and I fall back replete.

"Can't eat more. Might be sick," I confide. "Sorry. It's the shock. It was lovely."

"Ah," says Warbuckle. "I know just what you need. Just the thing for trauma." Moments later he's bring a bottle of high proof vodka and shot glasses. It has a fancy Russian crest on it as if it's been handed down from generations of Russian aristos. Perhaps bottled by Rasputin himself. Should I be worried?

"Um. I'm no expert but I've had brandy. Isn't mixing drinks unwise?"

"You're with Interpol. We ain't scared, Lovie dove. What our leader doesn't know won't hurt him and you, my darling peach-tree, have had a thoroughly shit day. Vodka on the rocks." He pours two shots and nudges one toward me. "Down in one. Boom yeah. Another?"

I shudder, then nod. I take the small glass between my fingers and follow orders. Then accept the refill.

"Atta girl. Think I'm gonna like you. You're just what we need here to brighten this crappy joint up. You bring some easy breeze to black ops bland."

The vodka burns my digestive tract like toxic diesel fuel. I'm coughing and my eyes are watering when I look up into the cold gray gaze of somebody who's just silently walked through the door to see me getting lashed on vodka shots.

"Having fun?"

Dan watches me, Batman-faced. He clocks the shot glass in my hand. He should come with the subtitle *unable to be sociable*. He's Wild Bill Hicock to my Calamity Jane. It worries me that he's just seen me drinking down Sasparillas, and he has a gun.

And marksmanship smarts.

"Ah. It's Sore Butt himself. Wanna shot, Bullet Man? C'mon—draw up a pew," Warbie baits him. Has he been on the cooking sherry all day?

"On duty," he spits out. "As are you."

I'm sensing an eggshells and tippy toes scenario. Dan could be about to blow big time. I watch his eyes dance, and the cord that tics in his neck is doing body-pops. If he has been chastised or hurt, he isn't walking strangely. But he doesn't look happy either.

"Settling in?" he asks darkly. "Warbie, you damn dillweed, get the lady triple-strength java pronto — I've orders to take her to meet the boss. As for you, my drama-stirring peace wrecker of a brain-frying female," he says, squaring me in his sights and it makes me gulp. "We'll chat later about things you won't do with Warbie. Or any male agent for that matter. Number One — alcohol — severely punishable at my hands. From now on I'm 'Sir' to you and you submit to my every command."

"Now, there's an offer," whispers Warbie, before vacating the table at speed. Warbie doesn't make anything better when he whispers over his shoulder. "Think we're in trouble. Jeez. Somebody's caught a major case of the crankies."

Dan fixes Warbie in his sights. "She's not like most people. She's not agent standard." Dan breathes fury flames like a dragon with a sore throat and an off-scale fever. "You deserve kicked asses — quit the besties chitty-chat and get the hell to it, *now!*"

Chapter Six

Kate

Dan leads me down a long, dark, rock-hewn corridor. I'm no geological boffin, but I'm sure we're deep in the earth's creepy bowels — I once did a news story on naturist potholers which made me avoid venturing below ground ever since. Naked men braving punishing cold temps by choice with their knobs out can do that to a girl.

I'm about to confide it to Dan but stop myself. These things have likely only popped into my head because I'm high on coffee and booze. So high, I'm ready for scaling the piped lighting like a radioactive ninja spider.

And I think Dan senses it, because he's staring at me strangely. "Why do you try to piss me off so hard?" he asks, grinding the words as if ventriloquism may be a new leisure time hobby.

"Exsqueeze me but maybe my actions aren't all about you?"

"Oh, I think you know exactly what you're doing. You're causing enough trouble to make me think involving you is a huge mistake."

I'm ready for sparring. Never start a fight with someone who's drunk booze too fast and been through too much high stress. "If you'll wind your ego in a notch you may just part your delusions enough to see the real view, Agent Narcissist."

Dan glares at me and shakes his head while his jaw does clench press-ups. I'm stuck here with this black ops cop, who's more than a tad storm-clouded touchy. His muscles are positively bristling. His body language screams fucking fucked-off to fuck and back.

But he doesn't scare me. Maybe I've a death wish that way.

"Jeez. Why do you lurch between okay and uptight so much? Are you bipolar? You should have assessments done and get meds."

"Don't fucking push me. I'm totally ready to do harm to something or someone," he growls.

Dan's aggressive attitude bugs me. As do the noodles I ate, now playing havoc with my innards. Probably wasn't a good idea to eat fast after high stress. I may throw up before the big bad international policing supremo I'm being led to. Perhaps on his shoes. 'Cos I'm acing all bases today.

I feel like singing—and that only ever happens with vodka, a reason I usually avoid it. "I swear if I sing down here it would echo back for weeks," I try to lure Dan into conversation. It doesn't help my plight.

"Please refrain. Unless you'd prefer I gag you. Could be arranged."

I blame the spirits combo for my rambling. "I could do a great rendition of the Let Me Out, You Nutjobs Overture? Why not tell me about some of this?" I mutter. "The police job. That there might be more to this assignment than was presented. A few hints even. This is all too much of a bombshell to cope with sober."

"You're not sober."

Which winds me up further. "And with justification. You've taken me back to bad places I don't want to visit. *Circle of Life*. Elton John wrote that song and Sir Elton knows stuff. *The Lion King* happens to be my fave movie."

Dan stops me with a large hand on my arm. "Nice window. Please just shut the fuck up. I've had a lion's share of bad day."

He keeps me held in his grip. As if he's scared I'll go AWOL. I've jumped from VIP Interpol guest to mistrusted ne'er-dowell. He takes cuffs out from his back pocket and closes them over my wrists, one at a time.

"Why?" I squeak. At the pinnacle of what I can take in the downers department.

"Technically, I'm not supposed to cuff you. You're a civilian and this is liable to get me in a shitload of grief. But frankly, my trust in you is completely kaput. So the cuffs stay until you calm the fuck down."

I pout. "So now I'm the liabloodybility?"

"You are. I couldn't tell you squat—strict orders. Doin' my job. Haven't we been through this, Katie? And FYI—the team are the best there is in life-ontheline situations, but put a woman with your ass and eyelashes in here an' things are gonna get loco. Six different agencies together—stray dogs at feedin' time. When the chips are down, I'm alpha wolf— just to be clear on the issue. You've made a hard situation a hell of a lot worse." He lets out a long breath that has his chiseled cheekbones doing overtime.

"Don't Katie me. I see the 'call me Kate' thing didn't last. It's Kate. How many times until you get it right?" But you know me and booze. I can't resist an ego jab opportunity. "And for your info, Alpha Wolf? In your dreams, *Wile E. Coyote*."

His nose meets mine, and he yanks the cuffs so hard I yelp. "Quit it. Damn straight I'm top cop here. They'll be flirting with you so hard it'll blow your tiny mind. Your orders from me are to avoid being alone with any of 'em. Warbie being an exception, but I'll give you rules of play. No drinking. No crazy stuff. In social time, you stay around me."

I bite because I'm pissed at his orders, and the alcohol doesn't help my restraint any. "Like I'll listen." My mind drifts like a butterfly visiting a rose garden. Maybe he's right and my mind is tiny? "Warbie's kind, not lecherous. My gaydar's flawless, and he's officially in the camp that prefers show tunes and sequins." Dan's eyes roll, but I'm on a verbal diarrhea roll. "Warbie's my only friend in this messed-up underworld where Havana hates me and I'm clueless, controlled, and now cuffed without sanction." I shake my wrist as proof. "You told him I'm 'not like most people' and definitely not 'agent standards'. Nice slice."

Dan stares then he sighs and unlocks the cuffs with reluctance. "I was reprimanding him, not you. I meant what I said about the guys — especially Rocco. Keep distance. As for Havana, she hates everybody. You really think you'd've come if you'd known the real deal?"

He has a point. I shake my head. "Havana doesn't hate everybody. She has a big, glowing soft spot for you that's somewhere censored." See. That's the booze talking. I'd never have said that sober. Not in a million.

I'm gratified when his cheeks burn. "You're more vital to this mission than you know. But I'm not the one who can tell you all. My boss, Redman, is. So keep your head straight and just go with me on this."

Dan stares at me. Gray eyes probing. Why am I such a sucker for pale-gray eyes and cow-like curly dark lashes on men? Ooft — loser. Maybe it isn't helped by the rippling muscles, the gun in a chest holster, like all my sexy action guy movies morphed into one man, and the fact that I watched him go to work like a crime-cracking ninja earlier before my very boggling eyes.

With the best pecs and tightest ass ever witnessed.

It's sexy. He's sexy — but I shouldn't let myself be affected. He's lied, he's cheated. He's probably going to be the cause of me doing awful things. I start breathing rapidly. He's seen me on the plane so he must know that this is a sure sign I'm about to spring a sob leak.

"Do not cry," he says. He's holding my hand and stroking the skin on the back of it. It soothes. But I wish he wouldn't do that.

"Why are you trying to be my friend when you're the one who got me into this shit?"

"Maybe I care how this works out for you."

I'd love to believe him. I really would. Especially when the way he says 'Katie' causes an entirely new enticing and comforting experience to skitter down my spine. This is new — scarily new. But I go over the top because it's too late to stop. "Stop being nice, you police bastard."

Dan raises his eyebrows. He's bulletproof to my insults and hissy-fits. I couldn't have expected anything less. "Katie suits you and I like it." He stops to tuck a strand of my hair behind my ear. "By the way. I really liked it when we kissed. More than liked. You carjack my mind. That's a fucking bad thing."

"Shame. All I want to do in future is kick you hard in the privates."

No smiles, but again those eyebrows say what words wouldn't. "C'mon then. Give me your best shot." He doesn't flinch or move aside. Just stands there wearing his black gear and high-necked sweater, with weapons on show as if to say — my *cojones* are made of steel, come and have a go if you think you have the mettle.

I figure I don't. I can't even shoot a water pistol straight at a pool party, never mind a gun. These expensive runningshop acquired training shoes were crap for walking in the woods, never mind testicle disabling. I'm a crap shot with the remote control, let alone something with ammunition trajectory capacity.

He's out of my league. I'd do well to admit it.

"I'm not going to kick your balls, Dan. Much as I'd like to."

"Thanks. There are other things I'd much rather you did to them." Fuck, he's blushing beet-red, but at least he had the bravery to say it out loud. For a hard ass he's way too bloody shy.

I grin. "In your dreams, pal."

Dan reaches out, and traces the side of my face with his thumb. "You will be. Oh Katie, what you do to me...you send me fucking wild and you don't even see it or try. I never cross lines at work."

This, I really did not expect. "What would Havana say? She's hot for you."

"Who the fuck cares? There's only one woman who's driving me crazy right now. You."

I narrow my eyes to block the flattery assault. "She wants to rub privates with you, Bullet Man. License to thrill."

He's closer than close. I feel his breath on my cheek. "No dice with Havana. But open offer stands for further investigations with you. Do you copy that, Joseph? I'm game if you are?"

Shit, wow and how the hell did that just happen? He's skimming my cheek with his fingers and making something go melty and warm in a very special place called my lady bits. Really, I should have left that particular pussy at home in Blighty in a cattery, under lock and key, if it's going to betray me so badly now. It's so hungry and lustfogged it's almost mewing to be stroked. Or given a catnip and kapok-filled sausage.

Dan's only touched my face, for fuck's sake. I only have one set of undies. These ones are damp at his hand and hot as the wrapper of a takeaway steak sandwich.

"I want more. I want it all. All the ways we can think of."

"Don't touch. Breakages must be paid for." Why did I say that? Brain fart. Booze blip. Why did I bloody blurt that? Brandy. Vodka. Shit. There I was thinking I was bad on Sambuca.

"I'd break you, all right. But you'd want every single stinging second," he brags.

I have no bloody clue why I say the things I do around him. It tends to be the first foolish, trite thing that pops into my head, and I just blurt it like a ratty drunk at a cab rank at midnight.

"Okay. Let's pencil that in as a future possible, shall we?"

Fortunately, Dan smiles. "You've no idea how cute you are when you're half-scared, half-angry and fit to throttle me. The brandy and vodka vibe suits you too." He goes into his pocket. "Here. Suck this mint. Don't want the boss man smelling booze."

He pops the mint between my lips. Then softly puts his

mouth over mine and slides his tongue inside it. My agent just gave me a minty candy. He really likes me—he does, he does. He's promising rude trysts for randy stuff in my future. Talk about winner!

Then, fuck me backwards with a pitchfork, but his lips descend on mine and he's kissing me again—hungrily. I've a mint in my mouth, but neither of us care. He's eating my mouth with nips and demands and entreaties by tongue. Yes, Sir. His lips are warm as toast that's been left for just the right amount of cool down—I'm a toast fan, so sue me. Believe me, his don't need butter or jam to get sweeter. He's like sherry wine plus tequila shots merged into one beautiful, oral mind bender.

I open my mouth under his and let his tongue tantalize like only a multi-skilled Interpol guy, who's qualified in the oral kissing alchemy module of his police work, can.

His tongue demands. His ramped breathing makes my vagina walls do rampant, undulating things. The touch of his fingers and the feel of his arms around me is a sexual curveball that every nerve ending responds to with a big flag emblazoned with the neon words *yes, more*.

And my sex drive is screaming like a siren to sign up for the course, if this is a taster. If kissing was a commando, he'd be the one made into a statue and honored on a yearly basis by passing troops.

I'm kissing back furiously and pushing into his body. My nipples are talking to his chest one-onone in a language all their own. I'm almost purring with avarice at his attentions. I'm guessing if I looked up an online dictionary, this would be my personal definition of displacement therapy? But when it feels this good in your sex parts, why not?

"Christ, you make me do bad things," he groans as he pulls away, acting as if I'm a bloody snake charmer with a flute, and he's some defenseless reptile. "I'm at fucking work here. This is breaking every code."

"If you wanted your mint back you only had to ask."

He emits a wry chuckle. "You are some suck tease. I love

it. I want to make you pay."

"Now I'm the bad one? Who kissed who? Who lied to who?"

"Do you know they say witches used to wear lipstick to tempt men?"

"What are you saying here?"

"You always reapply that damn lipstick—I've watched. You even have it back on now, is it in your pocket or something? Are you some kind of temptress? You and that Roseberry lip pencil thing. You override my better judgment with your lip black magic."

I shatter his 'sexy witch' accusation by doing bug eyes at him. "Doh! Not wearing any lipstick now. Not even gloss. How did you know it's Roseberry?"

"Interpol, sweet cheeks. How tough could it be? You smell great too."

I pull myself up, getting haughty. "I'm not wearing deodorant presently. Does body odor and the smell of fear usually turn you on?"

His hands tell me yes when they slide over my butt in a firm, slow caress.

"I wish you weren't wearing underwear," Dan says. I gasp. His tone is pure grizzly bear in need of a lumberjack snack. It knocks me for a cricketing century. "It's a thong, right, tell me that's a thong..."

I step back. "Given that I have no luggage, no hotel, no remit, no clue how the fuck to proceed—there's every chance I'll be knickerless by the end of the night. Happy now?"

He winks. His eyes sparkle with chemistry unleashed into fireworks.

"Hey Bullet Dick, LoserBrain," someone calls after a long whistle has split the air—and my eardrums. "They're waiting for you. What's keeping ya—other than your hardon?"

"Rocco," Dan says behind closed teeth, then yells to him. "Beat it, numb nuts."

77

"Bugger," I mutter. "This kind of interruption never happens in the movies. I think you need to tell the scriptwriters and put them straight. You're supposed to surprise the girl and have uninterrupted, if overly fast and passionate, but mutually satisfying sex, then move to the next scene. You're not fulfilling the promise."

"I'm not a spy, Katie. I'm a cop." His gray gaze makes a stark promise to prove it. "Do I kiss like a guy who wouldn't fulfil?"

Given that something impressive and loaded is pressing against my leg, and I'm still quivering for more of his kissy kiss stuff, he has a point. I'm still spinning in the aftermath of satisfaction interrupted. Dan has a spark, oh yes, and how. A spark that blasts through my ballsy barricades and leaves me covered in the rubble of yearning.

"We better move our asses."

I widen my eyes and follow him. Again I've no choice—dragging motion, big, strong boy who has me by the hand, you get the picture.

And while I'm following, all my brain sees is Dan's behind and I'm hypnotized. It is a very pretty backside. In the throes of passion it will be like smooth skin-covered steel. I bet he has muscles in that behind like an Olympian. In my mindscape it's a thing of beauty. Worthy of a whole lifedrawing course all on its own.

And I'm being held by the business end. About to be dragged before his big, bad boss of doom—slightly drunk, plus a measure of blurt-happy dangerous.

* * * *

"The movies don't lie, do, they?" I'm taking it all in and clambering over my dumbstruck awe. Checking it out—blinking some more. Knowing that after my brief adventure in Black Ops Wonderland I'll never relive this kind of experience again. Thank God.

It's techno flash-tastic.

"What movies?" Dan asks. He's so annoyingly blasé about his top drawer devil-may-care gun-carrying-license-holding Tom Cruiseness.

"Bond. Spies. Agents. Doing the do. *Mission Impossible*." I motion around us. It's more James Bond than a James Bond sound stage, with an orchestra playing the big brass theme tune, while Connery shushes his s sounds.

Dan doesn't answer. Which I take as a macho silent *I've no idea what you're on about, woman.* Hell he probably never goes to the movies — he's too busy polishing his guns.

"I'm saying, your day job is what the little boys dream about. All this is a movie backdrop — with me in it."

We're surrounded by high-tech bleeping gadgetry and more flash kit than a flagship Apple store in space. Dan says he's police, not spy league — I'm thinking otherwise from the stuff on show. I'm hazarding all these gizmos aren't for recording CCTV tapes or watching live sport over a beer and peanuts like the cops did back on my news patch. There are surveillance TVs to fit an entire wall and there is lots of activity being monitored on them by black ops minions.

"Wow," I breathe. I turn around to take in the admin agents at desks, manning monitors, with headsets and rapt attention. Like the highest spec badass call center ever. Call A Kill? Murder Dot Com? I defy anyone — even with my lack of IT ken — not to be bowled over at this, the pinnacle of all crime capture dojos worldwide.

"Just tools of the trade for catching hard nuts. These days policing *is* tech. Hardly a big surprise."

Then a profound thought occurs to me — it doesn't happen often, but sometimes I do have Einstein moments, and this is one. "With all this stuff, how come you were caught out when Tavi got shot?" See. I am a reporter for a reason — just call me Jeremina Paxman, I thank you.

"The villa security system was overridden. Bastards pulled a coup. Boy, are they gonna pay. Every system is fallible, Katie. Even the best of the best."

He's just popped my air balloon of wisdom, but I let out a low whistle at the impressive stuff that's going down here anyway. Which is probably the uncool response I'm not supposed to let myself make.

A shadow at the far wall in front of a stadium-sized screen turns with full drama. I can sense this must be *the moment*. He must be *the boss*. THE BOSS. It's almost worthy of a theme tune and a scantily clad dance troupe in silver leotards.

But a bizarrely normal voice says, "Welcome, Kate Joseph. I see our search party finally found you." The voice may be normal. The attitude is as commanding as an honored sea captain in a turbulent high winds squall.

I chance a peek at Dan for a steer on how to play this but his *Iron Man* countenance is fully in place. The 'what kept you' comment has me wondering if he's seen us snogging? Let's face it—he has tech. Wouldn't be a stretch for a snog cam. Then again, this man has bigger mad murdering fish to fry. Or does he? Does snogging on company time trump all sins in this subterranean spy world?

Will I or won't I get reamed out for not running to Bigman's summons and dallying with Draven's tongue temptations?

"Apologies for the delay. I'm a bit frazzled to be honest," I tell him. "Good to meet you at last Mr...er...I'm afraid I don't know your name."

Dan looks at me. His cheek is vise-clenched. I'm guessing this is not the way to talk to the Commanding big knob.

But the boss gets closer and smiles, affable charm personified. "Rich Redman at your service, Agent R. Sorry we've kept you waiting so long. But you realize we've had developments on the ground since your arrival. It's made a deep impact—but you're here now, good. Draven—try not to detain our guest repeatedly, won't you?"

He's seen us. I don't need to see Dan's expression now to know it. But what's done is done so I play brazen and straighten my spine. "Very pleased to meet you, Sir," I realize I sound exactly like Bridget Jones employing her 'faking professional voice'.

Renee Zellweger doppelganger. "And very pleased to be alive and not dead at this present moment. Alive, even if underground and with no idea what I'm doing here, is very much better than having no heartbeat to work with." See—full Bridget on parade. Complete with foot in mouth medals and a side of brain dead.

Both men are staring at me. Do I blame them?

I do a *Wallace and Gromit* slice of smile, knowing they're likely thinking I've been on the sauce, which I have, including buckets of coffee chasers.

My hand is squeezed—a definite signal from Dan to shut the eff up. So I do. After all, his job's on the line. I give him a look that says 'I'm done now, take it from here, Mr. Snake Hips Special Ops'.

The Big Boss before me is not what I expect of Interpol's Top Rank Supremo. He walks fully forward into a pool of light, and he's blond with a buzz cut do that wouldn't be out of place on a young and trendy vicar. Somewhat petite and dressed in a dapper fashion, with a tie and round spectacles. More like an insurance man than the big cheese responsible for all the licenses for killing peeps. Rich would fit right in at a *University Challenge* Final.

But then his smile halts. I notice the slightly crazed, Jack Nicholson staring eyes when he's thinking. Now I see why they're running shit-scared. In a second the mad look fades as fast as it came. But it's left a stark brand on my heart. New psycho boss on the block.

"Shall we move into the meeting chamber for privacy?" He directs us, and we follow his lead. Inside is a table and chairs and we cozy down. As much as you can with Interpol top brass in an underground stone lair with steel furniture and no tea and biscuits.

"So we meet at last. I'm sorry you've had such a stressful introduction. I'd hoped to do this with rather more finesse, at your leisure, but it sadly was not to be."

I stare at Dan's boss, thinking—frightened of him? Really—it's a bit like being frightened of the effeminate Geography teacher with the mismatched suits and spotted hanky habit.

Then he throws me like a boomerang by sitting back and crossing his hands behind his head. "So for the nuts and bolts of our operation, you, my dear Ms. Joseph, are key to our plans."

The screen behind me flashes up a face that sends my innards into freefall, because it's the last face I expect to see. Not here. Certainly not now.

"Oh God no!" I exclaim in dismay.

"Grey Donaldson," says Rich softly. "Though I don't need to tell you who he is."

Dan says nothing. Nor do I.

The air is redolent with the smell of raw shit that's hit at full speed mother of all fans.

Rich clears his throat. "Your AWOL, presumed-dead father."

The man doesn't beat about the bush. Even long-hidden gooseberry ones.

"I know who he is." Just would've preferred not to have a reminder flashed up on a screen. Did they have to create a PowerPoint for my destruction? Plus, I'm starting to get a bad feeling about this whole me being here at all thing.

"You see, Ms. Joseph," he says, and I recognize his smooth Brit Received Pronunciation tones are worthy of a National Theatre Actor, "what you perhaps are not aware of, given your estrangement from your father for many decades, is that he is Katsaros' key henchman. His partner in crime. His most vital 'plan-hatching' partner, nay, the very linchpin to this operation here in Santorini. He is not dead as you were told. The death was faked after he was released from prison. He is now a man who requires a joint Interpol task force and this elaborate base to trap. You are the woman we need on board to make this possible."

I have no words.

And right now I feel as if my intestines have melted inside me. In a sticky, ugly fashion. If I stand up my stomach might slide out of my knickers and puddle on the floor.

"I thought he was dead. I was pretty pleased at that outcome, so forgive me if I haven't sent Father's Day cards. Ever."

Rich does his scary 'Here's Johnny' smile. His tone turns to Daniel Craig facing a baddy and ready to blow him up with barbs. "We know this," says Rich. "We know rather more about you than you probably imagine. We know it all. Full security details as part of our process. We know what you had for lunch for the past three months."

"Not much, been on a diet." My answer is so quick I can't stop it. Though I should have.

Here's Johnny is back in a blink.

Fuck. Now I'm worrying about the confidential contents of my underwear drawer and the big thing bought at a drunken girlie party that buzzes and uses batteries. Do they know *that much*? What about my private preferences — what about that big tattoo nobody else knows about? I fucking hope to hell they don't know those!

"My father and I last talked when I was five. Him being unmasked as a bent copper taking hush money from Manchester's gangsters caused us to reconsider him as a positive parent example. We ran away and changed our name. I hate him. He's not really ever been a dad to me."

I feel Dan stiffen beside me. I'm guessing it's an awkwardness reaction. Or pity.

Rich fixes onto my gaze through circular specs. "The two biggest sex-trafficking pirates on this continent. You alone have the power to take them down. How does that feel — powerful? Preordained? Payback time? The best present you've ever been handed on a plate?"

I'd rather have had a decent parent.

So, shit. Not really.

I'd rather be back at home in Blighty not knowing this and never having witnessed a man breathing his last when all he was about to do was carry my bags for a work-based Greekcation. Especially now that I think my dad is at the back of it all.

My throat is tight as a concrete knot. "He's a pretty hard man to forget, but believe me, I've tried my best over the years."

I don't want to look at the screen – it's too big. I see the resemblance to my brother Mickey in the photo. But I push out feelings. I wouldn't help my ostracized father if he was drowning and I had the world's last Li-lo. I could do worse than drown him willfully, given a chance. He means nothing to me, thanks to his crime boss serving ways when I was young. He was a disgrace to the police badge he held. The fights. The fraud. The prison sentence. The shame of being in his family. I know this – Mum told me the history I'd overlooked in childhood. It damn near killed her, the disgrace of it.

"Sorry," Dan says softly. "You're not the contact lookalike. I improvised. I'm shit at it, by the way. I'm sorry I couldn't tell you more."

"Are you bloody really?" I deadpan, and my hatred for what he's done must show in my eyes because he drops his gaze. "Instead I'm the criminal's clueless daughter. Nice stitch-up. Why the hell should I help any of you, you bunch of lying bastards?"

"Good question," says Rich. "And why don't I help add some evidence with pictures as proof…"

I hold up a hand to stop him. You could hear a pin drop. I'm not saying something to make them feel better, so I let the pause linger.

And, with exquisite timing, he fills the screen with photographs. There must be hundreds. Girls faces. Some young boys. I know without details what's next.

"Missing presumed prostituted, at your father's and Katsaros' hands," says Rich. "You don't owe us – you might consider them, however. Being the loyal, decent, unblemished citizen we know you to be. This is your chance to ensure justice is fully served."

Dan segues, "We intend to lure him to a meeting with you." He eyes me. If he has emotional X-ray vision he'll see hate and hurt in Day-Glo shades of rage pulsing from every pore. "You'll be wired. Fully covered by marksmen every step of the way. You're key in getting him out of his lair — getting us in. Making him vulnerable so that we can blow his racket open. He has a very sophisticated operation at his mansion, Mone Dunamis — it's like a mini Fort Knox. We need a major distraction to infiltrate that."

To think I was worried about blowing open my past Santorini honeymoon shit fest with Seb. This is so much worse — revealing my private nightmare of a father before the world's high end criminal masterminding geeks. Showing the shabby underbelly of my ancestry — the Dad that scared us all rigid and made us flee.

"I haven't seen him in twenty years. I vowed he'd never find us. I never want to see him again. We took off for London — new life."

Rich is silent but watches his boots. "I realize you will have issues. That's understandable. But you are the kind of woman who wants justice. You will see sense — in that we trust."

I score myself high points for holding moral high ground. But my blood is still up. I'm not just going to simper and make it easy when they've been this underhanded. So I raise my chin and give Dan my worst evil stare.

"So now he's kidnapping children and pimping whores for mega earnings, good to know he's changed. Nice to know I still want to punch him hard. You know what they say, Rich? Once an arsehole, always a bad smell."

Rich clucks his tongue. "You're entitled to be angry — I get that. I'd hope that, given time to process and see good sense, you'll realize our motives are sound."

"Certainly, Sir. Three bags full, Sir. So glad you've mapped out my future without my consent. You set me up to face my nemesis, and get a bullet in the brain for my services."

"He won't get a single chance," whispers Dan. "Trust me on that."

And shit—it's only in saying that it hits me. What's going to happen to me? Will Dad be one step ahead and get me before they can counter-move? Or will the Spy Squad deem me surplus to requirements? Am I to disappear in the night like Tavi when I've fulfilled my purpose? Am I necessary collateral?

I gawp at him. "Then I guess my answer is still no. Sir."

"You have all the power in this one. You'll be at safe distance. Our plan is to have you lure him to a meeting—we know he has a desire to make amends. Ten minutes and every damn son of a bitch that works for him will be captured thanks to you."

"Why ever would he care about a visit from me after all these years?"

The men share a glance I can't read. They know something I don't, for sure.

"We have intelligence that suggests a reunion will be seen favorably," says Redman.

"Intelligence how?"

"We know he has regrets about the past. During taped conversations."

"Too damn late." Shit. But I'm not through yet. By a long chalk. "He's the last guy breathing that I'd ever want to meet. A bit like Mr. Stun Gun beside me."

Low blow. But pleasing nonetheless.

"You can lure him out so that we can make him pay," Rich concludes, ignoring the Dan jibe, and maintaining his offensive.

Dan turns to me. I can't read him. He's known this all along and never said a thing. "A meeting is all we need to get things rolling on the capture sweep. Grey is the heavy side of the team. With him off-site we can swoop. We'll have them all behind bars. You're the final domino in an elaborate and cleverly orchestrated showdown of the bad guys. Surely you can see why we've steered you here as our most vital weapon?"

"So what's it to be?" Rich asks.

I'd like to settle for slapping Dan's moosh. I'd make a run for it, but where would I get to? The kitchen?

"I need time. You're asking me to disregard my principles. The least you can do for me is treat me like somebody whose opinion actually counts. Permission to leave the room and process some of this shit?"

With shared looks and Rich's consent, Dan stands to follow me out. His fingers don't shake half as much as mine do when he tries to take my hand, I quickly slip out of his grasp. He is a pro marksman. He's shot me with his actions.

"My answer, Sir, is not fucking likely." I turn to leave. "I'd love to answer your prayers and say yes—but I hate my father, left him for a reason. He failed me and my brother and mother and abused our trust. We protected ourselves and changed our identities. Had our windows broken in a few times when the news hit."

"You'll save innocents and achieve justice for victims and their families. It's a big ask, but your influence is huge." Redman steeples his fingers and touches his chin. "You'll be duly compensated when you leave." He holds up a piece of paper—a check with more noughts than I've ever seen in real life. But truly—do they really think that's enough? "We know it is not without risks and sacrifice. You will be well remunerated. You're a seasoned reporter—use emotional detachment—he's primed to take this bait. You realize he tried to snatch you at the villa?"

Inside me an oxygen tornado's started and I'm failing to catch enough air to breathe. "They said it was a burglar!"

"We aren't entirely sure of the perpetrators of the villa attack. All we do know is that Tavi was targeted and the place was turned to matchsticks and mess, via raining bullets. But we're working on it. Katsaros and Grey are key suspects, naturally. He knows you're here and he wanted to intervene."

"Who's to say he won't kill me?" My insides going into

a cyclone-style freefall that makes my head feel light. In a blink, I feel Dan's hand in mine. His touch on my lower back, though light, goes through me like a lit taper on Bonfire Night, and I flinch away. He has that sizzling raw naked energy but he's toxic. He's brought me here, all along knowing what I faced and keeping that black truth silent.

I'm mad at my earlier snog willingness. Maybe it was just my lack of a shag for too many moons and being in close proximity to tight buns, loaded weapons and a man's double-barrelled biceps. I should have remembered policemen are the last guys I'd ever choose. How could I have known he'd lie all the way for his precious cop job?

"You can do this. But we know it's a big ask—we know you can pull it off," Dan whispers.

I'm not okay with any of this. I can barely swallow. "So I'm the reason Tavi is dead?"

Dan shakes his head. "Tavi died in the line of duty. We are still following enquiries about Tavi's death, and it's too early to draw a finite conclusion. But Tavi aside, your father is vulnerable with you here—he'll make mistakes, you're the prize."

"Trouble with prizes—one slip, they smash."

Rich's voice is commanding enough to make me flinch. "We don't slip. Nor will you—after full induction and practice exercises you'll be briefed in a carefully executed plan. In three days' time you'll pull Grey Donaldson into our iron web."

I should be repulsed still, but somehow I find a low certainty simmering inside me. My thoughts drift to my mother, and how Dad's been responsible for yet more violation, loss of innocence, murder. The least I can do is send him to prison and yeah, call me twisted, but that's a stirringly satisfying inducement.

Okay," I whisper. "I deplore having to even look at him again. But I'll do this to finish it for good."

Dan squeezes my hand, but I pull out of his grasp.

"Stay away from me. Right now I hate you!"

"Ms. Joseph. Agent Draven's my deputy. He's to work with you closely to get you ready for the task ahead. He's an expert in such situations. Outside of base he's the highest ranking agent on the mission."

He's rank all right — a full-on stink fest, Sir.

"I don't feel like I have much choice — right now it feels like a family memories Shanghai. But I realize how important the job is, and for that reason only, I'm prepared to listen."

I'm heart sore and angry, so I don't know whether to cry, flee or scream. But there's too much riding on this to follow those instincts.

"We'll reconvene for a progress debrief," says Sir Redman. "Dismissed." He puts out a hand to touch my arm. "Process and realize you're doing something crucial for international security."

I take solace in controlling my deep urge to hyperventilate as we walk away. We pass the agents at monitors with me not seeing them through my blurred vision. But I don't care.

Dan tails my fast strides, ironically acting somewhat submissive in all his macho gear.

"Don't speak to me unless you want to get a full-on kicking by a girl."

He follows in silence. But I don't know where I'm going, so eventually I have to turn back and let him lead me to my room. He tries to talk when we get there but I blank him so long Dan gives up and just locks me in.

And that's when I collapse in a heap.

And I crumple and just let myself cry.

Chapter Seven

Dan

I try to sleep and seek the chillzone. Empty brain, breathe—focus on breath. Yoda yada like the quack told me. But I still can't relax or rest. Or stop thinking about a certain pissed-off woman not too far away.

It's way past two a.m. Just like me, my brain doesn't take kindly to taking orders from dickwads. Katie's given me the dickwad award, complete with a framed diploma.

I don't even need my dream app tonight. The PTSD innovation one that regulates episodes and monitors my sleep rate. Usually it works too—reduces the crazed-out terror binges. Gently rouses me when I'm in close zone for a dreamed attack revisit.

But sleep evades me and right now, patience is in short supply. My guilt trip is big enough to keep me awake for a season. My futile attempt at enlightening Kate gently was nailed completely in an epic all-time fail that makes my skin feel blistered.

I pick up my phone and stare at the time. Again. Swear at myself.

"Move it, man." I rise and dress in sweats. Opt to head to the gym to beat the insomnia, knowing it'll be dawn before I'm done, but it's better than lying there defeated. First I take a moment to write a note, unsure if I'll toss it.

I shut the door, careful not to wake the neighbors. Pretending I'm not ultra-aware she's three rooms down, and my heart's not drumming as I near. I made Warbie put her close—further evidence of my dickwad status. I stand like a teen crush dweeb deserving a kicking. Absorbing quiet darkness, trying to gauge if she's awake. Or so woe begotten and buzzed with sorrow she's tipped over into oblivion?

I raise my fingers to knuckle rap. Then stop, walk a few steps, then stop again. What's with this fucking apology impulse thang? Why do I wanna see her face? Her hair and state of undress like Perv Central?

I grab the note from my pants pocket and slide it under the door before I can pull it back. Then walk. Fast. No thoughts permitted.

She'll tear it up. She hates me. But even a dillweed like I've been can do what he can to try.

* * * *

"What you doin' here, douche bag? No girlie mags left for a meaningful relationship tonight?"

My FBI nemesis Rocco's on pure hit form. I can tell once he stops the huff and puff of his workout I'm in for a full routine. The guy puts the G in Good Sense of Humor — providing the G here standards for garbage.

He's also mainlining fluids while he does serious damage to the treadmill. Like a rampaging rhino with the horn. He's sweating enough to have just completed an epic night swim. Mister Definition of Douche.

But, irony central, in a crisis he's the guy I always want to have my back. Doesn't make him easy to take. Something about the sin boulder on my shoulders tonight tells me the gym might've been my worst idea yet.

"How's you, Mister Never Right?" I fake a grin. "Take the silly-ass hat off and play nice. Gunna bro down and cut the crap?"

"Can't. When it's this much fun to make your uptight dick twitch. Almost wanna turn a hardy har hose on ya."

Yeah. He's a real white noise machine.

Just what I wanted to escape.

"So, to what do I owe the pleasure? You down here at silly o'clock wid nothin' but me for stimulation?"

"C'mon, Noneski. Jeez—you're gonna slip in a puddle of yourself. Don't you ever stop sweating or take a towel break?"

"No surrender. Beating my times. Nailed it—add to cart. Bang."

"So proud. Were you knocked on the head as a kid or is it just an act, pal?"

My chest is tight. Heart's heavy. Haven't even started. Now I'm wishing I'd kept the note. Shoulda left things. Fuck. Epic lack of street smarts on that one.

"Let's can the chat and just go for the zone, if you don't mind?" I urge.

But the son of a bitch doesn't copy the hint. "Would that be the butthead zone? Or the thinking 'bout your jump off zone? She's sweet, gotta give it to ya..."

Jerk gym buddy all the way. I cut our chat and filter his verbiage out. No way is he going to reel me in on the Kate thing.

My warm up's gentle—heading for light weights. Nothing like the burn of a bench press for cathartic torture.

Only Rocco's finished with playing nice. "So—the woman. Nice chassis. Skinny but not too much—stacked too. Bootylicious, workin' one helluva rear. What I couldn't do with summa that!"

Weird and tragic both. But I'm so not gonna bite.

"Run faster, man. Might help your brain engage. Or your balls to drop."

Rocco smiles. Tiger stalking my moves. "Said something about your girl to offend ya, ma bro? You two looked mighty sweet when we found you."

"Not my girl. Just doin' the job."

Rocco pauses. I wait for more. "Cozied in a cave, all loved-up. Lotta her buttons done up wrong if you ask me..." Rocco nods and ups pace. "Yeah. You want her so bad you're losin' it...sweet tastin' ass hard to resist."

"Get real, RocMan."

"So, did ya get some or did she flatline the loser? If she benched you, feel free to tell her I'm here, willing and ready."

His reflexes are hotter than I credit him with. He blocks my ill-timed blow and we both sense it woulda been a stunner. Literally.

He pushes me hard, and I fall back over equipment onto my ass and back. Taking a low thud *ooft* in the process. I catch my head on the way. Two head wounds, price of one. Not deep but still earns a flag up for tragic effort.

Though I guess if he'd taken my punch he mighta been in a worse state, and we both know it. For now we're breathing fast and I'm bleeding. He's just working out I've overstepped lines in more ways than Katie. I coulda killed him.

"Son of a bitch," he mutters. "Whoa. You crazy fuck!"

"Whoa yourself. Stop dissin' the lady."

"Man. You got it bad! If you ever land me a punch like that, you're dead meat and swimming in the canal. Job or no job."

I'm breathing like a boxer but acting like a brain-dead thug. I see Rocco's somehow got a split lip badge for his trouble—that means my ass will be fried come morning.

The noise of the door slamming makes us both look up.

"Yeah. Pair of crazy pricks, shoulda known! What the hell?" Havana stares and her eyes are laser-hot, she's ready to flay our hides. Our guilt is the big, fat, silent partner in the room too.

"Gentleman's disagreement," I say.

She punches the wall. See, I'm not the only one with anger management that needs work. There's a dent on the gym wall now—only room in this place that's plasterboard, not rock. She's lucky—her fingers would be fractured otherwise.

"I hate this shit! Civilians. Bring a girl on board and everybody loses the plot."

"Havana. You lose more plots than a memory-lapsed script team." Sometimes my best lines come in the tensest moments. Though she's toe-totoe and breathing fire at me for the slight.

"Fuck off, Dan. I so hate your guts right now!"

"See," says Rocco. "She's gonna screw up too—Hav wants you so bad she's gonna blow us wide open."

"I don't! I hate his guts."

Rocco does crazy face. "Like I said—probably has a photo under his pillow more nights than she'll admit, and that's as super-disturbing as it gets."

Now I'm the one grabbing Hav off Roc. What a night.

"Done here," I'm yelling. "Let's get the hell gone, and why we all here at two in the morning anyhoo?"

She grunts, shrugs. "Knew you'd end up chewin' one another's ears off. Civilians—toxic. It's a proven curse. I'm gonna talk to the boss."

Roc and I both shout as one. "Don't. Deal with it. Keep it tight."

Rocco's watching her and a light bulb flashes in my dense brain on why Rocco gets his junk in a funk all the time with me. It's not about me—it's about the woman watching.

Aha!

"Want me to walk you back, Hav? See, Bullet, some of us know how to treat a lady." Rocco says.

I squash my itch to out him, but I've caused more than enough harm for one night. "Great that you keep offa porn channels long enough to learn manners. Help him clean up that split lip, Hav?"

She's a shit-hot female agent. She's also our resident medic. Ironic for someone with zilch empathy and the bedside manner of a cobra.

Rocco's staring me down, not moving. She's tugging his brawny biceps and his voice is quiet. "Danno. Don't screw us all. She's civilian—toxic, remember? Don't cross lines."

"Copy that. Message received. As if I would."

But most things are toxic in this job. More lines have been

crossed than a celebrity coke party. I let my temper go—I never do that. Roc's a pal and the wit feud is usually a game. Why not here?

He's right, I'm getting this messed up. But the thought of him, or any man, touching Kate—especially her lowlife father—sends me punch-crazy. Loco douche wild.

Rocco and Hav cut out while I bench press. Nothing heavy or I'd have to use a spotter—just enough to keep my mind occupied. But it doesn't take edges off. The sharp corners of this pain-in-the-ass mission remain brutally jagged and the wounds bleed fresh.

Chapter Eight

Kate

For somebody who had very little sleep, I don't look as much of a troll as I rightly should. My room is small, with a metal bed, no window and minimal comforts, bar a small, spartan shower room.

So the supreme starlet duvet set is incongruous, with its silver gray sateen and piped splendor—but I'm reveling in that random touch of pamper. It's the nicest thing that happened yesterday and I won't forget Warbie's gesture.

And if my nose is right he's also behind what's got me dressed and ready for breakfast in record time. I already smell food. I splash water on my puffy eyes in the doll-sized basin, and even opt for makeup commando. I have lipstick and a few supplies but really, what's the point?

The delicious aroma of hot French toast tempts me and brings me out of 'dad brood' mood. I'm already planning toppings, and I don't know my way to the kitchen. It's truly *that* good.

I'm hammering on my locked room door by the time somebody comes. It's one of the guys from yesterday's rescue—can't remember his name, but I think it's Salchow. As in triple? The thing the skaters do? Either that or I heard wrong.

"Hi, you taking me for breakfast? All these doors and corridors are exactly the same. No idea where to find the food."

"Then let me show you the way," says the guy, allegedly known as Salchow. He's über tall. With a polar-white smile and crystal bling blue eyes that stare me out.

I glance away. "What's your name?"

He's handsome, in a male-model manner — not in an allman Dan way. But with the same agent-esque chiseled looks fit for a boy band gone badass. A dark boy band that does crazy things with guns. My mouth dries at the image.

"It's Falco. From the Norwegian Crime Squad, but my FBI buddies named me Falcon. I'm team climber and I aim to soar — rise like a bird. Then I swoop! In more ways than work." He smiles. Again with the staring. He's like a male robot chatting up a lady robot, and I don't want to do droid dating anytime soon. But I find myself robot-smiling back out of politeness.

"Here is the refectory, as requested. Want me to stick around in case you need directions again?" Stare, stare, intense ruddy stare. I'd give him the bird, but he may pull a gun on me. "I know this place backwards to frontwards." He's being serious. Not a glimmer of sarcasm in his clear, blue eyes that I swear could drill me through the wall.

I touch his arm in a chummy fashion. "That's sweet, Falco the Directions King. But I'll be fine. My stomach now has the sat nav manual."

He touches my arm. Ick. Kinda too familiar. "Make good with the fork, Katie. Today we have a fine breakfast selection." He smiles at me.

"How did you know my name?"

"Heard Dan call you that."

"It's Kate. Consider it a warning. Dan's on his last chance too." You'd think I knew karate or something, such is my stupid bluster. But there's only one guy I kinda let call me by that pet name. He has tattoos that make my lips auto-pout without permission.

I turn away from Ivan before he tries to stick English language words together like lumpy chunks of toddler Lego again.

But in turning, I see a line of grim faces. It's police line up gritty and hardass. They're all glaring at me over the long refectory table as if I just puked in their pool party, and one of them is Dan. He's no happier than when we last parted company.

Oooh. Shit.

"Good morning." When in doubt slap on the cheery.

Nobody answers. So I stare pointedly at Dan. At least I think it's Dan. Somewhere during the course of last night he had a brawl with a pillow containing a bag of spanners. Or his bed monster got out and smacked him like a fucker.

"Ooooh." I wince, then draw in further comment.

"Hey. Sleep okay?" he says grimly.

"Better than you, by the looks."

He has got a bruise on his head, as well as a scar from the Tavi scrap, and I'm pretty sure his lip is swollen, and that's not Botox. Speaking of lips, Rocco has the biggest trout pout I've ever seen. It's lip legend. He's more pissed than the Pissy King of the Piss Piranhas.

"Nice makeovers, peeps." I know I can't resist. "You doing this for reality TV? Or did the heavy weight poltergeists strike in the night?"

Thankfully, Dan ignores me beyond a swift, silencing glare.

Rocco pisses himself laughing. Told you he was super-pissy. I sense he's just that kinda guy. "She's so funny, maaan! So damn funny. Fuck. Somebody let me train her in body combat to pay for the comebacks."

"So what's been happening here? Night raid gone wrong?" Is all I can find to say before Warbie steers me away from the table end — and trouble. It's like a wake line-up with the worst mourners ever.

"No night raid. Just grievances aired," Warbie whispers. "Best not go there, Princess." Then he raises his voice in a theatrical dazzle, "So my darling, you sleep well?" Warbie's wearing a Greek flag bandana. Today, his black apron is covered with mini Spartan soldiers. If my gaydar's not scored another bang-on hit I'll go and do jazz hands while I shut the front door.

"Love that apron."

"I know, dolly duck. Rocks like my charm."

"Do you have gay joke aprons for every day of the week?"

"Now there's an idea." He grins. "I do have swim trunks in this print. I like a bit of flesh to wake me up for the breakfast run. Especially when I'm stuck with these long faces." He does a theatre whisper behind a hand. "The boys are all out of chat and chivalry today. So it's just you and me keeping the pep up. What'll it be...Full English, Pancakes, French Toast?"

"French Toast, *s'il vous plait!*" I've said it so fast I sound like a French Toast-addicted junkie with the DTs. But Warbie grins and wields his spatula like a fairy godmother — piling a glossy white plate with a stack fit to widen my eyes, as much as my belly.

"I won't eat all of these."

"Why not just try, girlfriend? I sense keeping your mouth filled might keep us all outta trouble."

"Charming. How do you know I don't talk with my mouth full?"

"Thought you were a lady, but do your worst. Surprising what a day of shocks and a good sleep can do for the appetite — fill your face 'til it hurts, girl!"

It'd be rude not to.

Given that I cried myself to sleep last night after the devastating news I've been drawn here via duplicitous means to lure my bastard presumed-dead father to prison again, I'm pretty impressed at my own resilience and my new-found appetite. But I always was a comfort eater. After one bite of the toast, I'm smitten. I'll have to count calories if I'm here for too long.

"Wow. These are amazing."

So ignoring my refectory mates, I'm getting into the groove when Warbie turns up the radio for *Xanadu* just to piss the others off. I'm laughing openly as I lose myself in lipsmacking bliss. Cinnamon and sugar. *One happy breakfast bunny for realz.*

* * * *

"Can I sit?" Dan's staring down at me. Lots of muscles in black cotton. I'm surprised to find him trying to cozy up, and feeling that he needs to ask me first. He is my captor after all.

"You're Sir's deputy dog. Do you need to ask?"

I look up at him as I stuff my third to last bite of French toast inelegantly into my greedy gob. More because I can't than won't speak, I don't. But I munch just to squeeze his angry knobs.

"You don't need to be like this. We both know the way it works. You're here because you're super-important to every one of us."

Instead of arguing, I shrug and nod. Hoping I'm giving the impression I really don't give a fig.

"I'll take that as promising."

I'd say 'take it as you must' but the toast isn't chomped enough.

"So...you get my note?"

I'm still chewing. *Note?* Ah yes. A letter from Dan apologizing for all the shit he's caused me. Quite nice handwriting too for a cop-slash-sharp-shooter-slash-lying-weasel-shithead. He said in the note that he recognized the error of his ways and he should've been straight from the off. Also said he should've been firmer with his superiors in expressing his view that I deserved not to be thrown into the deep end of the flaming pool of manure I was dumped into last night.

I hold my hand over my mouth while I'm still eating. "You asking me to mark it out of ten? Handwriting was nice but spelling was iffy." Like I say, this mouthful's taking work. I intend to make him work too. I flick him a glance and nod, getting back to mastication station.

"Do you accept my apology? That's what I'm asking."

Toast is still being beaten into submission here. I chew the last piece, putting my hand and fork in front of my mouth to indicate there is a process underway. Then I swallow. Then I mainline some coffee to enable me to swallow yet again.

"Damn, you like your chow."

"You'd better believe it. Okay—if it keeps your face on straight I'll overlook yesterday as one of those awful days when it all comes down at once. I still think you're a prize dick and you're going to owe me favors for a lifetime, but it's a start. You're so not forgiven or anything." My mouthful's gone. My stomach is now overladen with eggy bread, so I take a breather. I pick up my mug and chug more latte. Wiping my mouth, I fixate on his bruises. "Who rearranged your face?" I point to indicate his face damage. "Or did you do that to yourself out of a guilty conscience?"

He shrugs. Fuck, but my pussy notices when he does that. It's so boyish. So adorable. I've just been reeled in with a turned-on *zoink*. I blame the muscle T and the muscles therein. Plus a face any woman would cream over. "Karma decided to make me pay for stuff."

"Who?"

"You don't need to know. They both came off with wounds of their own."

I glance back, and from the grouch gazes I'm getting—start again and clarify—looks, that if they could, would incinerate me from the toenails upwards and leave nothing unburned all the way up to my hair follicles—it's Havana.

"She beat you up? She didn't really do all that to you?"

Dan makes a doh face. "As if."

"She hates me. She wants to take *my* face apart big time and feed my limbs to crocodiles." I suspect not just my face. Lots of parts of my anatomy would no doubt end up in jars. As trophies. I've read about people like her. She'd probably frame-mount my skin. Then lick it.

"She doesn't. She just thinks she does. She doesn't know what's good for her," Dan says, way too cryptically for my linking.

"Meaning?"

"I'll tell you some other time. Realized she has an admirer and she didn't know. Or realize how good he'd treat her. They'd be damn good together. Instead of taking chunks outta me as displacement therapy."

"Now you're being über-mysterious, and lying and hiding things from me got you in serious bad doo-doo before. I also shudder at the thought of you being anyone's dating counsellor. Ever."

"Why do you never gimme a break, woman?" Dan sighs and scratches his arm. It drags my gaze to defined muscles that I've never noticed up close before—they're hair-covered and strong, ridged. Watching makes me gulp. I'm thinking of other parts of his anatomy that might be wide in terms of girth and that gets me very hot and ready to combust with lust. The bulky watch strapped to his wrist looks as if any other man would need weight-training prep to adjust to wearing it.

"So if she didn't beat you up, who did?"

"Leave it." At that moment the most obvious perpetrator rises from his seat. A crown jewel shiner showing on his left eye, now that the light hits it.

I stage whisper, "You and Rocco had a big ruddy ding dong—does the boss know?" I whisper. "You're so in trouble when he sees."

Dan just fake smiles.

"Don't you have any sense? You should've used makeup. I have some concealer, I think that was in my pocket."

"Yeah. Right. Course. Used my Interpol Branded Color Me Beautiful boxed set. Maybe get my lashes done to divert attention."

I'm trying not to laugh, but it's so hard that I ended up giggling, and everyone in the room looks over. "I have makeup," I tell him. "You can both meet me in my room and I'll get rid of the dings with Dior."

Dan stands. "The boss'll have to deal. I'm not doing makeup even for you."

A voice behind us says. "Rocco, Draven. Boss's office in

five." It's Warbie who's answered the phone on the wall, and has just received orders.

"You're in trouble," I say as I watch Dan rise to go. "Told you. Make up needed — shoulda listened. Big trouble heading your way!"

Dan releases a long low sigh. His coffee breath is remarkably enticing, for such an early hour in the morning. He definitely has good mouth hygiene and great teeth. Big tick. My pussy meows for a sunrise spoon sometime. Shit. Poor guy.

Right now he's going to his doom for a big old boss ding dong.

"Rocco had it coming. Listen — can we talk later? Properly talk. In private," he asks me. How can I deny a man going to the gallows one last sojourn?

"Only if you and Rocco are planning a public second round. Or a big resolution scene with kissing. I'm backing him to win whatever way it goes."

He's angry fit to burst but I'm bubbling with the thrill of the wind-up. "Fucking can it. See you later," he spits out.

"Not if I see you first."

He goes off. Mr. Hot Holster Wearer of the year.

And I'm laughing along for several minutes after he's gone. Like a total bloody lunatic sitting on my own and unadvisedly full of eggy bread.

* * * *

I decide to help Warbie with the dishes and tidy up chores. It's not like I've got target practice or bollockings waiting. When I turn back, Havana and Rocco are gone, and when I bend to open the washer Warbie grabs me, a picture of rapture.

"There's gonna be shit to pay! What I wouldn't give to be a fly on that wall." Warbie declares.

I'm warming to him. Like a cat's butt warms on a south-facing window ledge, through double glazing, with the radiator on. He's spearing my affections too ably.

He has this grin and eye-roll thing going on I connect with on a deeply spiritual level. I get the feeling that Warbuckle has sway over Dan, despite Dan's Deputy status. He has Dan's back, or maybe Dan has Warbie's? Or is there more going on than I realize? Does it involve Spartan Soldier print thongs and joint sauna sessions?

Now there's a thought…

"Do you and Dan have a thing going?" I ask, grabbing my hunch by the short and curlies. Why shilly-shally on such eureka moments?

"Don't be crazy, girl. Listen, I have orders about you. Strict orders," he brags.

"As in what?"

"Orders to make sure Dan unhands you. Orders to keep you and Dan strictly apart for the duration of your stay. Straight from Redman—to be undertaken upon pain of death."

"You're kidding me?" I nearly drop a tea plate, but I juggle it into submission like Cirque Du Soleil at a tea party. We both sigh when I safely return the plate.

"Far from it. I've explicit instructions to mentor Ms. Katie and take you under my wing. I need to bathe and delouse you, and settle you into Her Majesty's Nuthouse, Santorini. Find you a locker—get you some clothes. Teach you base protocols, like how to use a knife and fork properly. Maybe wash your hair?"

I punch him for that one, but sense he's joking.

"Oh yes, big itinerary ahead. Aren't you the lucky one?" It's like *Pretty Woman*. But with chutzpah, and a fat gay fairy spy-mother.

"Are you always like this?" I ask him quietly. "So domineering? Or am I just your fag hag?"

"Definitely. It would drive anyone crazy to be stuck here with this mob, so I have mitigating circs. Finally, I have a friend who rocks my world." He draws out a chair noisily and sits on it back to front. "Listen, toots, Dan's hot for you.

Totes obvious. Rocco's hot on his heels. Statement of the abso-obvious. Havana's like a rabid cougar spoiling for a kill, because she's blind with lust for a Dan, who'll never want her back. Meantime Rocco has the jellybubs and a hard-on for Hav. You keeping up?"

I shake my head. "You lost me when you moved the chair."

"We haven't had this much drama action in eons. Consider yourself my new BFF. Given that I've a remit to get you readied in clothes for your big dad meet—I have free rein to dress you like the vintage fifties starlet of my dreams! I'm not bailing you out on that little treatette. I actually have a secret plan for pushing you and Dan together, and Redman will never know. It'll be our divine secret. By the time the mission's achieved, nobody will care that the big boss warned against it."

I slap my head with my hand. "I knew I had a bad feeling about you. I thought Dan was supposed to be called Sir? Aren't you supposed to do what he says? Or are you just a law unto yourself? You just said you'd been ordered to keep us apart? So, why are we having this convo?"

"I'm the guy who feeds Dan and washes his underwear. On my watch and in private he's Danny Boy and he's mine. Darlin', I want him to get what he needs most. A woman who can keep up. One who deserves him. So what the big boss doesn't know won't hurt him. But there can be no moves made until the perps are arrested and in custody. That's the vital part—Dan letting his cock loose at crisis point could fuck us up. Same applies to you."

"Me? I don't even have one. A cock that is."

Now he's getting patience-pissy. "Getting starry eyed with Dan's brand of crazy kink might just turn both your heads."

"What? Dan likes it kinky?"

"That's for you to find out and for him to tell you, not me."

My head hurts with this. But I think I'm right in saying

I'm not having sex. So I do.

"I'm not having sex with anyone."

"Gonna happen. Make sure it's after mission's end. Call it instinct. I'm great on instinct—and food. I even write a food blog. One day I wanna write a book. But that's another story."

"I really can't keep up now, Warbs!" I protest. Rolling my eyes in my head as I unload the dishwasher. "Haven't you considered you could just trust us to keep on the right side of safe and stay alive?"

"Seriously honey, you really think I can't read the stuff on the wall? He wants you bad."

Said on a purely estrogen-led Jane sees Tarzan and wants it bad level, I'm punching air. But I'm nothing if not oppositional. Even with myself.

"Please listen, you and Dan can do kissy kissy—nothing more. But Big Bad Sir can't know. That's the size of it." Warbuckle shoos me with his fingers, so I give up and perch on the counter top.

"Hate to spoil your plan but…cameras?"

"Mere cameras won't get your panties in a bunch."

"Well, Warbie—I'm planning no sex with your superior, and that is the end of it." I say, with a newfound certainty this man will be the future Chewie to my Han Solo. "But on a conversationchanging plus note thanks for my bed linens. Right now I'm not a great fan of your man Dan anyway. So it's strictly business all the way." The way I'm feeling, Liability Joseph will be scheduled for a strait-jacket before she'll give clearance to their carefully laid entrapment plan.

"You don't want to see your dad. I get that you feel set up. You've clearly suffered—as a child, then growing up with a secret you couldn't share. Plus, you thought he was dead—and now events are churning all those wounds up again. That's hard stuff to handle. But you've grown into this great, sexy woman with an amazing reporting job— I've seen footage. You're hot in all ways."

I turn away from Warbie, ware I'm starting to cry and

not wanting to show the soft, weak underbelly of my tough Kate act. Shit, I hate when this happens. Where's Izzy and Sambuca when I need her?

Warbie pulls me to him for a hug. His cologne is a mightily overpowering oriental but it beats eau de questionable hygiene any day. Speaking of which, I've had no deodorant in way too long. The hug feels damn good.

"Dan's a good guy. Cut him a break—there's sparks between you. Big, big supernova activity in the skies when you two are together."

"How do you know? No windows. No telescopes?"

"Stop ace reportering and answer."

I shake my head. Then spit out the truth like a wuss. "He's hot. Of course he's bloody hot. But you should never ask a lady such things."

He whispers, "He doesn't know about your tattoo—but I do."

I'm shocked to the core. Shocked. Totally. It's something I've kept hidden since it happened.

"How?"

"Sleep cam. Last night you got restless. That vest is short and revealing, too. Okay—I zoomed. Talk about a game changer." Warbie blows a *whoo*. "Just don't screw with his head or hurt him. Keep him sweet. Your life depends on it. Just so you know—he likes kink too."

If I thought Warbie was good before, he's now blown me apart with his hugs and his big heart. Could he be right about me and Sir Draven?

Could we really be perky kink pals on the side?

Nobody has seen my risqué tattoo. Not even my closest girlfriends.

"I'm tasking you to bring out a new slate and try to get along." There's a real *shit's gone down* look in Warbie's expression. So, I nod my comprehension. But he reaches for my hand. "You're a good kid. You're doin' a great thing— plus making an old gay guy happier than he's been in eons. You're my Barbie, Dan's special ops Ken and this is like Couture Christmas. We've so much to get you zipped into—prepare to dazzle and shine."

Chapter Nine

Kate

Together, we peruse Warbie's clothes suggestions for my Greek assignment. They'd be great—were I planning on a night in Amsterdam's drag discos, or assuming the guise of a fifties starlet by day. We're talking a veritable fashionista trousseau. Sequins, velvet and leather abound. Some of the dresses feature laser-cut keyholes fit for a high tech prison wing.

I'm thinking we're light years apart in the style stakes. But I opt for tact, shelving the 'Get Outta Town' putdowns in the name of diplomacy.

"Wherever did you find them?"

"Here and there—I have sources. I am stores super after all."

I finger pussy-bow blouses in a rainbow array of shades. Armani this isn't, but wherever he got them, it took his Interpol expenses allowance to the bank.

"You have a unique eye." The man's a style enigma. In more bad ways than good.

"Knew you'd agree," says Warbie by my ear. "Always wanted to be a fashion stylist—my true calling." Now I'm seeing the cracks in his crazy grouting. Having a civilian woman to cosplay dress here has unscrewed the linchpin of his sanity joists.

He stares at me like Bashful in a Seven Dwarves police lineup. "Listen. If it's not your thing I have boring options too. Normal work clothes and casuals."

I almost hug him in relief. "I usually wear trousers or

jeans. I don't do fussy." No way am I wearing a blouse with a bow under my chin like a cat being pamper tortured in a Japanese YouTube clip.

Warbie's face takes on an earnest cast. "But you will need a dress for your Mission Dad Reunion Meet. Surely we can work on that?"

The comment about the 'reunion' draws me up short. My stomach flips over. Unfortunately that gooey toast weighs me down like a goose prepped for *fois gras*. My nemesis meeting now even has a code name. I've never felt more like a number in my life. Or more inclined to run and wuss out.

"Shit. I really don't want to be here doing this."

Warbie strokes my arm with a comforting touch. Right now it's more soothing than he probably knows and I sigh so deeply that I realize I have the shakes. I'm a millimeter away from tears and that's so not me it's not true. Call it raw panic.

"Grey Donaldson is a lowlife bastard. I've spent half my life trying to forget him. Only to come here and have it rammed under my nose to relive yet again."

"It's shock."

"More than a shock, Warbs. He's my nemesis."

"I can see why you'd be resistant."

"I'm terrified. It's the thing I dread beyond all others. He's my biggest nightmare. He used to beat my mother. He was a bad cop on the take, who dragged our reputation through the mud."

Warbie's gaze holds me, steadying my focus and my flipped-out mind. "You're doing a worthy thing here. You're saving lives. You're making him pay. I figure you're the one who kinda deserves that honor."

"I'd gladly hand that over and have someone else do it while I stay at home and forget all about it."

And lo, but doesn't that just bring on the need to weep harder than a pepper spray attack. I'm sobbing in a noisy, sniffle-causing and snot-producing way, and I can't see there are that many tears, but Warbie rubs my back, and it feels so good to be hugged and supported and held in big strong arms.

Like the father figure I should have, but never, had.

I calm somewhat and begin to talk coherently. "You've got a deal. Dress me up like anybody you want—the less I look like the real me the better. As long as the rest of the time I can be normal. I need you to hold my hand and not tell any of the others what a bloody mess I'm in about this plan."

As much as I hate to think how I'll end up it makes no odds. I want to pretend and just get through it. No-one will see me. I'm in a Greek Interpol hideout and this is a throwaway episode of my life that I'll later bury out at sea. Plus, Warbie's a great guy and I have to throw him something re the dress.

"I'll make you so good you might even surprise yourself."

"It's kind you've done so much prep. If I ever venture into sparkle and cut out Lycra you'll know I'm finally over the edge and need therapy. Well. More than I do already with the Dad past from hell."

A knock on the door makes as both glance up, dazed.

"Yes," Warbie says but he's still rubbing my back like a vet would do to a dog that's just had a near miss in an eight car pileup. Come to think of it, I feel like I have and the mangled wreckage lies inside me.

Dan the Interpol man stands in the doorway. His black ops clothing makes my pulse hitch. The way I see his pecs and his gun holsters mold to his body make parts of me shimmy for sensual attention.

His jaw sets my ovaries to maraca rattle mode while his gaze sweeps over me. That makes me feel worse, knowing how important and vital and hot he is, while I'm a shabby, sobbing wreck of a no-hoper. Who hates him and fancies him at the same ruddy time.

His face is a mask of concern slash embarrassed horror. "Hey. You okay?"

"Dandy. Best holiday I've ever had, thanks for asking, when's the cabana boy coming by?" I have to be snarky, when I'm this much of a sniveling wretch. Fuck and sticky shit. Why the hell does it bother me so much that he's seeing me look this crap and acting this wussy and rubbish?

Why am I caring what he thinks? But I do.

Warbie scolds him with his gaze. "Sir. The woman's in shock. She needs time to process what's being asked of her. I have serious concerns about the way this has been handled. Sorry, Sir, but this is bad news."

"We'll talk. Point taken." Dan softens his voice and directs his comment to me. "I apologize. Are you okay with Warbie supporting you? Would you rather I assign someone else? Havana? A woman's touch?"

Robofemme? No thanks. No bloody effing way. I'd blowtorch my own Brazilian before I'd ever agree to *that* match. I'm a tad upset, but a psychopath, hate my guts mentor is the last remedy I need.

"Warbie's the last salvage of sense in a place gone awful."

"Good. We'll debrief shortly. Forty minutes." Sir disappears to go and do more daring-do.

"So. Guess I'll go fetch the jeans then," says Warbie, softly. "Run you a nice soothing lavender oil bath. You can soak and chill, then get yourself together with a cup of chamomile tea and start afresh."

I wish I had his confidence.

But straighten my spine. I'm no quitter. "No chiffon," I say softly. "I get rashy with scratchy fabric." Mission Mannequin is so not happening. "You know, Warbs, it would help if I had my own stuff. Don't suppose I could get my cases? We left them when we ditched the car."

He touches his nose and nods. "Leave it with me, sweetie. I'll get your bags. Katie...trust in Sir on this one. He's taking charge—debriefs and full training lined up. He won't let you fall on this, and he's the best in his game. He's taking your dad down and, most of all, he likes you. He's moved his room to the one next to yours." Then he stage whispers, "There's an adjoining door. Easy access. Minimal disruption."

Shit. Not sure how to take this revelation. "Oh, he loves me all right. Civilian liability with a potty mouth and a crime-boss father. Just his type." But I don't want to go there, especially when I'm this vulnerable, my past exposed for people to pity and prod.

A picture of my dad's photograph on newspapers slams into my brain—I'd found the old cuttings when I'd sorted Mum's stuff after she passed on. Rocked me hard, as I couldn't believe she'd keep them, because we ran. Had to. The cop on the take who'd fallen from grace and paid for his sins in prison. Our disgrace. No Dad figure in my life worth remembering. It's a memory parade I duck from.

"There's chemistry. I see it. I've never known him this way before either." Pardon me if I don't want to be a woman with a penchant for policemen.

"Good that I've always had a thing for overbearing, mission-obsessed, strikea-pose gun-toting control freaks then." I'm aiming for arid sarcasm. I'm feeling churned-up and in a mess.

"If I have my way I'm going to make you both realize it's okay to have the feels. Santorini Singles. Could be a new project?"

From stylist to dating pro. The man needs hobbies. Can't somebody show him how to French Knit? Or how to shut the eff up?

"You've been underground too long."

"Could say the same about you resisting the lure of a man."

Warbie scoots me to the bathroom. He could just be more right than I can take.

* * * *

I may have had a divine, chilling bath, but when Dan walks through the door that joins our rooms as I'm standing, pulling up my jeans zip, I learn I have a great aim. He has a super-quick duck response time.

Must be all that dodging bullets.

"Pillows won't hurt me," he says. "I'm wearing a pillow-proof vest."

"It's a bolster. Who says you can walk into my room anytime you like?"

"You're late."

"Ten minutes."

"We don't do late. We're waiting on your arrival. What did you want me to do? Let hell freeze over?" Dan stares at me deadpan. "My butt on the line. Figured if the mountain wouldn't come to Mohammed..."

"Fell asleep in the bath. Didn't sleep well last night. It caught up."

"You're not the only one," Dan remarks. "Figured I should say sorry, and we could spend time explaining things and ease you into what's ahead. Since we've no choice but to get on with this."

It's only now I notice he has one hand behind his back. He presents me with a pack that contains an MP3 player and some fitness leggings and a vest.

"What's this?"

"Might take your mind off things if you can do your mad dance fitness routines."

I'm kinda stunned at the thoughtfulness. The bad imp in my head is saying 'fuck exercise — let's just have sex'.

I blame Warbie's ear worm about Dan's kinky side. I can't get it out of my head now. I hold in my urge to question him. Even though it wants to pop out like an ill-timed fart at a vicar's tea party.

Instead I say, "You've not exactly proved yourself too reliable in the trust-me stakes. But thanks for trying to be nice."

Dan watches, with something dancing in his eyes, but I'm not sure what. Sadness? Depleted patience? Why does he have to get more handsome, smarter, sultrier with every passing hour? Not fair. He has stubble and it's early. How is this possible? Has he shaved in the night? Or does he draw on the designer stubble with a spy stubble kit?

So many questions. So little sanity left.

Dan goes into his pocket and hands me his warrant card. I flip it open and see his photo, his details. The badge of officialdom.

"This is the real me. Now you know the real mission. I'm sorry it's taken so long to get to the full truth."

"Bit late for this. I get you're the real McCoy." My heart bounces inside my chest while I'm smelling the spicy scent on his skin. Feeling the tension in the man, too. Bang, bang my ethics are dead.

"I feel you deserve explanations so I'm about to give them."

"No reason to tell me anything — just keep your distance and do your job. Cover my back and we're good," I say with a shrug.

"That's so not how we're going to play this. You and me putting up brick walls isn't going to help us solve anything, let alone crack my biggest career case. Tavi's death wasn't your fault. I know that's what you've been thinking, but you're wrong. So far — and don't quote me for divulging this — but so far top brass haven't got it right keeping you in the dark so I'm taking a chance here — we think he was a double agent."

"Wow! Truly?"

"Havana is undercover too, but she's doing it for us. She cleans at the Mone Dunamis, Katsaros' Mansion — twice a week. She's been our biggest lead in tapping Donaldson."

"Havana? You're kidding?"

"Hard nut but she's cool as a cucumber undercover. Tough as they come — the target thinks she's just a cleaning lady, and that the muscles are because she's a Pilates freak. Not for the black belt in Tae Kwon Do. She's a woman not to be messed with. Our chief intelligence gatherer Tavi was pretty good too — we'd no idea he was playing both sides."

"Or that Hav's in love with you and doesn't like me," I add. "Your intel skills could do with a refresher, come to think of it."

He semi-smiles. "Guess I was slow to pick that up, but yeah—don't worry. I've talked to her. She's not going to kill you in your sleep."

"We hope."

"She just thinks a civilian in the mix is messing up. It's hard for these guys to allow someone else in on this." Dan shrugs.

"And is it hard for you?"

He stares at me as if teleporting the answer into my brain. "Only if we let it be. We shouldn't get personal. But we should try for amicable. Whatever you might think, I do respect you." Dan sighs deeply, then steps near. "This is our major case of the decade and heads will go on spikes if we screw up. I can't afford slip-ups. I wouldn't pursue the idea if I didn't think it could work. You're more than able to nail this. He'll definitely take this bait." Dan paces, but when he turns, his gaze shows honesty. It's full of gritty frankness and determination.

"Lives are at stake, I get it," I whisper.

"Families are waiting for news. There's due to be a trafficking exercise end of the week and already women are hostage at the mansion. We're aiming to catch them in action when they try to move them on. It's as big as it gets, and it has to stop. I'm not at liberty to say more. But trust that there are teenage girls right now being held against their will on *this* island—ready to be shipped out to massage parlors and prostitution rings in five different countries." His giveaway ticking of the jaw is all the proof I need he's finally given me enough. "Of course now I've told you, I have to kill you." He grins at his own joke.

"You'll have to wait until I've turned in my dad first— being so crucial to your plans. Maybe I'll escape?"

"I wouldn't put it past you." Dan squeezes my hand, and my heart shimmies inside my ribcage. "You're smarter than you look, Joseph."

"You're braver than I'd've given you credit for."

Dan grins. "This is progress. See how good we are when we're civil?"

"I'm guessing that's a real shot wound on your back too — couldn't help but notice it earlier when you wore your vest."

"Not sayin'. Maybe I'll keep a bit of mystery in the mix yet."

Oh, and how the big tough guy image suits him. Adds to his stark allure. Makes me wonder and marvel at the surefire pure hit enigma that is Dan Draven.

A man I've baited and stereotyped — and none of it was right. I'd known nothing at all. Now I want to know everything. Including what rough stuff he likes most in bed.

In the full on flesh, he automatically stimulates my fantasies and attraction hormones. I like him. But he is possibly the worst kind of man ever to fall for, given my shitty past and his cop leanings.

Dangerous. Risk-focused. Married to his job.

The antithesis of what I need. Contrasting too sharply with my criminal father, but in so many ways just as driven. He courted danger and loved it, and had secrets and a dark side. Hell — why am I wondering about future options with the man anyhow?

"Don't be too blown away by all this — it's just a job. Ultimately someone has to do to this," Dan says softly, too close for comfort.

"You sure know how to surprise a girl." I find myself biting my lip, and suddenly he's watching. Close proximity to a wisecracking man who oozes maleness does weird things to a woman's sense of logic and ethics. The triangle of heat inside my knickers has, right now, scored a direct 'interest' hit.

And there is something about being here alone together that brings back the kiss in the cave, then the kiss outside the briefing chamber — and it alters the dynamic between us. To sizzle mode full gear.

There's intimacy hanging—like a fragile but alluring paper lantern on a tree. We're suddenly a team of two. The boss and colleague strictures have gone. They've been rubbed smooth to reveal human beings—just man and woman on the same side.

Scary thought. Though I'm pretty sure that randy man and gynae parts meltdown woman shouldn't appear in the room with a magician's flourish as quickly as it has in my brain. Especially as I'm wearing my skintight T-shirt, new skinny jeans, and my nipples are pointing the way.

I seize the moral high ground as my rudder. "You were about to say sorry?"

"Yes." He palms his hair. "Sorry. For everything. Yesterday would've put most new agents into the trauma zone. But you withstood. You're civilian—with emotional baggage on the line. I feel very responsible and sorry for the situation you were put in."

"Apology accepted."

He says, "Well at least we've stopped being adversaries— though it has been fun to spar with you when you get crazy about things—but we should move past that, Kate."

"Wow. You even called me by my correct name. This is serious. Do you feel quite well?"

"When it comes to you I'm very serious. All the way serious." He moves to close the space between us. We're toe to turned-on toe. "You make me off-road on the protocols script. It's frickin' out of order."

"Lucky me, Sir." My breathing has hitched, and melty middle zone is back. Purring pussy has sprung to life too. I don't want to start creaming as a response to this verbal teasing, because that would be body betrayal over willful resistance. But, hell, this feels good and it's been a long time.

Dan holds up his hands. "We're thousands of miles from the office. You're tempting in every way. But I can't risk chasing thrills with you when the action I'm here to handle is so vital."

I mouth an *O* in response that doesn't turn into words.

"I find you attractive, but I have to get real, Kate. I'm glad you enjoyed the bath I prescribed. For now, we have to get to work. I'm glad we're talking — can we go to the briefing room now? Or would you rather catch me up in five?"

Shit. I thought he was going to kiss me, I really did.

Thought he'd close the distance, and I was gagging for it.

He turns to go and I can tell I've lost something. It's something huge. He's ignoring the earlier attraction? Overriding the ability to connect.

And, hell, it's a loss that's hard to take so I stand up and grab his arm.

"Dan. What have I done to turn you off?" I bristle a bit, just because bristling felt warranted. It's never nice to feel like you've lost your luster. Mine's gone missing here. He kissed me and wanted me before — what's changed?

Then I feel a deluge of regret. Fielding all the blame on him hasn't been fair. He was responsible for the princess treatment from Warbie. He's trying his best to say sorry for the balls-ups. All I've ever done was blame him.

He turns, and it's only then I realize he has no gun on his chest. But through the shirt fabric that chest is more ironing board firm than I'd hitherto imagined. It reminds me of a sexy Spartan warrior, like Warbie's cartoons. I'd love to see that in cosplay soon.

He stretches worked-out arms, and his dark tribal tattoo taunts me. Is it my imagination or are his muscles more pronounced?

"You'll be safe from me," Dan answers softly. "I only pursue women who're willing and who like me. Who like it rough and play submissive to the rocks I have to crack. I won't ravish you in the night. Gentlemanly conduct above and beyond the call of duty, I'd call it. Job comes first from here on in."

"What if I don't want to be safe around you?" I whisper. Gad. So desperate. So piqued to be pushed off. Get me and my pushy 'take notice of me' vibes!

119

"You're playing with fire, Kate. It has to stop. I'm a big boy. Trust me—I can restrain my urges. Getting the perp comes first."

I get closer yet, and in his face—what's with me? My pulse fires into the crazy palpitation mode that happens when you're near to something hot and lethal, and it's a scary place called attraction. I know it and can feel it in my bones. But it's exciting scary too.

Especially when he looks as if he's about to grab me in those big, strong, brawny arms. Only his mouth and face are telling me he'd rather face grenade-juggling than me.

"You really know how to make an impact, but this is not the time," Dan whispers. He reaches out and brushes his thumb over my arm. The merest of touches. But, wow, the spot zings.

Dan gulps when he lets his gaze travel over me. It feels positively carnal, and it blows me away. Because his strong 'keep out' stance is melting my pussy and making my nipples peak more. Causing me untold heat and sparks to jive around my body like thrill-seeking missiles.

I have to moisten my own lips because my brain is no longer functioning on any thoughts beyond sex.

"Let me kiss you." Can you believe that's me imploring him? I need a slap. But it's hero worship. I blame action shows on TV.

And inside my head, as his lips meet mine, I'm yelling see—you were right to be nervous of this. This attraction should not be let loose because it messes with both of you. You clearly can't trust yourself with this magnetizing guy. Warbie should not have turned a blind eye to this.

Dan's hands are on my shoulders, and his lips travel over mine like warmed, honeyed wine. His tongue opens my lips, and I invite him in without a search warrant—or complaint. Wow, if this is kissing than any previous attempts with other men failed by a mile.

This is alchemy involving lips and entwined bodies. Even the lightness of his touch has me beseeching for more.

He roughs me up in the best of ways. Claiming me with a strong grasp that thrills me no end. Am I really this easy?

I kiss him back with craving fervor. Because I simply don't want this kissing to stop. It's hot. Addictive. Just like him.

Dan moves his hand to cup my breast and knead it with warm, firm fingers. In seconds, he's pulled up my top and he's inside. Fingering my breasts and teasing them and me to the point of no return. My breathing expels in jagged gasps of thrill. I push myself into those fingers that trace pure magic. I let him press me down on the small, single bed softly, trembling with need and completely in lust with him and this moment.

"Let's do this," I urge in a whore's lusty whisper.

"Katie...this is nuts," he pleads, like the marooned sailor warding off the mermaid queen.

Yes. I want him. Inside me. All of him. However he wants to do it.

He ravishes my mouth, and the feel of his strong hands and that muscular power in the man have me at his mercy. I revel in his fingers sliding down my torso to my abdomen, and I tremble as he skims toward my pussy. I'm lying back, opening my legs for easy access, because I so want this.

My molten liquid heat betrays me. He'll feel it—I'm almost sliding off the freakin' bed.

"Oh Kate...you drive me crazy, crap!"

I'm still in my top, but wearing it as a neck warmer and his mouth is on my areola, and I swear it turns me on so much to feel it and glance down to see him in rapture as he sucks. No way can this stop. His tongue causes sensory delight as he trails it there and nips lower, skimming a path to my navel and promising delights to follow.

But Dan swiftly, and with muttered curses, pulls away. Our eyes meet.

But not before I'd felt the long and hard length of him against my thigh. It's thrillingly enticing. That hard bulge isn't listening to Super Boss. There's only one answer to this at-work conundrum. It's driven by a motor called revved up unstoppable sperm release.

"Inside me," I pant. "Now! Don't you dare back out."

Dan watches me, and that solemn unspoken question of 'can we really go for broke?' breaks his spell. I see the barricades reerect even before the sentence is complete.

"We can't," he states.

I sit upright swiftly. His fingers were centimeters from being inside me. My apex of heat runs sweet for his fulfilment. I'm pretty sure there's a deep molten-fired desire raging in him ready to go.

But he's trained to resist. To bide his time. He's a man of his word. A man of steel.

Trained not to go over the edge when the job demands. No matter how much I want hot sex with Dan Draven, and I sense this was verging into 'gone crazy' by how much my body craved his touch, this moment is lost.

Sanity has prevailed. Because Dan the lover's been taken captive while Dan the Agent is back in the room on duty. With a gun and a stop warrant.

"We honestly can't," he says.

And I put up a hand but don't speak.

Would sleeping with Dan now have solved or proved anything — hell no. Wouldn't that just blow our problems even wider?

I hear him curse and sigh as he rolls onto his back and draws hands slowly over his face.

"I get the message — loud and clear. Not what we're here for," I tell him, as mortification takes me hostage. I long to kick it in the privates and run. I also sound calm but underneath my thoughts are like a freight train out of control. But this man doesn't want me. Why am I doing this? But I know. It's him. Him not wanting me. Him saying I've tried and I'm through. I'm so not good with that, and how.

Too many fucking rejections.

I implode with hideous results. I've only just realized why he's pulling away — I've changed. I have a shady dad.

I'm no longer a prospect—I'm beneath his contempt. In the cave, maybe I was just timewastingly tempting? But here and now shagging would align us when we're different polarities of moral ground.

In short, I'm too lowly to touch.

Yeah, I get it, finally. But a shard of steel stabs inside me. The hurt burning tissue and charring my good sense.

"You think you know me. With your clearances and vetting. But none of you know the real me at all. Think what you like—I'm past caring."

But I do know how to get his attention.

I'm standing and fully taking off the T-shirt. But I turn my back and pull it up high enough for the prized limited edition view. I've nothing beneath. I'm not showing my chest—this one's all back.

My brand in dark, irrevocable ink.

My tatt is more of a roar than a shout.

I know he stands and steps away—entranced or horrified? That raw, electric charge moment turns explosive as I offer a feast for his eyes to shock without words.

My tattoo is awesome. Maybe he hasn't got me so worked out at all.

Either way this is my best exit line ever.

He thinks I'm scum? Let him believe that. Showing Dan my most secret badass brand in ink says I can't be cowed. I force on a victor's smile that's hollow.

Then wait for him to unlock my door without raising my gaze.

"Sex would've been fun, but already I'm so over you it's scandalous."

Chapter Ten

Dan

The after image of Kate's awesome tattoo, in its perfect place at the base of her back, remains crystal clear in my mind. Like a visual imprint stamping our unclaimed link.

Erotic Enigma.

Erotic Enigma featured with a whip, cuffs and a belt around the calligraphic script. Could it be plainer? She craves kink. Goddamn. Would never have guessed.

A further line of tatt print beneath is an inked typographic stamp — *Property of Sir.*

Who is he? Why do I want to rip his throat out and erase every last letter?

I need to investigate the whats and whys. But I'm in a room with agents who'd jump down my throat if they knew my attention wasn't on the job. Shit timing. I've just blown my chances to buggery.

The only sound is my own voice and the ceiling fans driving my brain crazy. I'm going through the minutiae of the plan, yet my brain vacates the track for thoughts of bare backs and black tatts with erotic edges.

It's been a full-on three hours of initial briefing. I'm being driven in-slowlysane.

"So. Questions? We'll go over this again tomorrow. You'll also be given self-defense and rudimentary martial arts training for your protection. Havana will lead. Pays to be prepared."

"She hates me. The only thing she'll prep me for is my funeral — probably by peeling off my skin while on a spit."

My own jaw ticks. "She's a skilled, trained professional with a remit to ensure you are up to speed with basic self-defense knowledge."

She looks as reassured as a guinea pig watching a cobra slide into the next seat at the dinner table. My heart hammers like it does on a job suddenly gone south. Because I'm distracted by mental images of Kate. I should know better. Ignore my gut tightening every time she evades my eye contact with disgust.

The only ninja here is that inked woman — a black, intricate, temptation of a tattoo. Yet now she plays collected, taking notes in shorthand and keeping contact cursory. While I'm barely holding on to a few fried brain cells.

"Questions?"

She doesn't answer. Just shakes her head.

"Can I get you anything further — anything you need?"

Again. Blanked with a bored stare and a shut down.

My thoughts race. I've gotta get my ass together before I screw another mission. I can't get turned on by a woman I can't have, especially now. My brain skids out at the corner of fuck-fried crazy, knowing I've messed up on all levels.

* * * *

"Yo, Draven! Deaf ears!"

"Sir would fit better. You angling for a warning, or just fucking with death?"

It's Havana. For someone with the hots for me, she has a funny way of nailing my attention. She's head to toe in black, wearing a turtleneck and jeans so tight she must have used a spray paint or a shoe horn. She'd drive most men to horny distraction, I figure. She's more of colleague sister than sexbomb to me. Given her greeting, her seductive lines need work. I hold off telling her. I've made enough mistakes today.

"So, Hav. What ya after?" It's hot in here and she's offering me a chilled bottle of fruit water. I glug it down. "Thanks."

"Listen, I'm sorry 'bout last night. I got things wrong."
Apology. From Hav. Did not see this coming.

"Forget it. We're good."

She nods and narrows kohl-rimmed eyes that don't stay on mine. It's the only eye makeup she wears, but she more than makes up for it with the depth of application and Egyptian mystery. "Wanna say I won't get in your way. It's obvious you dig her. Kate seems an okay type for a civilian."

"Huh?" Exsqueeze me?

"You and whatsherface reporter."

I let a pause hang. Incredulous that Havana would ever talk of personal stuff. Especially to me. Appalled that I'm being called out at work about Kate.

She continues, "She likes you—looks mutual to me. Go for it. Rocco agrees. We've talked and decided what you two do, s'up ta you. We're backin' off."

"You're giving me dating advice? You and Rocco—did I miss the flying pigs outside? Has some alien landed and taken over your crazy mind?"

"Shut it, Bullet." She pushes me and near lands me into the wall. I suspect I'll be bruised, woman doesn't know her strength. Or her station. "I'm serious. You need a girl to soften your edges." She needs a course in staff relations and manual handling.

"Thanks. But there's nuthin' doin'—I'm all work, no play." I get back to working on cleaning my SIG. "You will look after her with the self-defense stuff. No catty female stuff. She's fit but she'd not used to our kinda shit."

"Course. She'll be cool. She's no wuss—for a civilian. I'm not gonna bawl her out. Or kick her ass in private as payback. Though come to think of it..." She grins to show she's kidding.

"Covering bases. Thank God she won't have a gun. She needs to stay safe though."

"She's cool underneath the fake 'tude. Bet she could take a decent shot if she had to. She's pretty smart." Hav grins, then it fades. "I'm stressed, hell, we all are about the mission. But if you like her, that's cool. I got your back."

Shit. I've never had talks like this with the team. I'm railing at myself for blowing things with being too obvious.

"You're saying I've blown it. If you're readin' me. I've messed."

"What you gonna do? Act like you hate her and kidnap her for a kiss session? You're a livin' breathing male with needs."

I shake my head. This convo is giving me ick in the first degree. "Shouldn't be doing this."

"Ever heard of the great sex stress reliever? Have to say I'm angling for some myself." Shit unlimited. I really do not want to be giving this airtime. I almost daren't look up at her, but when I do she's smiling. Havana Martinez — smiling like a goon. I'm getting her drift there's been developments.

"You tellin' me you're hot for Roc? Is this it?"

"Kinda like your blessing."

At least she's over her hots for me. Which is a relief. "Consider it blessed. I'm stoked you worked it out at long last. I'm cool with it as long as we back the hell up on talking about it ever again."

"Okay. Just wanted to be clear." A smirk twitches behind her pokerfaced stern suit.

"And since we're being so clear," I add. "The Kate things stays on the ice — mission first. But 'bout Rocco — he likes you bad. Give the guy a break — don't screw him around, Hav. I know you — you get all cool and shady when somebody comes on strong. Tell me the sitch? Say you aren't fakin' this?"

She swipes me just as hard as the first time. I swear. A bruise bonanza on the way. Embalming with arnica in my future.

"Quit the punches there. What's to hide?"

Her gaze doesn't meet mine. "Yeah. So I like him. We kissed. So what. It was awesome. There'll be more happening on that soon too."

I'm grinning. I never grin when Hav's around. This is a

first. Wow. Epiphany Central. Havana is *so* not the epiphany type. She looks at me with slanted eyes, but there's a spark, as if she's just woken up to a very stark fact. About him or her, I'm not sure which. Like hearing planet Earth is round or somethin'. Or the moon isn't made of spiced deli cheese. "Rockman doesn't have a heart. But he does have other parts that are taking my interest."

"Don't hurt him. His heart is tender for a tough guy."

She does that 'whoa brother' expression again. "Seriously, man."

"Plain as the nose on my face. It goes deep for him with you."

"You have a damn ugly nose. But your teeth are even, and the white smile makes up for it." She grins yet again. As if she's just been given a book of free grin vouchers.

"Can't be too perfect. Or they'd want me for movies. You have a guy with a big, ugly crush on you. Do something with that. Damn straight."

"We'll see. We're good now?"

"We're good. Don't tell Rocco I said…he'll hit me. I gotta protect these teeth."

"Need to go—cleaning duty at Katsaros' place shortly. Better go find my mops and crappy clothes so I'm dressed like shit again."

"Take care, Hav." We exchange fist bumps and Havana stomps away. Some days she looks like a badass model from a Paris runway—others she's the meanest assassin ninja harpy that preys on the criminal kind. If she takes my advice, Rocco's life may never be the same.

I carry on gun cleaning, realizing I've just had Hav's blessing. Not that I needed it. WTF? What is this, Agent Dates Dot Com?

But Kate's vulnerable. She's in my charge. I stopped the escalation on the bed. Maybe I am desperate to push deep inside her wet heat… Move beyond molten kisses, to tail chemistry strong enough to detonate a lab. God knows it's enough to make my nuts ache. Which they are again now.

Shit.

In a warped fantasy zone that appreciates a hot body and a dazzling smile, she rings bells. But my nuts can stay tight and flirt, and fuck ops can't be pursued, whatever Hav and Roc suggest.

I holster my weapon. Heading off to find Kate now, thankful that soon Hav will have her in hand. I'll be in control and out of her line of fire.

* * * *

Kate

Ivan escorts me to the refectory for tea when Dan is summoned by his boss. In contrast to Dan's grim reaper macho air, Ivan takes the escort thing to the next level. Hanging on my every word and being so attentive it's like having a Siamese twin butler who wants to win badges in excellence. But the touching my arm thing really munches on my irritable nibbles.

"Tea or coffee — we have a wide selection."

"Tea. Thanks."

"We have breakfast, Earl Grey, Herbal, Green." Ivan blinks at me, smiling beguilingly. "Or a great array of coffees worthy of any Italian barista's coffee bar menu."

"No coffee, thanks. An Earl Grey would be amazing. No milk."

Ivan smiles and stalls. "Biscuits, cakes or scones." He nods toward plates under domed glass display lids and doesn't budge.

"Seriously? Is this a five star hotel or a Santorini agent lair? This is a bit extreme."

Ivan gets way too close to my face. I can smell his scent, feel his breath too close. Ick.

"Can it not be both? We aim to please. Warbie stocks us with all our favorite items. Whatever you fancy can be arranged."

I jump back. I'm getting tired now. He's being overbearing.

"No, I don't need anything to eat."

Warbie comes to stand over me. Then flits Ivan away with a shooing hand. Perhaps he's seen my discomfort? Now his apron has poodles. His expression is hang dog. Kinda ironic.

"What's up, Katiepie? You seem tired and irritable, cherub, if you don't mind me observing."

"Thanks for that... Nothing like an encouraging chat passing on that I look shit to cheer me up. Didn't sleep much, if you must know, so it's allowed."

Warbie makes an 'oh I get it' face. "Let me make you a juice? I call my combo an Energy Zinger and it'll put the ping in your pep in no time. I'll add ginger, and tonight, I'll make you a sleep brew too. You'll be right as rain soon."

"Okay. The juice would be good. No to drugging sleep tea. I'll pass on the Earl Grey now, too."

Ivan's definitely miffed at Warbie muscling in, and he surprises us both by stamping back to the sink and throwing the cup noisily inside with a clatter. Somebody's having a crankywank.

"No offence," I add. "Just juice and tea don't mix."

"Sure you don't want a biscuit, we have many varieties? May I not fetch you a blanket or a heat pad for your eyes? Perhaps some chocolates or a fruit platter?"

Jeez. Ease up there, Norway Boy. "I'm fine. Thanks. Enough already. Go scale a building or work on your *Spiderman* stunts."

I get up, seeing a pile of magazines and newspapers on a nearby table. They're probably days old but anything from the outside world is seriously tempting. I notice Ivan moves with me. Is he going to be a shadow for the rest of life as I know it?

He doesn't choose a newspaper, but when I go back to sit down he does too. Then he sits down opposite me and stares.

"What? Stop this, will you?"

He shrugs. "Nothing. Just doing my job. Keeping you

cared for."

But I wasn't born yesterday. "What's up?"

"Nothing at all." He blinks at me and I stare, using my evil eye stare that always works in interviews to get to the root of a news story. Ivan sheepishly averts his gaze. "Orders from Sir. I'm not to let you stray too far… Surveillance at all times."

I throw my hands up, finally pissed right off. "I'm in subterranean prison. Where the hell am I going to sneak? The toilet? Heaven forbid!"

"Orders are orders."

Now I'm hurt too. Both at Ivan and at Dan. Sir is going to get a very large piece of my mind, and a good deal of shouting to contend with before I'm done.

Ivan knows he's vexed me and he puts a hand out to touch my arm.

"I'm sorry. Let's not fight. Come on, Katie, you're tired and stressed, and you've been hunched-up. Let me iron out your tired neck muscles."

Ivan's on me in a blink. Who knew he was a masseuse as well as the wall-climbing agent in the dream team? But wow — those digits are crazily effective. He works his fingers deep into the flesh of my shoulders and elicits a moan. Then he rubs and pounds.

I'm letting it all go and he's only just begun. I breathe a long sensuous sigh of approval. "Man — you really are good. You should do this for money!"

"Maybe you could just pay me in kind, mmm?" he whispers. More creep than a convention of creepy creepers.

My tense muscles and tattoo reveal incident regrets are melting away under practiced, able fingers that are inducing a magic relaxation zing.

"How did you get to be good at this? Part of the training?"

"Used to go out with a great masseuse. She taught me everything! In a great many ways. I'll give deep pressure sometime. Might involve me walking on your spine. Always better done fully naked of course."

And why are those the exact words Dan hears when he walks through the door of the refectory—looking right at me melting into a puddle of myself on the seat. He stiffens, death glares Ivan and stomps around the room like Attila the CarnageHungry Hun with a migraine.

Ivan softly instructs, "We should stop now." His fingers are gone. But the pungent reek of riled male on a path of mass destruction pervades.

"There's a dodgy, cricky bit in the center caused by an old trampoline accident in my teens that needs it most!" I say too loud. Every male head in the room turns and zeros in on me. "I've struggled with my left shoulder for years—you have my permission to get on it and give it welly!"

"Guess the massage is over," says Warbie, righting my blissed-out state by pushing a cold glass of water before me. "Wake up call for Katie."

"Ivan, we need to talk," says Dan. He's modelling the pissed-off mask of death to max effect. Like a nasty fight could kick off anytime soon, involving skull cracking. Ivan's already scarpered from the room with Dan pacing behind, and Warbie's now coming back at me with an enormous green gunk drink, looking like the most Hell's Angel cabana boy in history. The straw in it is pink, with a flamingo and a parasol.

"For me—you shouldn't have." I'm going to need to hold my nose on this one.

"Sort you out in no time, drink!" he orders. "Get rid of all those toxins."

"Keep watch with Kate," says Dan over his shoulder. "No disappearing acts. No funny stuff." Then he departs.

What does he think I am? A clown escape artist? "This place gets freakier by the second."

"You don't know the half of it," Warbie replies.

I've woken up in a Subterranean Spy Spa. Where massage turns to fraught feuds and everybody's so nutso my sanity's on the line.

"Drink up!" says Warbie nodding to my brew.

I close my eyes, tip it, and it's every bit as gruesome as I've dreaded.

"Renaming your recipe in honor of this place," I splutter, "Viscous, Venomous and Vile."

* * * *

She has the grace of a gazelle. The strength of a tiger. The ferocity of Beyoncé with chronic PMS, plus the ability of a very active and bouncy cricket. "You're a Tae Kwon Do champ. How am I supposed to compete? I'm a hippo at this stuff."

"It's a simple stance and kick. It's not rocket reinvention." She's standing there like Angelina Jolie's stunt double. *C'mon. Get realz.*

"It is to me."

Havana places palms on hips, then nods and shows me her move again. She grabs my lapels, then leg-strikes me to take me off balance. I wobble and fall on the mat with a loud slap and much winding.

She laughs. "You ain't even tryin', girl."

"Yeah, regular hyena moment. Thanks for your support. Who did you teacher train with? The Spanish Inquisition? Jean Claude Van Damme?"

I defy anyone to withstand her techniques, unless they have a cannon and a flamethrower as aids.

"Have confidence in yourself. Balance and mean it. You're convincing yourself to fail before you begin. I figured you were better than that."

She kicks out at the punch bag near us and near sends it through the wall.

Easy for her to do. I try to mimic but mine's more *Hong Kong Phooey* than Bruce Lee. I don't need more Body Combat classes—I need a week with the Martial Arts Triads and iron limbs.

Havana puts a hand out to pull me up. "You're way too hard on yourself. Why are you so scared of stuffing up?"

Her expressionless face is its usual mask of no giveaways.

Wow. There's a question. Why am *I* this hard on me?

Having a dad linked with shame develops iron armor and a desire never to earn negative attention again. Living a life in secret, hiding from the past that scares you, does that too. So failing makes me fall apart inside. It's why I've always striven to be as good as I can be. I need to stay strong, to make things a success. I need to be great and show the word I don't care and I can do this.

Then, when I know I suck, I back off.

Like with Dan now. Game over.

"Let's just say, as a kid I had more reason to prove myself than most. To keep face for Mum."

Hav nods. "Me too. Single parent, huh?"

"Yes, she went through too much for me to ever show it when I was hurting. But I did. At school they bullied the newcomer. Then somebody spread a rumor."

It's always been my secret mantra. My fight song — my heart's plea. Keep it inside and don't show weakness.

Just get through it. Don't admit you're hurting fit to fall.

"Katie. If you apply and let me show you, I know you'll nail this. For what it's worth, my brother got in with a bad lot — neighborhood gangs. Mom took it real bad and he wound up dead — made me be a cop." She stares at me hard. I'm so shocked, I put my hand to my mouth. "Trying your hardest can't hurt, can it?"

I try it and it works. Possibly because I've just pulled up socks majorly and given Hav her full dose of double respect. She nods, but I see a tiny flicker in her features that tells me she's jazzed I'm getting it.

I reach out for her hand and we do a clenchy handgrip thing that they do in movies. It's a nice moment. Hav and me bonding. Don't quite think she's ready to blast The Eurythmics though.

But, in an instant, I'm back on the floor, being pressed into the mat as she pushes her face into mine like the antichrist.

"Yeah. We're buddies. But if you ever hurt the Dan Man

on my watch I will hunt you down and drink your blood at sundown. Feelin' my realz?"

She's pressing on my windpipe so hard I can't answer. I just nod. Loud and clear.

Wow. I'd commit harakiri before I'd ever face Hav in murderous mood.

I stagger up to my feet. "Glad we're buddies now. Because you scare me rigid otherwise."

"Makes sense for us to be kinda okay around together. I'm not gonna watch chick flicks or do your hair or anything. I'll still bust your balls if you're outta line."

"I'd never ask different. Suspect you still hate my guts deep down about the Dan thing."

She gives me that sidey glance thing she always does. "I don't hate you. Have to admit you kinda pissed me off when I saw the way he got around you. But I'm woman enough to wake up about that. The better person admits defeat."

"What happened to no surrender?"

"We agents fight tooth and nail, but we know when to refocus. Question is—what are you going to do now? Responsibility is on you."

"I don't get it."

"I'm backing up on Sir. But you'd better not bail out. You're exactly what he needs. Even though he's on a mission—you have every right to what's going on between you! Job or no job."

"I don't think so."

"It wasn't a suggestion or a question. It was a damn order." She breathes out steam like a bull at a fiesta. It's thoroughly unsettling. "Right—let's repeat the move again. Then back to the first sequence—over three times without fail."

"Hard mentor."

For the first time ever she falters. Then bites her lip. "Um. Maybe you could teach me a few things back."

"Like?"

"Scaling down makeup." She has a point. She's got more kohl than the kohl master using his kohl discount during kohl centenary week. But I don't want a kick in the jaw.

"When I get my bags back, I have natural makeup. I also do a mean smoky eye."

"Good plan, copy that. It's back already, your case," she tells me. "I was the one who hauled it to your room. What the fuck you got in it?"

"Hallefuckin'lujah!" I say and do a mini-disco dance. "Just bits and bobs."

"So, let's get to it. But this time, no ruddy mistakes. When the guys see you do this they're gonna realize how bloody great I am at teaching. You'll be my star trophy!"

"And what's in it for me?" I pout.

"I'd tell you, but I'd have to…"

I sigh. "Kill me. I know this. Then start at the bloody beginning, yet another time already!"

* * * *

Today's done me no favors. Warbie's lunch smelled delicious — but it was so notdoingitformynervous-belly. I couldn't manage the juice, never mind a plate of food as a follow-up.

Today's activities, and the preoccupation with preparing me to meet the dangerous criminal, A.K.A. my dad, have left me in a clenched ball of nerves.

Sir's rejection bent me out of shape completely too. I'm left ego-crushed and stuck here alone, and up against it. I've no bandages or sexrejection recovery tonic to nurse it better.

The only sunshine in my day is the welcome return of some of my long-lost luggage. I'm rearranging stuff into neat piles now — OCD, thy name is Kate.

I'm actually waiting for another summons for Mission Prep. I have a plan, a script, Havana's moves and some idea of how to use them. Only a brief summary tour, via CCTV footage of the locale and the baddies' hideout, left for my full day's tuition to be complete.

Just as I pull on my favorite soft red T-shirt and super-worn gray jeans, here's a tap on the door. Thank God. I'm saved from death by clothes pile stacking.

"It's me," says Dan. "Can we talk?"

Why do my insides do a mambo at that deep roughed-up voice? Dark as an NYC alleyway and as enticing as a kiss in the back of a yellow cab. I want to smile in excitement but won't let myself.

At least I'm facing him in my favorite casual clothes combo. I know I feel normal and look more relaxed dressed this way.

I clear my throat. "Why ask—you have the key, don't you?"

The door clicks and opens a crack. "Trying to be a gentleman. Being the good guy. Can I come in?"

I shove my hands deep into my pockets. Damn—feeling way too much without guile before this hunk of cop God. He *is* a cop God—this time in sports clothes that make my pulse go pitapat.

"Not as if I'm doing anything useful. Don't fancy your chances re the gentleman passing-out ceremony, though. Gentlemen by the Brit definition tend to tell only the truth."

He's fully in the room now. So big and muscular in his clothes, it hurts my impulses not to just stand and drink him in.

"I tell the truth. When I'm allowed to," he parries back.

"So what did you do to Ivan earlier? He won't even glance near me now, and goes to the other side of the room. What happened?"

Dan breathes slowly through his nostrils. "Orders from above."

"Isn't that your answer for everything?"

Dan's jaw tenses. A sure sign I'm on the nose of the truth. "We had a chat. He's been assigned other duties. Massage is not in his remit. His lines got blurred. Won't happen again."

"He's an okay guy. He was trying to be friendly."

"There's friendly and there's missed the mark and landed in a pool of reprimand. He's fine. You're fine—topic dismissed."

"You're so commanding, Sir." He's so fucking hunky it's criminal.

"Because that's my job. Get over it."

Then my conscience starts to rag me—why am I milking this?

Dan is one of the only two friends I have here and I'm still doling out the snitty. That won't win me favors, or save my skin. Or help me cope with my meet-up with the one man I hate beyond all others. The person best qualified to help me with that is standing beside me now.

Dan shuts the door and moves closer. His sporty, black fitness gear is fit for a soccer ninja. Every time I see him, I'm aware of his height and muscular but athletic build. I deny the presence of awareness that's goosebumping my skin. Betraying urges be gone!

"What's up?" I ask him. "You bored out of your mind too?"

His gaze oil-drills my retinas. "Checking on you. I worry you're not eating. Noticed you've barely had anything. What's with that?"

As usual he's just being all anal agent with the whistles and bells on. But his voice is soft. He's looking at me with a gaze that doesn't tempt a fistfight. Maybe I should be saying sorry for earlier—is that why he's come? I was pretty pissy and petty, now I recall. But then, he rebuffed me and told me to put my clothes back on. Then got all heavy on Ivan as a calling card. "I shouldn't have showed you my tatt. It was totally over the top. If I was shitty earlier, don't take it personally." Not an apology, but as close as he's getting. "Sir Who Must Be Obeyed must learn that I'm the girl least likely to play Obey Orders Beach Ball. I have history on that."

He shrugs. "You do tear me down but, I admit this at my peril, you actually make me like it."

"You have a strange way of showing it."

"Nobody else has the balls to really nail it." He sits on my bed. Uninvited. My bed. Him. Big, muscly and very fit. My bed is not the most helpful place to put himself. Especially when his muscles are revealed at close range and it's where we did intimate things before.

Perhaps sateen trim has that effect on him?

So I blurt it out before my brain can tell me to do a U-turn. "I'm sorry for blaming you and kissing you and launching myself at you when my blood was up."

He stares hard. "Tatt was a shocker. But not in the way you think. Total power move with *badittude*. I didn't see that coming."

I narrow one eye as I watch him to see if he's being serious. "Seb, my ex-fiancé, was too much like you for comfort— makes me react. He was Mister Command and Make It So. Including when he worked out I'd outstayed my use to his career. I lash out at rejection. But you're not Seb the Bastard. I also figured you pushed me away because of the Dad thing. That kind of hurt me too."

"Your biological father is nothing to you. Why would he matter to me?"

I shrug. Because he shows the family shady side. Reveals that Perfect Kate isn't so perfect when you dig deep. The thing I struggle with most.

"My dad isn't someone I'm proud of. I figure agents like you would prefer the people they tangle with to be pretty squeaky clean."

"You think I'm that shallow?" He's offended and it bounces out in waves. "Was Seb the Sir on your back?" his voice is low.

I shake my head. "No. He was strict vanilla control freak—my rebellion in ink was the Sir who came next. Seb was a guy who thought he was in control—as an antidote I went for one who truly was and who wore that well in the bedroom. He went only by the name of Slash."

Dan is watching me, saying nothing.

Which is something.

"Shocked?"

"Not as much as you probably think."

I like it. Because he's not judging. He's just listened, which is more than either of them would have done.

"Sir is history. After Seb I *really* wanted to let loose and tap my wild side. Turns out I did — only to be bummed out when he found a new interest. Shame he didn't dump me before I committed it to ink."

Dan's eyes darken and he reaches out to link his fingers with mine. "So, Sir is not your steady?"

I shake my head. "Sir wasn't the steady type. He went on to first-time submissives new. Saw my tattoo and did a dump and run."

Shit — why am I sharing my disasters?

Dan lets out a low breath through his teeth. "Quite a tatt to claim for someone with a short attention span?" He's nailed it in one sentence. "But hopefully you'll find other Sirs who can live up to the position."

I stare back. Shake my head. "Why do you care?"

"Because a tatt like that nails attention. I'm thinking you just need to find yourself that new Sir."

Is he teasing? He's so unfazed by my stuff — a cop thing? It's so bloody refreshing not to have guilty baggage. Not to feel like I'm a kinked-out reject.

"Plenty more Sirs in the sea," he says.

"I live in hope." I do. But I'm choosy as hell too.

I stare at Dan, who stares right back — irises on fire. The sparky vibes crackle like space dust as a gourmet dessert topping.

Dan whispers, "Forgive me, but both guys sound like idiots. Don't sweat the sorries to me — I dig the tatt. Wish I'd thought of Kink Ink myself."

'Kink Ink' — how does he manage to make that statement sound like an intimate proposal? Why would he want kink

ink too? Unless…

"We're friends, aren't we?" I say. But I'm wondering if friends who match in the kink stakes can stay friends?

He answers, "We can try. But we both need to work on control issues. You need to learn to trust me. I need to stop letting you fry my brain and make my dick go crazy." He smiles. "So—let's loosen up and treat one another like project partners."

Ah, project buddies.

But, *woomph,* the oxygen in my lungs doesn't work, because I've already imagined him inked for kink. Causing a distinct lack of breathing ability and dizziness. Dan is in his muscle-back gym vest, tattoos as sidekicks, and in shiny loose shorts that display legs that could cause seizures, is too much of an open invitation not to imagine him naked. If I could pick, it would be a massive black snake circling up his inner thigh…

And the word 'partner' takes on an entirely new fixation in my head.

One my greedy brain grabs with relish. It doesn't help that his gym-ready clothing isn't good for my healthy pulse.

I softly repeat a mantra I really should be taking more heed of. "Sounds like a good plan, Dan. I'd sworn off dangerous men. Given my heritage, I should be sticking to that like glue."

He stares from under dark, curled lashes. God—so unfair at how blessed he is with those! He rises to go.

"Heading to the gym, Kate. All this flight time and briefings eat into my training schedule. Gotta pay with sweat."

"Thought I was getting another briefing?"

"You've done enough. Time to get sweaty and kick back."

I nod. Watch his mouth—that's just formed a word I can't release. Sweat. What's with me? He slowly winks.

"Maybe you should forgive yourself for that tattoo for starters, huh?"

I jump in seizing my chance. "Can I come? To the gym,

being here is driving me nuts without exercise. I need to escape this room."

"You didn't eat—you sure you can take that?"

I let out a breath. "I need a workout so badly it's criminal. Endorphins always help my equilibrium. I even have fitness gear now." I snatch my pile of Lycra and a towel, and my shower gel, and I'm good to go.

Then I realize what I'm putting myself through in choosing Dan as a gym buddy—in the six-pack stakes, he's buy one get one free phenomenal. It could turn a girl's head. He shrugs shoulders made for martial arts. He stares at me. Gray gaze boring into mine. I really have to work not to stare at that very fine chest. That dusting of hair—who knew I'd've liked that so much? Even his neck cords are so cute I want a collection in a cabinet…never mind the legs that make mine shake like an earthquake's hit.

Hey sista. Step away. Sweet Jerusalem, don't puddle on the floor.

I guess the whole abducted by Interpol situation is getting to me, re the lust attacks. But I'm still going to grab my chance to escape to the gym.

"If it'll cheer you up let's do it."

"You can let me beat you on the treadmill," I answer.

"I'll cuff you up and make you watch my work out before that happens."

I follow him to the gym faking huffy. But we're smiling, and inside I'm quivering thinking of cuffs and sweat.

And that body. With a new snake tattoo.

Plus the revelation that Dan isn't deterred by my kink ink. In fact he seems not to mind it on me at all.

Chapter Eleven

Dan

When it comes to fitness, Kate is my match plus a foot floored on the gas pedal. A kissable smile in the mix — which ain't allowed.

Sure, I like that she's hot at fitness, but I hate it in equal measure. The competitor in me can't stand the showdown. Will she be that way in bed? My terms? Or hers?

The urge to stride over and plant a smacker on that mouth grinds inside me. Even without glossed lips she vibes me — can't get my head around this spell.

"How do you like our gym?" I'm breathing hard but I wanna play normal. Talking lightly. Focusing on the run. Not letting my gaze latch on to her fine ass in full spray-on activewear high definition.

"Fine."

"Just fine?"

She grins. "I'm in the zone. Talk later."

I block out hard-ons and force my attention from her ass in gympants and the impressive curves of her biceps and breasts. For a slim girl, she has undulations that a man likes. She causes craziness to my libido and brain cells.

We push ourselves to our limits. Treadmill, kettlebells, bikes and a full range of machines that ends up a full-on workout stretching us both. My legs shake, and that's rare.

We get to the locker room drenched in sweat and endorphin-pumped, mainlining water like Rocco does sports drinks.

"Nice workout, Joseph."

"When in Rome...can't have these agent types showing me up. I'm a fitness hobbyist — makes me take it personally. I was kidding about the gym — it's great," she remarks, between gulps of water. "Full of surprises."

"See, you're not the only one with all the moves," I let slip. Damn. It's that tattoo's repeat play on my brain track, so I hastily cover. "You're fit. *Really* fit. You don't give in. It's not about the running to show your butt off either. Or to look cute in kit. You push."

She stares at me, ensnares me, and I have to work not to falter.

"From you that's a compliment, Sir." She fakes a military command tone.

"Do you have to deflect every damn compliment?"

She shrugs. So I go back to her original statement. "Yeah — we smuggled some perks in. Without the gym work we'd go crazy. Rocco already is." I slug water. But I'm trying not to notice the sweat patches on her intimate areas and wishing I could peel layers and push her down for more action — then really make her head turn with my moves.

She throws me completely with a random question, "Tell me about Warbie. I sense you're his blue-eyed boy wonder. He's fun, got charisma — I like him a lot."

"I'd put a word in but he's gay."

"This I knew. So does he just idolize you or fancy you?"

"What's not to love?" I grin. Shit, I'm sounding like Rocco. I know how much that slimes me. "Nah. He has my back. I also got his. Worked a lot of jobs together. Seen a lot of stuff."

"Ah, you captain for that team too?" she says, and does a Jack o' Lantern smile.

"Straight as a very straight line. Women all the way. Thought you'd have twigged to that by now." I try not to stare at the droplet of water on her lower lip. Or the sweat beads heading south to her valley of no return. The nipples showing through the top are my undoing. Wow — the thought of tasting spins me on mental skates on a lake. I'm already on my butt and doing Bambi legs.

You want this you doofus.

Stop playing high school games. Go for what you want.

"Warbie and I have worked together before. FYI, my eyes are gray, not blue. Hurt you hadn't noticed. Clearly my mind control hasn't worked. You have Warbie right—he's a great guy to have around in a crisis."

"Been too busy insulting you to admire your eyeliner, Sir."

I fake a cheesy smile. "Keep that up and you might get promoted to favorite journalist."

"You have others here? You collect them?"

Sparring with Kate is fun. But annoying as hell too. "Warbie was one of yours. Maybe that's why you gel—hacks together. Drama queens and lushes all, I'm told."

I watch as she towels off her sweat—*can I keep that as a souvenir?* "You mean if I play my cards right I could apply for a job making Interpol's beds and suppers? Hold me back!"

I'm properly laughing, and I never do that at work. I rarely laugh hard at all. Since Nathan. Since Gina. Losing two people who get you in close succession can do that. I may be a hard ass but I do, I've found, still have a heart with a spot that leaks fuel.

"Shower, sweet cheeks?" I ask her, feigning Warbie's accent. "Summon me, mistress—should you require anything to improve your stay?"

She laughs, then looks at her disarray. "Sweat cheeks fits better. Industrial strength power washers and a loofah with disinfectant to go."

"Take the wetroom. I'll wait—you go first."

"I'm moved beyond words." She does a hand-swirling courtier courtesy pose. I'm grinning like a boy. Together we play so High school it needs its ass kicked. So I launch a fluffy towel and point to the door. She enters, closes, and I itch to follow so badly I root my feet.

So why don't you do it?

No cameras. You knew this.

Jumping into burning buildings, scaling sheer faces and throwing grenades is one thing. Taking bad guys down face to face—perk of the job. Facing women you're attracted to head-on, and throwing risk at the wall during work time after what happened with Gina and the fails I made with Nathan—well, give me a grenade between my teeth any day.

Can I handle getting close to a woman when falling for Gina blew apart in all the wrong ways?

I smell hot disaster and inability to stop my feet. I suspect head-turning sex is not in my sanctioned Interpol plans. But fuck it.

To use agent code—gun me up and live life wild—because we can be dead before we're ready.

As Gina learned to her cost.

I've survived in the wreckage of this lesson, so I know.

* * * *

"So—I'm in here. Because I want you. Sound doable?"

As sex-intro lines go it's crud. This, I know.

But I'm inside the wet room and it's because I want to be inside her. My dick is loaded with need and a hankering for action.

The door wasn't locked. Did she know? Did it matter when I have a master key anyhow? Would tasered wild horses have stopped me?

"Come in, the water's lovely," she says. Her voice is a gentle enticement like the soothing H2O cascade she's under.

Inside, I'm cheering for joy. Mostly because I can see the black blur of that tatt, the shadow of her pussy. My lust stupor leads me to the shower—a clear screen that's steam-fogged, and the hot steam swirls Turkish bath style. I shuck off my shorts and vest. Move the damn screen.

"So I can join you and you won't yell and attack me? Not

sure if this was my plan or yours — or neither?"

"Get in, Dan. What did I say before about talking too much?"

Kate stops moving, but she's in silhouette. A very lithe and wet-hot silhouette.

I want to rain on her with my greedy, wild kisses. I want to do it long enough to explain this impulse without words. So she'll know I'm more than just hot for her — I'm brainlessly gone. This isn't just a sex pit-stop. This is something we can't ignore and not follow.

"Sounds like you're not as pissed with me crashing your shower as I feared you might be."

"I'm only pissed it took you this long."

My hardon's become an untamable thing with a mind of its own. Proud as iron between my legs and rampaging to get at her. It knows where it wants to go and I don't want to stop its fast-track aspirations.

"I can't get your damn tattoo, face, your hot body or sexy ass out of my brain. Were you waiting? Or am I totally wrong in this?"

"We both know the answer." Kate slides out and into my body space. Wet. Glistening. Naked, and even better in the flesh than my dreamed-up, brain-airbrushedportrait version. "Waiting can heighten anticipation, can't it? Thanks for asking first, Sir. Thought you'd never climb down off the high and mighty principles code. Glad you did."

She welcomes me to her, wrapping my head in her wet, slithering hands. Wow. As lines go hers rock.

Especially when her tits stand to such ready attention, peaked just for me, rubbing at my chest to say hi — and she smiles as her mouth meets mine and teases a welcome.

She's glistening like a nymph in a moonlit pool. She's here ready for me to touch and feel and kiss. *Let me at it!* I touch everywhere I can with fingers, palms, mouth, tongue.

I claim her mouth, paying special homage after snatched kisses that could be improved on with privacy and no time limit. Man, is what greets me divine! She's a tongue ninja who's just got her Frenchies black belt. Fuck—she's going to blow my mind. Backwards. Then flat on its back.

"So sue me, I want you. Can't believe I'm saying it but I do..." she whispers as I kiss her neck and shoulders like a ravenous desert wanderer at a full banquet table. She's all over my body too in the most blissful of ways. Will I stay the course or do a spurt of shame in this fast-speed, surprise shower flesh orgy for two?

"I'm in meltdown, honey. But this has gotta be consensual—you gotta know the full score and be okay with it."

"Meaning?"

"No freak-outs after fucking."

Wow. I'm being blunter than a rough-hewn brick, but I guess that's the power of a nuclear dick that's just found where it most wants to be and won't wait. I have to think with my brain for a minute here. It takes concerted effort.

"I don't want my mission jeopardized by any of this."

She soothes me with her kisses. "Won't be. Why would I freak out when the sex will be as good as I know it's going to be?"

"Even if it's vanilla sex? No feasible kink in this place? No time, not enough sex shops with decent opening hours for starters..."

She laughs against my cheek. "Do you hear me complaining? It's all in the execution, Sir."

I whisper, "Just so happens erotic is my brand. I like my girls in cuffs. Leather usually. Sometimes rope. Ankle bars. When it comes to sex play I like control and experimentation. Even women who'll treat me bad."

"Sounds divine. I've never tried being bad with a Sir, but now you bring it up, it could be workable."

"What's your fave kind?" I ask her.

"Men who know what they want and aren't afraid to take it."

I smile and hold her in place with hands at each side of her face as I kiss her like I've wanted to since I met her.

Inside I'm singing — and it's a hot sexy song that makes me feel joy and power. Especially as I dick-press against her and she widens to let it slide where she most wants it.

"Fuck, Katie!"

Bastard and Sir shelved her. I want to show her it can be different. I may have a pedigree of callous job smarts, but I want to show her it can be good and a guy can only go on for so long repeatedly mentally undressing her and replaying that cave kiss on slow-mo.

Finally she's mine and naked, wet and showering is part of the party trick too.

I touch that delicious, dark delta of curls at her pussy and find it hot and wet and ready for me. She gasps as I finger-lave her there — giving her due warning of what's to come. Enjoying her breathing and tiny squeaks of appreciation, I rub her clit as I kiss her mouth hard and get her panting good and hard. Nice. Her dirty tongue tells me this is just the tip and she wants way more.

I pull a condom from my three-pack. That gym locker stash was my savior today. "You like?"

"Try...find out."

I'm smiling as I slide my finger inside her, and she grinds onto it and grins into my kisses. She clenches strong muscles good and hard, that have me panting in anticipation.

"I think you're packing more ammo than that, Sir."

I growl deep in my throat as my dick pushes my foreplay out of the way. I'm in a condom in seconds. My tip at her pussy is being promised a damn good time.

"This trying to be a gentleman thing ain't all it's cracked up to be."

She kisses me. It's not the way you'd kiss politely. Wet and demanding and hard with a tongue that's carnal and explicit in each move. "Then don't be shy. Be Sir. Fuck me."

I pull her ass up and raising her as I spear my dick inside in with one move that takes us both hard and fast against the wall. She yelps, but her pleasure's clear — it's a fun, 'give it to me now' sound and, man, she's excited. Climbing me like a tree at the sensations of being joined. Hard's exactly the brand of sexual self-expression I need right now.

"Sir. You got me. Consider me under arrest."

She's moving on me. Claiming her control. I pull out, then ram back home, deeper. Her approving moan is all I need to know she likes being lawfully detained.

"Let me set the pace."

My fingers tease her nipples as I slam back and slide her up the wall with the ferocity of my thrusts. But I sense she wants it hard and fast, so I speed up to fall in line with her demands. Damn, it's the fastest action, full throttle, blast-it-on-turbo fuck I've had in a while. She's loving every nanosecond.

I'm pounding, pumping hard into her pussy and taking no prisoners, and she's grabbing hold so tightly, it's probably leaving nail marks. She's slamming back, jolting up and down on my dick with cries of an oblivion-ride to match. Such obvious enjoyment—it's liberating to watch a woman so at home with how she wants it, especially when I hear her pussy making noises that tell me it's having fun all on its own.

And it turns me on in a way I haven't been. No boner turning flaccid here—no job regrets. No visions of crime scenes. No Nathan lying lifeless. No memories of receiving news from my NYPD colleagues that my regular woman has just been pronounced dead.

This is steel cock that can go on, and is ready to rocket with wild woman unleashed. Kate's grinning as she's coming.

"Come for me, baby. Come for me, Katie."

It slips out. But it's her name I'm calling, nobody else's. I feel her tense her muscles, then release on purpose. Is it punishment or approval? Again, and again. It blows my mind. I wanted to last and show her some good love, but I can't steer this. She's grinding on my cock, using her hold on me for torsion, and she's coming hard and fast in explicit Technicolor—I hear her pleasure moans and sounds and it's manna.

"Yeah, baby. Man, you're good."

She's such a wet dream to watch in action. Now I'm lost — losing my control inside her as my climax rips me to shit and I fill her pussy with my cum. Our friendly Mr. Condom is our only barrier here and her pert, glossy breasts promise me future wet dreams. I may have come, but there's a lot more that I want from this chick, and soon. She's a legend and I want it all.

Kate looks at me, licks my lips, and clings onto my neck as the water beats us, but we'll never be clean after this future-altering action. Just hooked.

"Okay, you can call me Katie. Kinda like it. Now you've earned your fuck stripes."

I lift her, but her legs are still wrapped around me, and my dick is inside her. It likes it there.

"My muscles have gone. Think they're asleep. A bed to lie down on would be nice — do I ask too much? Could Warbie impro?"

"Shower — take it slow. You'll come down in time. No way is anyone intruding on this spot of heaven, Katie mine."

She clings to my torso and I've never felt manlier. More brimming with the thought that 'For Now I Want This and More of This'. For me that's big. Larger than huge.

"Thanks, Sir. You were awesome." She kisses me, eyes fluttering open.

My mouth's gone dry. Dry as my thirst on Planet Hot after everybody had been doing a twelve-hour highenergy workout without water.

Our gazes slowly meet.

"Full points for fucktastic."

"I win," I answer, and she shakes with low laughter. "Thanks to you. Next time I'll find us some toys."

Whoever her past lovers were — they were jackass dickwads. They didn't deserve her, and are owed time inside just for messing with her head. I turn her round and sweep her hair aside. Thinking of the impact this woman's fine ass made in an airport, I revel in the fact that right now she's mine! Talk about ego promotion. I kiss those shoulders and pay attention on her neck until she moans afresh. Then I let my eyes fall to the tattoo. The one that had me at a glimpse.

Thankfully I'm a guy who is practiced in putting things right in the long haul. At making sure justice is served. She needs ego-boosting – and I know the best therapy man has. This and more of it.

"Guess there's a new Sir on duty around here – if it suits, I could take over your personal needs duties?"

She wiggles her smooth, sweet ass over the greedy tip of my pleading dick. Then gives me cartoon chick eyes and my cock's so zoom-charged it might've been bitten by a lethal tropical bug. There's no telling it 'down boy' now.

"Oooh," she answers. "I'm not sure. Maybe we should try so I can judge?"

Kate sighs and pulls my hand to stroke her. Katie. Knew it. Proved it. Claimed it.

"More please. I promise I'll come willingly." I think that answer is a definite yes.

Equals one happy but code-busted guy.

* * * *

Kate

Dan touches me, and I implode inside in the nicest of ways. Just a flick of my clit after orgasm and I'm ready again. The point of contact tingles and surges with intense heat and power throughout my entire body, and I shiver at the way he kisses me from behind. Something inside fizzes and melts, and I yearn for more. My pussy wants him. All the way, *every* way.

He can be my stand-in Sir, no question.

Any old time he chooses.

I'm smiling as I feel his dick slide behind me. The breath shoots out of my body – he's so big and long. He takes me deeper than any man has. He's already in a condom. The packet's tossed on the floor. Quite a guy.

Dan moves, and it spins me into happy-mounting-thrills-zone. Back and forth—hit my spots then slide. Deeper, so far I cry out. A spot that sets my neurons on fire. Deep, holy G. The sensation is a sublime hit but this is the tip of our action, merely suggesting adventures to follow. What will he be like with toys and tools and full Sir on parade? I can barely wait.

I moan when he bites my neck in a way that says he's about to get heavier than before. For vanilla straightforward—this hits my notes.

"More...you really want more?" I'm a kidder. But why stop when it can be this much fun? "Don't you have work to do?"

"Work can wait," he growls into my neck, then flicks me round and he's on my nipples, seizing them with his teeth and staking his claim to parts of me, not fully versed in the ways of Dan.

"Ow," I protest playfully as the passion verges on pain, nipping, sucking, grazing. But it feels damn good and I force myself deeper into his mouth, and revel in sensation when his hand claims my sex again. He's rough with me but I like it. My clit wants him—my whole pussy craves his dick. But there's time yet. He's fingering my folds, and I'm nonverbal with pleasure as his finger goes up inside me.

I tongue-kiss my approval at his handling of this second ride of our day.

"Shame we don't have a bed," I whimper.

"You like it in beds? You keep talking about beds..."

"More room, soft landings."

"And here was me thinking you're a girl who likes it hard?"

"Very hard. You up to that? Those cuffs have been on my mind...often."

What a tease I sound. But something about Dan Draven wires me to flirt and get pushy playful, and crave all he can give.

"Can you handle that I like it rough back, Katie?"

I stare at him, trying to discern his meaning. "What kind of rough?"

"I'm pretty great at control. But I like it rough in return. You up for being dominant?"

"Never say no." Just then the wind makes the door rattle in its frame, spooking me and springing me right back to the moment. "Shit. What if somebody opens the door?" I'm whispering. "It'll cause a scandal."

He's working my clit with immense skill to make my breath quicken and my pussy yearn more for his hardest part. As water beats down and we drain Santorini—and one another—dry.

"What if we're interrupted? Doesn't that turn you on? The view from here is so worth not stopping."

And to match his words, he rams inside me. Ramrod dick that drives me so it scoots me up the wall hard to his body. He pounds inside me hard, again, again, again. Filled so full I'll never recover from the perfection of this.

"How about I flip you over again? I want you not knowing which way is up after this…"

"You wouldn't…"

"Wouldn't I?"

And in a swift sharp turn he has me against the tile. This time face to tiles and dick pressing into me, hard and long and entering on one firm steady thrust that goes right to my deepest place and makes me moan out in joy. He holds me there as I pulse my muscles against him as hard as I can.

And his groan of desire buoys me like a dingy sailing home after a storm.

"You said you liked it hard," he teases softly.

"You listen, don't you?"

And I'm so nearly undone on one thrust I can barely talk, let alone stand to think. He plunges back out and back in, and repeats the move over three, four times at a speed that leaves me seeing stars, and I'm slapping back onto his balls with force, but it's all the more sublime. We start to come together. Panting and groaning in our joint fight for the summit.

It's heightened even further when a strong, commanding finger claims my clit and takes no prisoners. He flicks me hard and fast, and ceaselessly presses that spot of flame until I'm molten and coming joyously with unabashed moans of full rapture.

"Fuck, Dan."

"You got it!"

I'd laugh if this wasn't the biggest, most life-shifting, fate-altering, world-on-its-axis orgasm of my entire life. I had great, wild sex with Slash. But I never experienced this utter, forceful possession. The other was play time with props — this is hungry, dark man's fulfilment.

He's staking his own climax and nailing it, and I'm limp and spent and taking all he has. Wanting what he can give. Wanting to give this guy the pleasure he's surged through me so ably and relentlessly. Just wow.

My privates are liquid honey, and internally my body's temp spiked, then mellowed to seduced nirvana. I can smell Dan's musky male scent everywhere. Like a keeper signature scent.

"You're bad for me," I whisper-slash-whimper. "But so good."

"You think this is something I can help?" His eyes plead harder than the words. He touches my forehand so gently it's a featherlike caress. You're bad for my resistance, Katie. If this was a police course I'd be failing and sent back to college. I vowed not to go here with you — let's just say I've been avoiding personals since losing close buddies in the last couple of years."

I turn and he's holding me in his arms, and it's good because I may well slither into a heap of myself at his feet.

"Sorry for your loss. I'd come back to college with you — as long as I could keep coming that way with you. You could keep me as your shower pet. It's kinda special. Best Sir for the job."

He grins. Then kisses me, and his fingers move on the flesh of my shoulders and neck, and I can feel the heat from his body. It feels tantalizingly good. Tantalizingly tempting. I like that hand on my shoulder, my décolletage, then his lips on my neck. Hell. I bend my head to relish the closeness. Submit completely to the touch, the intimacy and connection. This is a crazy, dangerous and highly affecting thing.

But so is this man.

"We really can't do more sex in here..." I whisper and push on his chest.

"There is no can't," he says.

But I mean it. "There'll be a search party soon. Somebody's bound to come find us here." Even if right now what I yearn for yet another good, soft, enveloping fast orgasm. Followed by a slow deep kiss-andspoon head spin chaser.

I touch Dan's arm to make him stop. Just as a very loud attention-stalling bleeping noise comes from somewhere close by. It's a ramping tone that gets louder, yet in only the four rings it takes Dan to get to it.

"Shit, speaking of called back to real life," he curses and strides butt-naked to retrieve his clothes as he answers.

Monosyllabic curt words ensue as he's speed-pulling on his clothes faster than I can switch off the shower and find a towel. He's already at the door. And I'm with him — still showerdamp and my clothes in dampspotted disarray

"What's up?"

His face is grim meets the grim reaper one-on-one. "Shit's gone down. Agent injured bad after an attack."

"Who?"

"Havana. Cleaning job took a nasty turn."

I already miss the heat of Dan's torso against my body. But the moment has gone. My stomach's just pretzeled into a million Chinese knots. I feel like I've been naughty in high school, and we've been summoned after sneaking off. Yet, so much darker.

"Let's get you safely back to your room," he says.

It's over. My Secret Sexy Sir's gone. To be replaced by the Sir who clicks into full-on serve and protect mode and living his life on a way too dangerous line.

Dan stares at me, his face is somber. "Don't revert to type and push me away, Kate. This isn't over." He pauses and lets his real-time tone linger. "I know you've been hurt—I won't do that. I'll stop Donaldson with my bare hands if needed. You've so much potential you spin my head around. Don't push me out anymore. That's exactly what you mean to do, isn't it? Because they all did that to you?"

I wobble but I don't answer. He's so close to the truth his toes are on the parapet of my destruction.

"We will reconvene. When things settle."

"Okay. If that's what you want," I answer.

Dan's linking his hand in mine and it's time to head back to reality. We kiss deeply—before we dive into the shit pool together. Me and my steelhard asskicking Legend of a Sir.

Chapter Twelve

Dan

"What the hell happened to Hav?"

Rocco's a weird mix of gray and white pallor that isn't good. If he's gonna fall, I'm yelling timber and leaping away. A dead weight of Rocco could cause loss of life. "She's been fucking shot."

We look into the room she's been taken to. She's on the bed – her face a tapestry of grazes, gashes and a bouquet of bumpy bruise promises to come. The dark blood spot on her shirt would go unnoticed were it not for the wet telltale signs of the stain on the bed. Her eyes flick up to mine in a silent *'kay, Boss. Keep the faith.*

"She's exhausted. Too shocked to talk," says Rich. "Emergency medic coming in to operate. Should be here shortly"

"Thank God," says Warbie. "I'll go get stuff ready." He softly tugs at Kate. "Could you help?"

She nods. She's as ashen as Rocco. This blood loss – shot agents thing is happening with way too close regularity. "Of course I'll help. Tell me what you need." They go off and I'm glad Kate's otherwise engaged. It'll stop her fretting. I force away my brain's urges to think about her or what happened downstairs in private, and the ramifications it has on us going forward.

I shrug off the lapse and walk into the room. Rocco's by Havana's side. He's shaking – the big guy totally gone to fall-apart bits. Twisting her fingers in his hand while Ivan looks on broodingly, as if he's about to kick shit out of something as revenge. Can't say I blame him. Maybe I'll come too?

I'm guessing they've developed more than a just friend's appreciation.

Rich talks softly. We're in the room of a sick patient, after all. In a hospital we'd have a strict beds numbers rule. "Says she knew something was off as she got near the mansion. Felt like she was being watched. Instinct made her flick a U-turn to get back. Then she was tailed – car tried to force her off the road. She ended up shooting the car off the roadway and leaping out. But took a slug in the process. You know those roads, take a pro rally driver to keep a car straight with a jackass pushing you for kicks."

"Jackass with a gun too," I state. "So what's next?"

"We'll talk of this later, but I'm sensing our mission needs re-planning and civilian input is off the agenda. Way too dangerous on top of Tavi."

The relief that washes through me speaks louder than a loud hailer. I've gotten in way too deep. She matters. I'm protecting her above all else. What the fuck? But I'm still über-relieved.

"How'd it pan out, how'd she get back safe?"

"You know Hav. Did the do and threw herself clear. Hence the scratches. Think that arm's a sure break. Leg isn't too clever either. Hopefully the shot is a flesh wound. Doc on way."

"Katsaros' orders? Is that your intel?"

"Not sure. He has enemies. But it's smelling to me like they're wise. The Kate thing can't go ahead."

Yep, I'm still so damn happy about that I'm damn pissed-off too. This could set the mission back by months.

Rich can read my mind better than anyone. "We will go in tonight. Night mission. Surveillance, reconnaissance. Then we hit them with our Plan B when we're prepped."

"And Andreas? Any word."

"It's gone quiet." Rich's face is grave enough to suggest the worst.

Three agents impacted is bad news.

I feel my jaw flex like vised iron. Because I'm running way close to the wire here. My first thought was for women in my charge. I'm not caring enough that the entrapment plan is blown apart.

I know it so hard the knowledge causes a painful, searing twist of anxiety in my belly. Because I felt like this before when Nathan died. I cared more about him fleeing a siege than the collar. It ended up with us both taken hostage. These fucking lapses ended up in a double jeopardy because Nathan was gunned down.

Detached control must be all in this job and I'm ballsing big time.

Perfection is my watchword. But tonight I've already bent my codes and taken risks with Kate. Correction — got involved. Given her orgasms, promised more. Staked a claim and branded her.

But alluding to futures to come? Really?

What's with me? As if?

My window for doing the right thing and being detached is blown. When I scrambled to dress and gun up I was swearing at my own foolishness full tilt.

Redman walks with me in the lower corridor. If he suspects what I've done, he pays it no heed. So I'm figuring he's clueless.

"Change of plans, Sir. You'll reconnaissance at one. We sent Andreas word to get out — if he's still alive and able to meet you, he'll have intelligence and a USB to pass. Boat trip at nightfall. We need ammo stored at strategic points. Some work done on door locks and prep. You're on this — and we're down an agent, so I'm relying on you to fill Dockery in. He knows he's on duty but he needs to be briefed."

So we have a plan. Andreas is our guy on the ground at the mansion. At least Andreas is sharpeyed to opportunity, even if I'm missing markers by a mile mooning over Katie. Flagging and sidestepping protocols at every turn — I curse and walk into the Troika-launching cave where the speedboats are housed.

"Can we ensure Joseph gets a sleeping aid tonight? She's wired, traumatized. Antsy as hell," I say.

"I notice she trusts you. I think involving civilian intervention with this level of challenge would be foolish now. Warbuckle will deal with her in your absence."

Which has to be good. Retreat. Back off. Recognize error and sort it.

My jaw ticks. Tending to her needs. Haven't I just? What've I started?

"We'll reconnaissance the Katsaros mansion periphery. Count on it."

Getting me back on the job and back in the game is the best thing for us all. I head off to find Dockery. Already working out what I'm going to say to Kate before I leave.

And that troubles me greatly — that already I'm still putting woman before mission. Fool that I am.

* * * *

I call to my team as I step in the boat. "Mone Dunamis for one a.m. Troy, coordinates please?" I jump to Troy's side at the wheel of the boat and he flicks me a nod. The two Greek aides in our team who know every inch of the island discuss arrangements as Dockery arrives on board.

The team's on course, as is the boat. Even if I feel more at sea than sanity should allow.

"Issues with the civilian, Sir? Sent the base into freefall, I reckon." Ivan looms behind me, his too-snarky jab on target. His bulk in the dark light looks reptilian. Always something I haven't trusted about Ivan. Too damn perfect, pensive. Too much watching every little move of mine.

His angry, narrowed-eyed expression is the full pissed-off python deal. Where is his big objectivity and hard to faze chip now?

"Paying her personal attention, Sir. Is that regulation?"

"None of your goddamned business."

"But you get sidelined—we all fuck up, Sir." The way he Sirs me raises my hackles.

"Now is not the time," I grind the words out. Pissed he'd dare to question.

"I understand, but I don't trust her."

His tone alone sends my 'calm and collected' to 'about to rip him to ribbons.'

Then he pushes my no-go button. "What if she's a plant? Partisan to her old man?"

"Trust the intelligence, Agent. I do." I note he's clenching fists. I'm grinding my jaw fit for a dental visit.

"Enough to risk the game?"

"You're out of line." He may be taller than me, but he's wiry where I'm built. I can take him and he knows it. He stands back, then moves aside.

I hate rising to his bait but I'm antsy. Hav's in med bay and Kate's on watch—playing nurse as if she has a choice. The whole Kate thing messes up my brain with recriminatory ear worms.

I'm more pissed off than a very pissy definition of the word angry. So I snap.

"Get back to base, Ivan. You aren't coming tonight. I don't want someone I can't trust at my back. Send Tomas. Doubletime."

Again, I curse my instincts. Because they tell me Ivan has a point. As much as I keep affirming that they don't know Kate like I do.

I curse my hang-ups, fuck-ups and hormonal flaws. While against all my training and experience, a bewitching tattoo still brands my brain.

The memory of a hesitant Kate. A new fearful spark in her eyes when faced with the control room and Redman, makes my neck hair prickle. Is Ivan right?

Was bringing her a mistake? I'm starting to think choosing her was a grave error. Plan changes never bode well, and getting intimately involved is a big, shitty disaster. Especially not knee-jerk decisions to kiss her, or take her in the shower room…or promise future trysts for more…

I see my catastrophe in true Eureka moment style. Then a gremlin says—*Ivan is a career cop climber. You know damn well he's after your job. He's playing you.*

Kate is now tangled in this assignment's nitty gritty barbed wire. Knowing Ivan, he won't give in without stripping me—and Kate—down when he can.

Tomas hustles on board. "Let's go. What are we all waiting for? Katsaros to hand himself in and send us flowers?"

The speedboat slides out of its quiet, inky-black hiding place, and I force my unease down, but not before Kate's words ring in my ears. *'I'd sworn off dangerous men. Given my heritage, I should be sticking to that like glue.'*

Kate has no idea how fast I'm pedaling below surface. I've brought the wrong mission buddy to Santorini to solve this trafficking scam. Or perhaps—*double damn it to hell*— my instincts are right. I've picked the right woman. At the worst possible time?

Dangerous?

Too right. Every which angle of shitty.

* * * *

We have to get the mission active without disruption, and make up for lost ground. Period. Tomorrow we'll strike and tonight is about a perfect set up.

Andreas is the best undercover agent I've ever known and I trust him with my life. Thanks to him, we have a full routines rundown and layout map of the place. From where the girls are held, since being shipped in from Eastern Europe to the Achilles heel for entry, via the cellar's compromised door hatch.

The Katsaros Mansion appears more like a movie set prison, with its barricaded perimeter than something from an architect's show-book. We've technobugged the place out with cameras at strategic bushes and gulleys.

I catch Andreas in my peripheral vision and I leave the

boat to join him by the rocks. We climb together stopping at intervals to exchange info. We're not talking much near to the water in case the sound will carry. All I can see are his eyes, but that's enough to know he's concerned. That and the rasp in his quiet voice.

"Your news via a fish peddler was surprising even for you."

"Had to pull you out. Shit hit fast and furious. We're upping the strike to tomorrow."

"Civilian here?"

I nod. "At base." I'm about to tell him that the original plan is screwed when he lays surprising new info on me.

"Shit's been going down big time. One inner circle dude shot dead for a perceived insult, and another shot in the hand last week. Can't risk a civilian is my take."

The stomach muscles that had cramped at his words relax. I fight to keep my voice at a whisper. "First Tavi was gunned down. Havana tailed and shot at yesterday. Too much happening to risk it."

"Havana?" Andreas's gaze reads spooked, and that worries me.

"You didn't know?"

"My legitimate tasks take me away too often. I miss stuff. Think the daughter meet won't work. But Donaldson could change his mind again. He's worse than Katsaros sometimes for mood swings."

"She's not setting foot there. She's spooked as it is."

"Dangerous situation."

"What if she's taken hostage?"

Andreas affirms. "You have two of us on the inside. We can do this, Sir."

"Hav is not going back. Neither are you. That's my gut instinct."

Andreas shakes his head. "I'm going back. I disappear now and Katsaros will disappear and blow this."

I grunt because I know he's right. "We hit tomorrow."

"Before the second shipment from Romania next week?"

"We hit hard, there won't be another shipment. How are the girls?"

"Bad shape. One died in transit."

I shake my head. This climbing body count is worse than bad.

"And there's one girl who took his interest so she's been given special treatment. Hard to watch."

We moved quietly in towards the brow of the hill for a good view of the mansion layout. My agents are deployed setting explosives, as arranged. I focus night vision goggles on the fortified property. There. A thermal hit. Someone waiting under the trees.

A small whistle—like a low birdcall—rends the air. It's one of mine. Shit. Why the noise?

I scan the area and get another thermal hit, a guard on slow patrol. He's smoking a cigarette—the glowing tip evident as he paces. He tosses the butt to the side and goes into a crouch, gun up, ready. Why did our guy whistle with the guard so close?

Andreas shook his head. "Guard's spooked," he whispered. "One of the ransoms hasn't materialized. Katsaros does not deal well with failed plans."

"Poor guy. Heart bleeds. You know why Havana was rumbled?"

"News to me. Cancelled payments a problem? Give him the cash and stop the bastard."

The guard on the high perimeter post lays down a heavy stream of fire in our direction.

"Fuck it." A bullet whips past my left ear. So close that I almost have a new natty piercing. Andreas rolls one way and I the other. We tumble down the hillside, rolling at speed. It's a bigger drop than I'd've predicted, and a jagged rock, unseen in the dark sand, swipes a hefty slice at my neck. A boulder just misses taking my balls for dessert. I'll so take a cut neck over any crown jewels emergency any day.

Ten seconds later we land in more rocks than would be

sensible, were it not out of necessity. It's arid and dusty and I choke on the throat-clogging sand storm my descent's caused. This job may pay well, but it sure as hell ain't restful. I'm sweating buckets and not just from these clothes in this dry heat.

I give Andreas another chance to reconsider. "You can come back with us and bail. Why not leave now? Come back with us?"

The other guys have been setting up traps and incendiary devices at strategic places for tomorrow night's bust out. Two appear, nodding their success. We can feasibly take Andreas now the mission's on for tomorrow.

"I'm not coming back until that bastard is under lock and key. Wanna be there when you take him down. Let's nail it."

I dab at my neck with my hand. I'm making too much of a habit of losing blood in the last few days. "What the hell? A shoot-happy guard? Hope I'm not a man down out there." I won't settle until we're all back in the boat.

"Rabbit probably. With Katsaros in a foul mood, they're shooting at shadows. Rabbits are the scourge of the place. They take the flack."

"Hope you're right. We'll make sure he's fed salad nightly when he's inside. For the rabbits."

I part ways with Andreas, having received his USB, and I skirt away to the coastal pathway that leads towards the boat. Andreas will lurk until it's safe to return. Reconnaissance objective nailed even if I'm bleeding over my shirt and hurting like hell with a face like an opened crate of catastrophe that crashed on a cobbled street.

Chapter Thirteen

Kate

I'm shaking when I leave the medical room. I'm no natural nurse and tonight I've seen my seven shades of hell.

"You okay?" Dr. Lekkas has amazing skills that make me feel my own job is a faked rubbish waste of time in comparison. Saving lives. Sorting out mortal mistakes.

"I'm fine," I bluff.

"You can assist my operations in future any time. The shaking hands have almost stopped now."

"Only because we're almost finished. I think if I had to do that again I'd pass out."

But I glance over at Hav, who is lying there, still anaesthetized, but looking so peaceful and serene, with a machine that tells me her heart rate seems fine, and Rocco guarding her like her very own avenging angel. If he wasn't in total love with her before, he definitely is now.

"I think there's a man who'll be forever in your debt."

Dr. Lekkas grins. "Keep an eye on our patient. I'll be sticking around for a day or so to check on her. For now we both need rest."

All I'd had to do was keep the doctor's tools close at hand and ensure that the light was where he needed it to be to undertake Havana's bullet removal and stitch up. I didn't dare open my eyes during most of the procedure.

Or think about anything. I was just super delighted she pulled through, the bullet came out, and she's been stitched right back up good as new.

What's Dan doing now? asks a voice in my brain.

But I quash it.

Doctor's right. I'm exhausted. Dead on my feet.

And I'm just heading toward my room—I can just about now work out where to find it by myself—when I bump into Ivan.

He grins. "Fancy meeting you here, and this time, I'm giving you directions whether you need them or not."

Ivan's smiling down at me with glassy, glittering eyes. He's tall—almost seven foot I'm guessing—a basketball coach's dream. Some women would likely go gaga for Mr. Tall Gunned-Up and Gutsy. But he's *so* not my type.

For starters, my jokes jar in translation—never a good sign when you feel even less funny than you think you are. Our dates would be awkward meets bored. For seconds, he's a great, skinny beanpole with prominent teeth and no tatts or personality. I smile—politeness making me aim for friend over harsh-tongued harpy. I need pals in this place, and if I ever need escape without an available ladder I sense he'll be a great guy to know or climb onto.

"Hey, Katie. Boss said I should give you another briefing. Ready for a quickie with me and some one-on-one fun?"

So wish he hadn't just said that.

My grin is now a grimace and turning that back to happy zone is a near impossible feat.

And shit. I've just stood in on a long, grueling operation on a shot woman. I'm still wearing stores' scrubs and I'd kinda hoped bedtime might be soon. As in alone bedtime. Not yet more agent demands, agent detailing and boring bullcrap.

Do these people ever frickin' sleep? Are they robots? Workaholic weasels without apology or intention of ever calling it a day?

"Kinda tired. Can't it wait for morning, Ivan? Seriously. I'm the walking dead here. Need my zzzzs."

"Afraid not. Sir was very specific before he left. He wants photos and fingerprints taken. You need to get on the system. Protocol, but I won't detain you for long."

My mind flicks to Dan, wondering where the hell he is and what he's doing. There's a tiny coil of worry tightening inside my belly. It's next to the part of my anatomy that sits up like a frisky puppy begging for a biscuit at the mere mention of Sir's name. I hope he'll be okay. How would I cope if he came back wounded like Hav or worse? We've shared intimate moments. Showered and swapped sexy maneuvers. In a manner that will have me having solo fun just reliving it in my head—seriously, that hot and good. Yet there's so much that's uncertain. So much more to be discovered.

Does he really even like me? Sometimes I'm hardly sure.

And is there even an us? Am I being a crazy lovelorn weird wisher just imagining such a thing? Do I need a get-agrip kick in the crotch?

Ivan disturbs me from my in-head doodles on Dan. "So. You ready to come with me? Or you gonna stand here all night yawning and looking delightfully dopey on me. Man, you're some cute kinda squeeze, aren't ya?"

"Um, can you lay off? Do I have a choice? Can I substitute a me clone to take my place?"

Ivan stares at me oddly. With Dan he'd've realized I was teasing and come back with a line, or a glower that slayed me back. With Ivan he's too gullible and we don't align.

Which dings my tolerance. "Of course I'll come, I was kidding," I clarify.

Then he takes me off guard completely. He walks along the corridor where there's some sort of laundry trolley with a big basket on wheels contraption and slides it back to where I stand.

"Your carriage awaits."

"Yeah. Great joke. Ivan. Never kid a kidder."

"I need to take you in this. It's quite a walk. Hop in here and I'll do the hard bit." He opens the basket where there's room enough to sit, if you curl up super-tight and pretend you're a squirrel hibernating.

I do my 'as if' face. "You're so not being serious."

Ivan nods his head, then bodily picks me up in a fairytale damsel move that shocks me rather abruptly. Mostly because his hand is tight on my arse.

"Nope. Hop on—seriously. We won't detain you too long—it's quite a way, and it's uphill to the security office. Just following orders, Miss."

I sigh, but let Ivan drop me into the cart's basket. I sit very uncomfortably, thinking any minute the bloody thing will collapse in a heap of trashed bits. But it doesn't and Ivan merely shoves laundry over me as if I'm buried alive by washbasket blues.

"You okay in there?" asks Ivan. Not that he stopped to check first.

"It's lovely in first class, thanks for asking," I sass back, muffled by a king-sized duvet and a set of towels. If anybody's slimy flannel comes within an inch of me I think I may scream my lungs hoarse. "It's bloody ridiculous actually."

"Oh, quit with the drama already." Ivan stuffs yet more linen on top of me, drowning out my complaints. It makes me shout in surprise, but the trolley is now moving at a fast pace, making further discussion hopeless.

Why do I feel like the bearded lady waiting for the big unveil at the freak show fair? Come to think of it, maybe that's what he's planning? I'll wake up in some Nordic illicit circus act surrounded by Norwegian dwarves on stilts. Shit. Not funny. I have the creeps just thinking about it.

Bring back Dan and his grumpy stuff—all is forgiven.

Bring back Dan, because he'd never shove me in a laundry cart or squeeze my butt in a way that made me feel bleh and itch to scram. With Dan I'd follow willingly.

So why am I feeling so uneasy? Where is Ivan taking me? Why the crazy trolley cloak and hide under the airing cupboard contents daggers? I'm thinking I'm so not going to like the answers.

* * * *

It turns out that Ivan is smuggling me out of Troika in a laundry cart. As in properly smuggling me out of the place that's been driving me nutso, but in a way that's making me think of spitting frying pans and roaring lethal fires.

"Hey, I'm struggling to breathe in here."

"Quiet. Shit," he commands

And for some weird reason I draw my cell phone from my pocket and set it to record. Some bumping around happens then a long period where it feels like we're in some strange mineshaft type elevator. It's amazing what you can imagine when all you have is your ears dulled by duvets for sat nav.

Eventually, the clothes that are piled on top of me — they'd better bloody well be clean — are pulled aside. Ivan's head appears, and he grins.

If this hadn't really been happening to me I'd've sworn it was a cheesy plot from some terrible film I'd've walked out of and demanded my ticket money back for.

If this is how spies operate in the field, then the future of our secret global law enforcement service is totally screwed and then some. I know he's smuggled me out as soon as I feel the breeze and smell the ocean.

I'm so overjoyed to be out of my underground prison, I almost forget to get pissy about what's going down without my consent.

"I'm out."

"Yep, angel. Thought I'd give you a surprise. Great isn't it?"

Is it me or has he just got a bit smarmy 'angel' step-back-and-mind-your-place Misterish with me?

My too close to me hackles have risen and I feel the need to keep a healthy distance, but he's got his hands on my waist and he's lifting me out of the basket he'd thrust me in. The Police's song — *Don't Stand So Close To Me* — is already playing in my head — I can't turn it off. Especially as his hands stay on my waist and back, pissing me off, so I step away.

"Why are we here? Where is this?"

"Welcome to Jenny's Taverna, the Achilles heel escape hatch from Troika Base, and if anybody knew I'd brought you here my career would be blown to shit. We never use this exit. It's hidden in the vending machine behind the bar."

Ivan's face is way too close to my own. He holds out a hand to assist me and I grab it, making sure I hurt his fingers in the process, like a mad wife in labor taking contractions pain out on the sperm provider and ruining his future hand function.

"Jenny's Taverna?"

"Yeah, she's Rich's wife, she runs a dating agency from this place," says Ivan as I dust myself down, trying to find my equilibrium. "The lady herself is heavily pregnant and is staying with friends until the baby is safely here, so this place is temporarily closed."

It's only then I realize that the Santorini dating story wasn't as much of a fiction as I'd assumed. Jenny Redman really does exist after all.

"But why are we here? Doesn't look like a security office to me." I feel his hand slither to softly caress the small of my back, and it's a private *eek* moment. So I take control and step out of his reach.

"I lied about the photos and prints," says Ivan. "Figured while Bullet Man was away you and I could have a play." He slowly smiles and it creeps me to creepy town by the creepy ville back roads paths and turned-off and needing distance broads.

The very word 'Dan' lights a flare in my heart.

"You like dicing with death? He'll have your balls for cufflinks. They'll probably end up in space or something. He strikes me as the out-thepark revenge type."

"You and he poke pals? Is that it?" The sneery look on Ivan's face shows he's a man of jealous emotions and questionable ego. Shit. Hadn't quite pegged him as this bad.

"Nice turn of phrase. Isn't that my business, not yours?"

He grasps my wrist tightly. I may not know agent protocol,

and might not have known Dan that long, but I do know he doesn't wuss about when the shit's going down. And my shit radar's bleeping like a mother, with an arrow pointing at Ivan. The words "vacate any way you can" spring to mind.

Again, his other hand is on my back. While I'm kept captive by my wrist.

"Maybe you're worth it? Maybe I don't care?" says Ivan. "Maybe I'll take any way I can to get you alone and see where things can lead?" He says it way too close to my ear. I get the creepy creeps with a big dose of person-aversion to go. I don't want him getting so up close to me. I'm not sure I want to be broken out by him, even if this was Alcatraz and I was bunking with the mad Taxidermist Head Boiler Killer.

What the hell's he planning? To get me drunk? For us to bunk? To force me to jazz dance to *Uptown Funk*? Is Scandi Man a thrill-chasing stalker on the side who forces his foibles on ladies?

"We are going back, though? I mean, you don't wanna lose your job."

"Never fear. Falco is prepared. Nobody will know. We could be here all night if you wanted." Ivan goes behind the bar. "What would you like me to get you?"

A cab.

He watches me again. "A drink? Anything you want, honey? Falco can bring what you most desire."

Never trust a man who talks about himself in the third person.

A Tarzan vine to swing on and escape might be nice.

A phone to call a Danbulance with full flashing sirens is my final choice.

"I'd like to be taken back, please. Then we shall never talk of this again."

"C'mon. Live a little, angel," he smoothly entices. Yeah right. Then he sings, "Dance…a few kisses…caresses in the moonlight…"

"Seriously. I made my wishes clear, didn't I? Let's get back before this gets any more stupid for either of us."

But Ivan has swooped to holding me even tighter before I register. I've no idea how. "I've liked you since we met. Didn't you realize I hung about that corridor for hours waiting for you to come out that day? But that prick watches you like a hawk. Gives no chance to any other man. Loser."

Holy restraining orders.

But I have to seize control. For sanity's sake. "It's a shame I'm in love with him. There really can never be anything more between us. Not when Dan breathes oxygen. I crave his body like no other."

Ivan's face veers from euphoric to psychotic. Knew he was a psycho. Something just told me. Maybe watching too many episodes of *Silent Witness* and noting down Jack and Nikki's processes in three shades of highlighter pen has helped my crime deduction skills and psycho spotting.

Or I'm a Miss Marple-Jessica Fletcher doppelganger.

"You're not going back," he says. "Indulge me. I want to chill here with you. I haven't even kissed you yet... You aren't going back until I do."

And my stomach falls twenty elevator floors of doom. Shit. Where are a girl's nunchuks when she needs them? Why is Havana wounded and recovering when she should be dropping in through the ceiling to pulverize Ivan's balls?

Ivan slides his hands over my body, nauseating me beyond bearable point. I can't free myself from him and a violin squeals a movie horror requiem in my ears.

"So..." he begins. His mouth nears mine.

"Didn't you hear? I like Dan and he'll be mighty pissed off at you."

"You think I'm scared of the Dan man?"

I sense if I let him start the sweet talk I'll be lost and he'll be doing things to me I really don't want to witness. The thought of him touching my skin makes my knickers turn to instant-set concrete. So I stall with efforts to psych him the hell out.

"And here was me thinking you're a career-centered guy. You're kinda keen on promotion aren't you? What's gonna happen when the CCTV guys catch evidence of you and me AWOL?" I nod toward the cameras in the three corners of the room.

"Taken care of." He grins like he's been so very clever and devilish. Hands down a Jack Nicholson scary face. "My friendly neighborhood aerosol skills happened to come by for some prep graffiti. Nobody can see a thing. Smokescreen."

Now I'm really scared. "Your superior is a clever guy. He'll get to the bottom of this eventually."

"You think I really care what Cockface Draven thinks? Or Redman? They've no proof. Dan hates me anyway. I hate him. But on this one—and on the promotion when I stitch him up—I'm gonna win. I'll be promoted and he'll be out when I have my way."

"He's your superior. You should show due respect."

"In Norway I'm equal rank with Draven. We're same grade, only here the Yanks run the show and it pisses me off. He's got the bad stuff coming to him."

I figure we've just struck the raw seam of Ivan's deep set gripe mine. Dan and job envy. I look around the dark taverna. Desperation and self-preservation dance an unwieldy polka in my innards. Even the sea view of inky ocean lapping and tantalizing can't sweeten my soured unease.

I want to escape.

I need to stall him.

It's then I notice the bar's quirky décor. The bar's a romantic, pink-tinged idyll of love in the guise of an outdoor garden, with an ornate dining area. A huge fountain features Poseidon and dancing nymphs as the central feature.

Jenny's Taverna has a flower-filled gazebo-covered grotto with statues from Aphrodite to Venus. Cupids in abundance flank a gold leaf tableau of dancing nymphs. Stuffed caged love birds hang from the gazebo.

Cocktail specials of 'Just Married Margaritas', 'Pina Colada Hot Crushes', 'Lust on the Beach' and a toxic punch named 'Honeymoon Horizontal Homebrew' are advertised in neon colors on the bar's chalkboards.

Wow. Said in an ironic internal voice. If it wasn't such blatant craziness, this place could have been mad, bad and dangerous to know. The clientele of honeymooners must have a rose-tinted aversion to good taste décor.

And I'm here with a stalker crazo agent licensed to kill, and quite possibly go off fully loaded in pervy directions.

I have my eye on the nearest bronze cupid bust that I could possibly knock Ivan into next month with, if I managed to wield it like a samurai.

"I'm gonna make us some drinks," he declares. Ivan stalks to the bar, and I move over swiftly to check out the fountain. While he's pouring, I take the medium-sized cupid and set it close behind me.

His focus on making me consume a drink I haven't asked for makes me think he may be planning to drug me, and that's just not on.

"So? Come on, have a drink? Gin, slammers, Jägerbombs? What's your poison?" he asks.

As much as I've been through already, I fear this strange creepy experience will stay with me for years. May even leave me a worrying, traumatized, wreck.

"Why don't you put on some music to dance?" Ivan says, motioning to the jukebox on the far wall.

I shake my head. I'd rather clean toilets as a career choice.

"Pretty please?" Ivan slips from behind the bar, leaving the drinks behind. He yanks me into his arms so fast that I slap against his hard long length. I'm nauseated. The cupid is within easy grabbing distance.

His hands seize my waist. Then they slide up my ribcage, making me squirm. He's millimeters from my boobs, and if he touches me there I might just bite his face like a rabid dog.

"No. This isn't what I want. Listen, Ivan," I tell him.

"You're creeping me out. Big time. You and I aren't *ever* going to happen. If you don't take the subtle hint I'll tell Dan everything and get you fired. I'll go to Rich Redman myself."

"Didn't you hear me when I said no evidence? Your word against mine. Who do you think they'll believe, huh?"

Thankfully just happens I've recorded everything on my cellphone. But I'll keep that as a later surprise for the busted wise guy.

"They'd believe me. Sexual harassment part of the Interpol training nowadays?" I point at his chest and narrow my eyes. "Take me back and realize you're being a dick right now — I'll let it slide. You've made a mistake — but if you back off we can get past this."

"Knew you had baditude. But you really think I'm gonna back down that easy?"

I grab Cupid, counting on love's power and the weight of plaster.

I sense from Ivan's look that there's either a gas mains leaking somewhere or perhaps dripping petrol near a just struck match. Maybe I'm that scary and impressive when wielding a cupid as a weapon but I doubt it. My muscles are shaking.

"I think it's time we left," says Ivan softly and backs up, his gaze targeted on something or someone behind me.

Wow. I must be good. Cupid wielding — I am a mighty warrior

Ivan's hot glare doesn't waiver. I turn to see Warbie and another agent watching us. Warbie makes a small gesture, and the agent grabs Ivan roughly by the arm, forcing him back into the soda-machine-disguised portal to Spy Haven.

Whoever would have guessed that one? These guys are good. I lay down the cupid in relief because I'm about to drop it in exhaustion.

"Close call."

"You're telling me, Katiepie. That was damn near a human rights violation."

I fall into the large warm cave of Warbie's arms for a hug. "He's such a wanker."

"Went to your room with a nightcap and you weren't there. Nasty jackass—never liked him a bit. He'll pay for this."

"I honestly thought he'd assault me. I kept him talking, trying to maintain arms' length."

"Dan will kill him. Tear him apart in a slow fashion, using methods that would have weak stomachs lurching. Totally justified power move, might I add."

"No he won't. We won't let him. We're not going to tell him, are we?" I stare up at Warbs. "Please? Hasn't Dan enough on his plate as it is?"

I know Ivan is out to dis Dan, but I'm pretty sure he can be effectively persuaded otherwise. I squeeze into Warbie's hug and he reciprocates. It's the warmest, deepest hug I've had in eons, and I not only enjoy it, I linger and stay there, sucking in this man's marvelous energizing friend's embrace of hope.

"You're a beacon in a very black place, Warbiebuddy. Let's not make another drama. Haven't we had enough?"

"Sir will string me up if he ever finds out. If that dweeb kissed you maybe you should get a tetanus jab?"

I shake my head. "Give me some credit for taste, Warbs. We'll make sure Sir won't find out. His team are falling like flies."

"Hot damn. You care about him, don't you?" says Warbie, his eyes glittering in the dim light. He gives me a warm smile.

"Yeah. Crazy as I am, I do. He deserves to have somebody in his corner, don't you think?"

"I feel the same. Our DanBoy picked me up when I was low. Hurt by a guy and the way I was going I was gonna end up dead with spiraling depression. Dan didn't give up on me."

I stare. "I'm sorry, Warbs. But glad he's such a bossy Sir who won't take a no."

Warbie's face takes a grim cast. "He's honorable. But he's not that straightforward, Kate. He doesn't ever mix work with anything else, which makes you a very special exception. He has scars. He's lost people and has shouldered all the blame. You'll have to tread gently and take care. We will talk, we really will. But if my pressure cooker explodes in the refectory, I think it'll be my firing line execution at dawn, not Ivan's. Let's go."

"Go get your cooker fixed, Fairy Godfather."

"Hang onto hope, Cinders. Not all the princes out there are bastards."

The comment hangs heavy, because I know he's talking about Dad. Not past lovers. Or relationship mistakes. The man who first let me down. The one who made me stop thinking a man could save me.

My eyes fill with tears. God knows why. I'm making way too much of a habit of this. Personally I blame Warbie's influence or a complex about the Dad I never had.

I watch him and that makes it worse because he looks at me with pity.

"Don't be kind, Warbs. Please don't talk about that man again. I do not want to discuss him."

"Okay, Princess. Back to your broom cupboard."

"My friends call me princess," I say softly.

"Course they do. Your regal charm shines out. We're spiritual twins now."

But I don't feel very regal. My charms seem very distant, too.

"Why don't I fetch you a bracing nightcap to get you into a deep sleep tonight? Sir sanctioned that move." With a forced smile Warbie, leads me back below ground. To keep me captive and confused to the max in this Godforsaken hole from hell atrocity scenario with knobs on.

Chapter Fourteen

Dan

I'm back, and Geezer, the IT guy with the Will.i.am styling and nerdy ways, collars me with info that's as shocking as the intel from Andreas.

Middle of the night and the kid's been hanging out, likely with matchsticks under his eyes, java in hand, a flickering screen for solace. His face is heavily drawn as an iron carriage with a killer load and brakes on. "Geezer. How goes?"

"Need you to see somethin', Sir. Activity caught on cameras."

My heart rate's zooming. I'd be tempted to call time and ask for a reprieve 'til morning but we're only an hour or so until sunset and waiting wasn't in the job profile I signed up to. Geezer intel can't wait.

"Course." But I see the images before I'm ready for them. Ivan. Hands on Katie. Her backing up when he's getting in her face. Hands on her arms. Her body.

"Seems he underestimated the level of CCTV cover at the Taverna exit. We also have it alarmed. We used to use it for taped insider briefings. He outed three cams — as in dry shampoo spray over the lenses — that means they've had it and we're gonna have to replenish kit."

"What's the latest? Kate okay?"

"Fine." He swiftly switches to a screen to show her lying sleeping. "Strictly off-limits but just to set your mind at rest, Sir."

"You think he's a plant and was out to spring her back to

Dad?" I'm barking questions while I'm watching the run again on rewind and again on slow.

"All's back to normal. Warbie intervened. No reason to think it's kidnapping, Sir. Maybe just a nasty civilian crush rash?"

I'm breathing like a fiesta bull when the cape unfurls. "Maybe. But it won't be cream and antihistamines on his prescription. Something a little less soothing." Nasty-ass creep needs a testicle-kicking party in his honor. I'll be the star turn compere on proceedings.

I watch Geezer fast frame through the necessary. I discern Kate's stark discontent and body language that suggests this was no come-on party trick. She's straight as a surfboard and resisting and pulling back from the body contact Ivan's out to serve her way.

"Was she shaken up?"

"Warbuckle intervened and gave her sleeping meds. I alerted him when I caught it on the monitors."

I could almost crack my own teeth with my jaw tension. I take it down a notch for my own sanity. "Thanks for this. I'll deal with this tomorrow, but keep this low key for now. Geezer — you've done a great job, appreciated."

"No problem, Sir."

Ivan's balls are so fried they're cinder dust mixed with carbon. But if I had little chance of sleep before, it's now completely nixed. My blood's up from seethe unvented, and too many vexing scenarios have raced through my brain. I head for the bathroom when I get to my room. Not too much the worse for wear since I've cleaned up the neck gash — it's a scratch — and checked myself out in the bathroom mirror. Lookin' pretty badass, like a dog that's been in a few scraps. Feeling pretty gone on principles scotched — and that's just not like me. I'm usually cucumber-cool Bullet Man. Or I was — once upon a time, before a certain civilian came to stay and caused this level of complication.

But is she hurt? Did Ivan overstep in unseen ways?

I head to my room, throw my shirt where it lands. It's gone

three a.m. and I'm beat. So how come the crazy questions kick in, making me too wired to sleep?

In a heartbeat, I'm not thinking through the reasons not to, and just heading for that connecting door that links my room to hers. My heat's drumming my actions, but I'm not listening to my own thoughts, so a few heart bumps won't stop me.

I'm only wearing pants. No shirt, no guns, no principles either. What am I doing?

Making damn well sure she's okay.

She's not crying. Or lying staring at the wall. She's sleeping like a child, and deeply, too. I stand frozen. Not breathing, just watching.

Feeling bad for stealing in here like a stalker in the night. Yet so privileged and glad she's okay and I've a sneaky chance to just watch.

So I do. Drinking in her soft breathing. The sight of her chestnut hair, displayed like a silk robe on the pillow, her shoulders so stark and bare, with only tiny straps keeping her away from the X-rated zone.

She's safe.

I turn. Then stand again. Because I can't damn well bring myself to leave. Which is so beyond stupid, but it's the thought of Ivan. Him taking her, against orders, out of here. Him pawing her. Was it my fault—revenge for me calling him off the job?

I don't trust myself to walk or to leave. How could he? How could I have gotten this so badly wrong?

Am I fucking this whole thing up as much as Ivan is? By letting it all get below the skin where it should never be allowed to penetrate. A whole half hour passes, with me just standing like a crush-assed mannequin watching the girl sleep. Am I playing stalker tag too? Am I up there with Ivan?

As soon as that wake-up nudge hits me I focus. Enough to walk away.

I take small, silent steps out of there. I need to retreat.

Reverse the attraction and get a grip on the job and my head. The mission can only ever come first.

* * * *

Kate

There is a heavy pounding when I open my eyes, head still on pillow. It's like the loudest, mournful drum orchestra from the abyss of hell and behind my eyes, someone has set my neurons to silent vibrate, explosion mode.

And who had the authority to make me feel this bad, pray tell? Then I remember Warbie's sleep meds nightcap. I would go and blame him for every sin under the sun, but I sense my head is so bad I may never be able to walk again. I'd say no Kates were hurt in what I went through yesterday, but I'd be lying.

I hurt like shit.

I wince. Steady myself for another round of head-based stabbing. I would groan, but making any sound is beyond me. If I wasn't very much mistaken, I have a hangover from hell, but I know I haven't drunk a thing since I went before Redman having downed straight shots.

At some point last night, a very large double decker bus ran me over, accompanied by a gang of marauding elephants wearing clogs.

My eyes snap open and see a sight that makes breathing normally tricky. Warbie is sitting on the edge of my bed, making me feel decidedly awkward. It's only then I remember where I am — mystery Santorini secret location surrounded by real proper spy policemen — and the full surreal nature of reality is especially hard to digest.

"What is it?" I croak. "Why are you watching me?"

"It's gone two p.m. You've been in bed for twelve hours now. Figured it was time to wake the sleeping princess."

I don't feel much like a princess, but I've no time to ponder that.

He adds, "And Sir is nagging me to get you fit so he can

183

visit. It's been one hell of a morning, sweet cheeks. Figure you'll be glad you missed it."

I'd ask more, but my head's so sore it's made me nauseous. I just stare at him like a stoned garden gnome.

"Sir and Ivan. Clash of the Interpol Titans. The swear box would be full, but I haven't dared asked Bullet Man to pay his share."

Then logic and memory click in. It's in a very painful area of my brain that's thrumming at me having to use it. It's not a good thrum. I suspect I'll be seeing the wrong side of the toilet soon.

"Ivan? About last night? You told?"

Warbie shakes his head. "Not guilty, mistress. Somebody else got in there first. Sir has this place running to his pissed-to-the-pinnacle tune, and Ivan's gone already. Career aspirations bye-bye."

"Shit."

"And then some. On the upside, I made you breakfast. Late breakfast."

"You shouldn't have. But what the hell did you put me out with last night?"

"It's known in the trade as horse tranquilizer. That's just a nickname, of course. Merely a mix of natural herbs."

I'm thinking he's lying about the last part. I'm feeling like a horse they tried to put down. Why, in the name of good sense and intellect, is all this happening? I slide up in bed. Even that hurts. "Why are you watching me?"

"Just checking honeypie is still alive," says Warbie. "We were a tad worried you'd OD'd."

"Were you hoping for an early demise? If you want me gone you only had to ask me."

"The sleeping draught worked. You chilled and you got great rest."

I'd shake my head, but my migraine is such I may throw up on the bed. "Please just give me a drink of water, if you have one."

"I've better than that," says Warbie, with a flourish to the prepped wheeled trolley beside him that I hadn't noticed before.

"All the trimmings. Cooked goods and continental on the side, just in case you're from the posher side of the sheets."

If posh means in danger of projectile puke, then I'm there. I leap up and launch myself at the cupboard that serves as a toilet and fortunately I make the basin in time. Let's just say it's more about retching and gagging than Technicolor shows. But still not pretty.

"Poor dear. Valerian can have that effect. I make the possets up myself."

"You've poisoned me," I say, and heave again. I'm thinking Warbie belongs in a *Game of Thrones* evil plot. He probably has dragons in his lair.

"We'd do well to save Sir from this pleasure."

Like I care a flip flam. I'm busy feeling like death warmed up slightly, then laced with arsenic, at his orders.

"I so don't feel well."

"It's okay," says Warbie. "I have anti-sickness pills. Drink. We want to improve you before Sir returns to prep you for baddie-wrangling, don't we?"

I can't keep up. I take the water and force down the pill. Then, reluctantly, take his small shot of green gunk chaser. Then I throw myself back on the bed and wish for a cool flannel. I'm just about to suggest it when Warbie provides one.

"I've gone off you."

"I'm not exactly inspired by your gag reflex either, Miss."

Then I think of Dan. Tattoo revealed in its blatant shiny glory, chest moving in tune with his breathing as he stared into my eyes through the shower's spray. I remember all the things he did to my privates with his mouth and his fingers and another important area...

"Where is he?" My voice is rusty.

"Can't tell you. I would, but I'd have to kill you."

Why do all these bastards here keep saying this? "Maybe you should. I feel like it would be a release from having to hear that phrase and feel this shitty."

"Sir would kill me. You're his key to cracking his case. You're gold bullion, baby. You're his hot bit of stuff on the side."

And it's only then that my orgasmic, sex interest euphoria dies.

Warbie's just given me a wakeup call. Sir is just using me as collateral — keeping me sweet. A fuck on the side is just part of the service. He wants to screw over my dad — he's done the next available person on the way.

I have what he needs most for his precious work. He probably screws his accomplices all the time. I'm just one of many. Bastard wanker shitface.

"He's a lousy piece of vomit."

"He's no such thing. If you knew what he'd been through, you'd never say such things."

I sit up. Head pounding, flannel falling but I'm past caring.

"What? So what happened? Why does everybody seem to act like he's the guy who can't be sneezed at?"

"Because he lost important things."

"What like, his marbles? His virginity? His key to the poison drinks cabinet?"

Warbie's eyes are angry and he's never looked at me that way before. It hurts. But I'm too far gone to leave it.

"He lost the two people who were his closest in the world."

With a gulp of air I falter. "How? Who? Why?"

"His partner. Guy he'd worked with for a decade."

"How did he die?" My voice has softened.

"Mexico Heist gone loco."

"And Dan survived?"

"He took that hardest blow — taken captive, but survived. Crazy thing is Nathan had his back and Dan had taken a couple of falls on duty before. Nathan used to give him flack for being the liability injured party as a joke. But Dan's got some idea the 'liability' line is wedged in his brain.

Blames himself. Had PTSD counselling. His first mission since return to duty."

I feel bad for the things I've said. For glibly quipping that I'm just one of many, when Dan's issues are so much bigger. "Was this recent?"

"Year and a half ago. But there are other recent wounds — a woman. I don't think Dan would want me going there with you. Maybe he can tell you himself?"

I'm flailing at this reveal. Spinning in the aftermath of feeling guilty and heartsore at what I've just learned. He had my respect and sympathy.

Ironically my headache's improving and the nausea is ebbing like a Li-lo floating out to sea. But it's scant consolation. The slug slime must be sucking up my heave juices. While guilt pulverizes my braincells. Dan is so not an open and shut case.

Warbie rises from the bed end. "Don't ever tell him I told you."

"I won't."

"And for all you malign him, he's asked me to give you special care. You're causing a big bloody rumpus here at Troika. I've never seen him more challenged or less in control, and that isn't good. Though don't let on I said that."

"I'll take great joy in dobbing you in," I whisper.

Warbie's hand goes up and his face isn't listening. "He's more beautiful than a display at The Museum of Manhood In Its Prime. You'd jump on him like a skipping rope. Surveillance guys are keeping it mum. Shower stuff." He touches his nose. I'm more beetroot than a big one at a vegetable show prize-giving.

For seconds I regard Warbie. He's bald as bald can be, but he's a great-smiled-slice-of- humor with a Machiavellian evil glow that's addictive. His eyelashes are envylicious.

"You really do care for him, don't you?" I probe.

"What's not to love? Kinda like you, too."

I feign a light tone. "Have you never thought of theatre? You're great looking after the boys, but you're so wasted here. You'd make an ace pantomime dame."

"The smell of the crowd—the roar of the greasepaint. Tempting, but this job's in my blood and bones, sweetie. There's something magically stirring about playing nanny to black ops boys. All those muscles and trigger finger sharp reflexes. But once this job's tied up—Copacabana Beach, watch out! I'll be living my dreams soon enough, hon. Maybe you should indulge your own instead of worrying about me?"

"So why is he here? His Lord and Master—Darth Vader with a cop badge? Why is this mission so vital?"

"Katsaros. It's a personal mission. Dan's out to prove himself—or get himself blown up."

"You really only going to give me that? Has he had his heart broken?"

"Nathan died on duty on Dan's watch. Dan had a girlfriend, who wasn't exactly squeaky clean—taken out at point blank range. I said I wouldn't tell you, so you're totally sworn to die before you'll ever let that go."

"Shit. But yes, it'll stay incarcerated in my brain. Won't breathe a word. Wouldn't dare."

Just. Shit.

"Yeah. He's kinda never been the same since. He has personal points to score—that he's back on game and can take this particular bad guy down. Let's just say the sex trafficker thing is his personal *bête noir*."

This is my life as a spy mole. Gritty shocks and measures of reality, and revelations that make you feel so tiny and insignificant, it's humbling. I'd rather work on the checkouts, frankly, but at least I'm alive and being well looked after. I feel intense guilt at being such a diva burden to all these guys who put their life so ably on the line.

Except Ivan. He got what was coming. Dickwad.

But all the others—especially Dan. Just shit. I'm not worthy—totally unprepared for these reveals. Totally unprepared for the wobble of empathy that's gone way too deep inside my heart.

* * * *

Later, once I've showered and dressed in my freshly laundered clothes, Warbie takes me out of my room for good behavior.

"Time to get your head back in the game," he says.

I'd clap my hands and say goodie, but I resist. I'm grateful just to feel okay again. "Where are we going, anyway?"

"You need a fitting."

Does he mean for a coffin?

"For what?" I squeak.

"Clothes. You meet Donaldson soon. Can't go appearing like Orphan Annie went to a thrift store and only had twenty pence to barter with."

"But I thought that was on hold."

"In this place plans change more than a burlesque dancer's wardrobe."

Warbie stops in front of a steel door, then presses a button that slides it away. He nods for me to enter before him, like the crazed psycho gentleman than he is.

"Your Bibbety-BobbityBoo moment. Where I turn you from a bumpkin to a beauty."

"You're really pissing me off," I grind out. If petulant was a lip color I'd have it as my signature style.

"Honey. There are no full-length mirrors in this place other than the one we're about to use on you. Trust me — you look like shit."

I glance over and there is a huge mirror and I jump. Not at my reflection, though the hair is Lady GaGa after a fight meets Zombie Apocalypse. It's the scowling woman staring me down beside it.

"Do I know you?" I say.

If dislike was a person — this would be she. She's doing a gorilla face. I don't know what I've done.

"You don't know me. I'm Havana's replacement. You can call me Dee."

Shit. Come back Hav, all is forgiven.

"Why the hell they've sent me here to help you with dresses I'm less than pleased about."

"Is she crazy?" I ask Warbie.

"She's sane. Utterly sane and lethal. She's gunned-up too, so tread with care. She knows how to kill a man by touching his neck in two places."

"Useful," I answer and evade the fiery daggers she throws me, glare after glare. Instead I swap attention to the pile of clothes and hangers before me.

"Get behind the screen. Get your gear off and let's get this show on the road."

Warbie's going to dress me up, and I'm going to hate every goddamn minute almost as much as Dee the female wrestler spy hates me.

"I really have to?" I plead with Oscar eyes at Warbie, but he doesn't answer and just gives me an indelicate shove. Bastard.

Chapter Fifteen

Kate

I now have an outfit decreed as Interpol appropriate. The downside is it's for a meeting with my dreaded crimescum dad.

I'd hoped to avoid this, but like an appalling scratchy outfit you hate in childhood, it's on again for reasons outside of my control. I'm left squirming with the discomfort. So this is just a nasty stinging nettle I'll still have to grasp and bear buggering blisters from.

"Stop scowling, you're totes hot," says Warbie.

Even Havana stops by, with her IV fluids tripod in tow, to take a peek. Man, there's nothing that'll keep that woman down. Today she's sporting the toned-down smoky eye and I'm hugely impressed.

"Great look, Hav," I whisper.

"Thinkin' just the same thing."

I shrug. "Thanks. I can think of better guy dates to use it on, but them's the breaks." At least the silky, cobalt rockin' it dress suit is gameon, even if my insides will be carved into inch-long bits of terror. So Warbie has hidden style talents after all.

I go back to my room for an hour of wall staring, when Warbie returns like a boomerang footman and, smiling, presents me with the half of my lost luggage that was confiscated, presumed security checks and laundering. Apparently it's had to undergo clearance, I mean, get real.

"Shit, Warbs. You're amazeballs." I throw my arms around him and I think he's shocked and a bit awkward with my manic display of affection. But the comforts of home bring untold joy, even if slightly over the top.

I flip the locks and run my eyes and excited fingers over my things.

"I have connections." He winks. "And a very fit young agent who wants to please at my bidding. So does your Sir. He'd put in an order before I did."

I feel like Sir's vanished without due warning. I've not seen him. "Did the mission go okay?"

I feel like I don't have grips on the lingo yet. How do they talk about such things and is there appropriate vocab? I suspect I'm missing the marker by a country hectare. "Did they get in and out like they wanted?"

"Objective achieved. Sir's busy with unexpected strategy planning. The other part of my messenger duty right now is to take you down to G wing. He's waiting for you there. An update and another briefing."

Zing. But doesn't that cause an internal shimmy. It's somewhere warm and welcoming. That enjoys spooning and slow dances. Shit.

I'm so easy it makes me wince.

I act normal but am probably blushing like a teenager in puberty with her first blushers variety box ready for experimentation. "G Wing? Don't I get time to change into real clothes first?" It's probably a cellar and a dungeon, but if it gets me out of wall staring, I'd take cleaning duty or worse.

Warbie hides his comment behind a hand. "Rooms at G wing have no camera surveillance. I'd suggest you opt for decent underwear, too. Go, get changed. Good plan."

Shit, the man doesn't pull his punches.

"Nice slice, Warbs. I can't imagine what you mean." He's laundered my things. He's seen the full horror. "Is that all you can think about? People at it?"

"We don't get much down here, chicken. Covering up your shenanigans has turned into my full time job. Ten minutes to get changed, then I'm taking you as directed.

'Kay?"

I wreak my subtle revenge on his baldy head. "Keep your hair on. Laters."

But I'm left thinking I can't believe there's a team of crackpot IT wiz crime-crackers who've probably hidden condemning evidence of my arse and tits as their day job.

I caress my clothes, towels and goodies to take my mind off Sir's plans and past indiscretions. Today, they've made a kidnapped, confused and sleep-drugged woman intensely satisfied. That's not something I say lightly.

Warbie leaves me to my luggage comfort break to prep for a visit to Sir.

* * * *

Room Three in G Wing isn't some awful torture chamber or sluice room. It's a very small billet with a low bed and a light and that's it. Except right now it also has Dan lying in it under that gray dim central light.

"You okay?" I whisper. "You wanted me? You sleeping?"

The lump in the bed moves and turns to face me. It's a handsome, breathing, awake lump with muscles like a Spartan and a face you'd kiss until you cried.

"Katie. Nice wake up call. I should take you on all my assignments." He's grasped my hands in an affectionate display that takes me quite by surprise.

"No fear. I'd rather be a pirate. I hate boats. I get seasick crossing a puddle. Don't think I'd pass your entry tests."

"Oh I think you underestimate the strings I'd pull for you." Dan shakes his head at my rambles. But his grin gives me hope he doesn't hate me that much. "I'm fitting in extra sleep recovery time — haven't had much recently. You do that to a guy, d'you know that?" His sparkling eyes crinkle in a way that tells me he won't be aiming for more siesta. Or polite hand holding. "Kinda fancied another close inspection of that highly arousing tattoo."

"Presumptuous, aren't you, Sir?"

"For defs. I am the deputy boss guy. Deal."

God, how did he get to be so gorgeous with all that stubble shadow, and when he spends all his time in ops clothes ready to do the daring do? I see the slash marks on his face and neck, and I let out a sharp gasp.

"What the hell happened? Not another Rocco fight?"

"No. Long story. No damage as such. A scratch."

"Other than your boat race." I nod toward his previous head gash. Now, added to the neck wound they're not quite Freddy Krueger, but he's suffered a few dents to be sure.

"Boat race?" I forget he's a New Yorker, and he won't get my Cockney slang for face. So I change tack, closing the space between us when I smell his macho male just-back-from-maneuvers scent. "Kinda like you roughed up and ready, Sir. Dirty and dented around the edges."

"Kinda like you any which way I can get you." He rises in the bed to lean on his elbows. "Listen, we have to talk." He stares at me. A crooked smile, that delectable chin dimple and lips designed for first thing in the morning sin. Killer combo. My tongue is glued just watching.

I unglue it enough to react. "Talk about what?"

"Last night I told myself I was going to back up from you. I realized I'm getting in deep. Which is bad for the mission and for my mental state," he says softly. Like I'm absinthe or crystal meth or something. "Then I found out what that freakin' asswipe Ivan did to you, and all bets were off on the back off. If I can't have you, then nobody can."

Wow. He's gone all action man. Primed and powerful.

And I find I like it. Especially when he growls, then seizes me for a kiss that tells me he means it. I'm gasping in nought to four seconds.

"I hadn't planned to tell you about Ivan," I pant, when we eventually part lips for long enough.

"Why the frig not?" He's a thunderbolt of anger in a blink. "Huh?"

"Didn't want to start feuds on campus, Sir."

"Seriously, the man has been an ass licker creep out to

sabotage my rank. But last night was the limit. He's fired, *hasta la vista*, dumbwad."

"Wow." I nod. "I've never been responsible for a super cop's career collapse — nice résumé add, though. Was that why you asked me to come here? Details about how I'm the thistle in your day, making you fire your staff at a rate of knots?"

"I asked you to come here — mistress mine — so I could get my rocks off before I explode into suicide sex bomber shrapnel."

"Sounds fun to watch, but painful to experience..."

But Dan shoves a hand over my mouth. It's a forceful hand. A strong, warm and not-takingnoforananswer hand. "Stop talking, woman. You're on my bed — I want you in it."

I squeak. It's all I can manage. "You really think that's a good idea? Thought you were backing up?"

"There's a penalty for the way you make me feel. The way you've taken control of my thoughts and my body." He grabs my hand. The next thing I know it's been thrust onto his man-ofsteel cock. I don't dally either. I rove his plains of promise with an eager hand. It's a very impressive member. One that's just been on maneuvers. I just didn't imagine I'd be manhandling his primed privates quite this soon without instructions.

Whoa! Talk about curveball with benefits.

"Dan. This your version of a dick pic?"

He gives me a wolfish grin. "This is how you make me," he grinds out. "Fully loaded." His accent, with a roughed-up desperate edge, agitates the suds out of my easy to oust sex drive. It leaves me lathered and ready for a whirling cycle, followed by a fast spin. I'm creaming, wanting a full cottons high temp seeing-to with a man who could service all my stains in a blink.

But there's a kink in my 'insults' drainage pipe...

"You said you don't want me. You can't want me. That's not exactly flattering. Doesn't exactly make me inclined to oblige."

"I said it. But the voice is being ignored to hell and back. I want every bit of you and more. I want it *now*."

His lips press to mine, and he devours my mouth in a long series of plundering, mouthwracking kisses that go deeper than the submarine diver who got the bends. I love it. I kiss him back. Tasting him, touching him wherever I can. The touch of his scar—still tender, but warm—is an unexpected turn on. Who knew?

"God, you drive me wild. I don't want you either—I'm trying to resist here."

"Ya think?" He's smiling, but his moves are claiming.

He tweaks my nipples. His hand roves to my pussy through jeans, and I'm grinding into it like a wanton strumpet in heat.

He's unbuttoning my T-shirt top and manhandling my breasts while I'm on him, wanting to ride his stallion any old time he cares to open that stable door.

"What's with us, Dan?"

"Who fucking cares. Just get it on."

My pussy is ripe for him, my breasts alive with a need for more attention. His hands and mouth are on me. Fortunately, I don't have to wait, as he already claims me without waiting to request permission, unzipping my jeans and getting inside like a ninja briefed him for the job. Maybe that's because I'm kissing him back in a carnal way that's a first for me. I almost can't get over it.

With Slash it was all yes Sir, no Sir. Submissive lover who knew her place. Told where to sit and what to say. I'd quite enjoyed that for a time until it became a 'thrills for him' tick list.

But this is so very different—has Dan unleashed my lady-beast?

Then, swiftly, he pulls back and lays the covers aside.

"I got this for us. You like?"

"Wow. Talk about premeditated. I should tell your officers to take a statement. Where did you get them?"

"I have my sources."

My eyes widen. Desire is still thrumming in my veins, and this time they're championed by excitement and yearning. Woo—what a party. It's like a small showcase from the cops' Argos catalogue in kink.

"Call me Sir?" he whispers. "Your only Sir."

He clicks on the cuffs. They're big and bulky. They even gleam in the light.

No modern fancy tech kind of cuff these. We're talking FBI vintage for serious offenders. I kinda like this retro raunchy edge. Weighty, proper steel cuffs especially for me. With real keys that will probably scrape in the lock.

"Giving me toys now?"

"The best kind, sugar."

It's every submissive kink craver's dream. Two pairs. A matching set. There's even coiled rope as an extra side to go. Black, plastic-coated rope that'll tie anything up tight as tight.

I avert my eyes. My previous Sir liked me submissive, quiet, doting—eyes to floor was his preference. I guess the habit's stuck—even if the man didn't.

"Look at me now," Sir orders. "Don't dare to divert your eyes."

And I obey. We lock gazes when the cuffs click sharply shut, and they feel heavy, cold, and they're already making me horny. I know they're going to hurt like hell, with a bite like a bitch in less than five minutes, but I don't care. Because I won't mind, in fact I'll crave it.

"Please, Sir, do your worst. I must be punished."

Dan takes out a black blindfold. "I'm not going to punish you, Agent K. I'm giving you what you most deserve. Putting you through your paces because in this we're on the same side of the kink line."

Fuck. I think I'm going to come. Before he's even touched me.

He smiles. Like he's just read my mind.

"Count on it. Count and don't miss a single beat." Dan

leans over and seizes a coil of rope. My insides jiggle at the sight, especially when he binds it slowly around one ankle and then the bed. He grunts softly as he does the same to my other leg. He then pulls the rope tighter yet before he slides the blindfold over my eyes. All is blackness and I'm bound to the metal bed end, face down. The sound of his breathing is suddenly very loud and I'm gulping air, unsure if excitement or acute angst makes me do so. This is new, Slash liked it with my back to the bed or on my knees. But this is Sir's private pleasure preference.

"You okay?"

"Yes. Would it matter?"

"Everything about this matters. *You* matter," he states.

"A civilian in your charge. You'd so get the sack."

"I'd rather have you in the sack."

"Fired. You could be fired."

His tone is liquid caramel. "The only thing I want to fire – is you."

The cuffs have me tight to the steel headboard. Then something ice cold – holy shit – journeys slowly up my body from my inner ankle to my pussy. I yelp, I can't help it. It's hard, but like ice.

"What?"

No answer. Just the light cold, pressure of some thin implement that's tracing tantalizing paths of destruction across my skin. It teases me and has me under its crazy spell – like he's trailing a giant icicle and I spasm in response, cuffs clanking already and we've barely begun.

"What is it, Dan?"

"Sir!" he barks. "You forget my rank." He sounds shit hard but I can hear the smile behind the words.

"My master," I whimper.

"Oh yeah. That I like. Nice job, Agent."

Yus! I'm an agent now.

"Agent Provocateur!" I whisper.

His agent of passion. I giggle. It starts so suddenly and leaps out as I'm unable to keep that thought on 'neutral' but he silences me swiftly. He kisses my arse so fiercely and thoroughly I can't help laughing. My giggles soon become rapture gasps, because he gently starts to nip and bite me on the backside. All the time something is moving against my clit.

I groan and quake. What the hell is this?

I've no idea. It's too cold to be him, and the effect multiplies the intensity.

I'm coming, straining at the cuffs. Already panting hard and squirming with the ecstasy he's so quickly incited. Wow. But it stops as soon as it started leaving me hanging — my rollercoaster dip has a tease pause in the program. I'm flailing a mile high and dangling with desire.

"You will wait until you have my permission," he growls.

Then the bites get harder. My buttocks will be in no shape for sitting around later. But they'll probably be a great psychedelic shade of scarlet and scorch.

"Nice work, Sir!" I moan. "You hungry there? My buns on a bap to your liking?"

Without warning he slaps my arse fully hard with his hand.

I squeal out. Half in pique and half in shock, with a tad of 'holy hell this is hot' for good measure. Slash was never a spanker — this Sir is proving to be my biggest surprise. The implement from before — I'm thinking it's some kind of crop — is now being lashed over my backside.

Again, again and again on steady rhythm.

"Too damn right, Agent. Shut your damn mouth or I'll eat you alive. How do you like your punishment for daring to keep Ivan's misdeeds from me?"

Wow. Now this is a head spin.

"You have got to be kidding me."

"Not a bit of it."

The lashes get faster. My cuffs jangle and I feel the rope my ankles are bound with chafe my skin as I writhe to escape his torturous touch.

Then it stops.

"I think that's enough punishment for now."

"Thanks for small mercies, Sir."

Wow, but my heart is pounding, and the thrills that are running through me right now I can't even hope to describe. It's like a champagne cocktail, mixed with the euphoria of a recent rollercoaster vertical rush.

"You ready for the next stage?" he whispers by my ear.

I nod. If I talk I might just lose it. Coming with absolutely no incitement other than horseplay, banter and restraints is a cardinal sin I will not commit.

And the cherry on the sundae is his 'Interpol Sir' guise at full throttle on me in the bedroom, and I find I love it. His coercion tactics have me at his mercy. I'm like a tired toddler being nap-prepped by a pro nanny. Only sleeping is the last thing on my Sir's mind.

He still hasn't told me what implement he's using. Seconds later I've a clue when it thwacks across my buttocks deliciously hard yet again.

"Is that a crop?"

"Well done, little one. This one's made of steel."

The action makes it hard for me to swallow. Hard. Like the thing in his combat pants that touches my thigh from time to time, when he bends over me to stroke my arse and back to soothe me. I'm hoping it'll soon come out to play too, because I'm greedy that way.

"You're aroused," I whisper.

"You caused it."

"I wanted to tell you the bets are off too…"

"I beg to differ… Maybe we're not in control for once?"

"You don't understand. It has to be the worst mistake ever — you and me." He presses his hand on my buttocks in a series of deep pressure moves. Movement and breathing aren't doable. Instead I blink.

"You don't care?" he whispers. "And what I want goes. Right now I want to take you from behind."

From the sounds I'm craning to hear he's pulling off his black ops vest and pants. The waiting almost makes me whimper.

"What I have for you is long, rigid, fully loaded and about to detonate. But first I need your safeword. What do you choose?"

I lick my lips. His dick against my thigh is telling me in uncertain terms that he's feeling very recovered.

My voice sounds tight to my own ears. "Jericho."

He pauses and I feel him swirl his fingers over my naked back and buttocks. "The lengths I've gone to, to find us a stash of condoms," he whispers, before kissing the back of my neck so delightfully I swear I could fly.

I find I'm keening for release. I want to touch him and kiss him and savor myself. All this keeping me in place is making me antsy.

Dan's hands claim my hips to tilt them, and I feel something soft slide beneath my belly. It must be a pillow.

But the familiarity of the position makes me freeze. All the horny, vibed stuff skitters away leaving behind a chilled, stark fear.

Fuck. Seb used to do this—he used to cause me physical pain. For all his vanilla ways, he was the only guy who figured sex to the point of painful was just part of the game. Ironic that my other partner was a BDSM freak but never ever 'hurt me' in the way my 'safe-tastes' boyfriend did.

A memory of the time he bruised and left me raw inside catches me so sharply I almost have a panic attack.

"Jericho," I stammer.

"What?" Unlike Seb, who didn't do empathy or care in the bedroom, I trust that he will stop at my safeword. "You okay?"

No. Not okay.

Not with that.

For all my bravado and erotic enigma branding, when it comes to this kind of doggy style that once left me crying and shaking I'm all at sea. I've never done this since Seb. Because he hurt me. Every time. But that didn't stop him.

"I can't," I say and I know I'm so close to crying it's

inevitable. I bet Sir's never had car crash sex like this is turning into.

"You're shaking. What's happened, what's wrong?"

I thought I was over it.

Turns out I wasn't. Turns out my tattoo's boasts are half fake. Because I'm not as game as I'd figured — when the wounds of my past are laid bare.

Talk about spoiling the moment. Just when I was about to have the best sex of my life.

"What happened, Katie?" he asks me. Already I can feel the cuffs and ropes being removed. When my hands are free I take off the blindfold myself, but I can't meet his gaze.

"You probably think I'm a 'been there, done it all' girl — the tattoo. I'm not. Slash had me under a spell — he liked domination but in a cosplay and toys way. Kink for turn-on over pain. Seb, on the other hand — he hurt me without it even being part of the game. I've never done that position with anyone else since. I guess my brain is wired to reject it."

"He hurt you — the one you were engaged to?"

"He liked his own way and he got rough. He was enthusiastic, sometimes to the point of ouch. Especially when he'd had a drink. It's given me an aversion."

Dan palms his hair. "I'm so sorry. But what I don't understand is why you'd settle for that?"

"Oh for God's sake, don't get like this. It's me who's ruined things. Mea culpa — let's leave the inquisition there."

"You haven't ruined anything. But I promise, I would never have hurt you. Never could, never will. When you voice your safe word then I stop. No question."

Dan kisses me. Gently, with exquisite care and tenderness. He exposes my neck, taking time to smooth away my hair, and gently kisses my neck — soft as silk but twice as sinful and so moreish I can't help but let my mouth open yearning for his kiss there instead. I turn then revel in feeling him enter and explore my mouth with his tongue and I gasp with the enticing delight of him.

"I'll never let anyone hurt you again. Especially me."

"You haven't hurt me."

"I could have. I never want to do that."

He is heady as a potent cocktail with a pure hit of thrilling chili kick.

When he takes my mouth, his kiss is like no other I've ever experienced. My breathing comes in shallow gasps as he gently pushes his hands through my hair, then strokes my neck. His kisses move to cover the flesh of my shoulders is, suffused with the passion I've long craved yet never quite found.

Desire pools between my legs and it thrills me no end.

Dan moves his hand to cup my breast and knead it with warm, firm fingers. It makes my breathing expel in jagged gasps of thrill. I push myself into his fingers that trace pure magic. I let him push me down on the bed softly. Loving the feel of his strong hands and that muscular power in the man. He explores my pussy with his fingers. I want it — oh how.

"You drive me crazy, don't ever think I don't want you."

"I'm scared I'll hurt you."

"You won't. Maybe next time you'll teach me how what you planned can be different?"

"You trust me enough?"

I sense the blossoming connection, and feel equally ensnared. Soon, he kisses my thighs, and he claims my clit with his kisses. It takes my breath away. But I don't want him to stop. His tongue causes sensory delight as he trails it there and suckles me. Then he pulls back only to return and to tease again. Our gazes lock and intensify the thrills.

"I thought this was punishment?"

"I think you've been punished more than enough. I think you deserve only good things."

Soon, before I even know it, my legs are tight around his waist. I feel him long and hard and close, and thrillingly enticing. He rolls on a condom, then comes back to where I need him most. Sliding into my moist heat, in a long pleasuring ride of a move. I gasp out his name in wonder.

Dan looks up, and that solemn unspoken question, checking if I'm okay, breaks the spell.

"Stop worrying. I won't break. Dan. Please, I want you. If you're worried, let me go on top. Though I'll struggle being quiet." I smile.

He moves me on top. Badass even in bed. His jaw is titanium-flexed.

"Soundproofed. No cameras. Copy that."

Dan

Not only is she über hot, too sexy for sanity's sake—butt naked with handcuff marks—but the irreversible damage is I've no damn right to take her or even aspire to this.

She's suffered enough. Why would she want more letdowns from another loser bad news guy? What can I give Kate? Except a marriage to my job and fucked-up sex tricks.

But I'm at her mercy and my strict focus on the job in hand has suddenly got mussed, messy and hard to deal with.

I'm inside her and she's riding me hard, kissing me as if these are our last seconds in time, and she's nuclear-hot meets pressure cooker of turn-on.

Plus, she has a rare knack for some wild, rampaging alchemy that makes me want to rip clothes off with my teeth whenever she's near. I watch her breasts jiggle as she rides me, feeling the waves of promise that tell me I'm on the verge. Yet, still she rides harder and faster, and it's only as I'm here about to experience this stellar orgasm I realize I've had more vanilla sex with Kate than I've had since things went tits up.

This is new.

Can I leave the kind of play I usually opt for? Or risk it with Katie?

Since the Mexican mistakes, I've opted for hard, hurting. Pain to rid me of the bugs that crawl beneath my skin about

Nathan—partner deceased, guilt indelible. Yet, something about being tied, restrained and hurt helped fill the dark void that's always there about Nathan being dead, and clears the memories of that night gone wrong.

Or is it that it takes me to the edge, where I feel punishment payback gives me the release?

Kate pulses her muscles around my dick, and I cry out as I fall into spiraling waves of 'yes'. It briefly overrides the grief that usually overtakes me at the mere memory of my failings.

I'm kissing her hard, grazing her lips with my fierceness and pawing her with demanding, crazed fingers. Shit, but if that doesn't make me feel more of a monster yet. Even though she's kissing me back with a raw, carnal hunger I dig.

I pull back swiftly, breathing harder than I had in any gym workout.

"Fuck. Katie—what's with this?"

"Don't stop."

"But. No. I should be gentle...you need...deserve gentle."

"What do you want, Dan? One minute you want it? Next you can't get away fast enough."

I'm grinding out words I don't want to share, but I can't hold in. "Because all I have is hard. Fast. Dark. Crazed and messed-up, so I can't think. Sometimes, it has to get to the point of me howling in pain. You really don't need that—do you?"

She's silent. Point taken.

"Who was she?" she asks.

And inside me turns to crimson lava boil. "What?"

"Clearly this is about a woman."

I shake my head. She so doesn't need this. Has somebody told? Doesn't need me in her life nor to hear any deets I'm not willing to give.

"Her real name was Gina. But we didn't do names—she was Mistress Miscreant."

She's staring at me in horror.

"Fake name. She was a hooker. Not so nice, when you get up close, am I?"

Yeah. My masochistic therapy isn't pretty. But then, it's only to shed the reptilian killer by default's skin. To offset the night terrors. So, I take some of what I deserve for letting Nathan die.

Does Kate really need a messed-up beast? Answer, no. So, now she knows the full gory glory.

"I usually like candle wax. Crops. Nice things to ask of a lady, huh? Crop Mistress Miscreant was her fake name. She didn't mind. Turned out her time was up sooner than either of us were ready for."

"Are you trying for shock factor?"

"Honesty is all."

"Beats sex trafficking and pimping—that's my dad's example. Or making love to me, whether you're hurting me or not—and I nearly married him. Hell, the last guy I wanted didn't even want me at all, after designing his preferred tattoo on paper. Believe me—I've seen my fill of guys whose needs come first."

And in that stark sentence I'm lost. Her scars are substantial—who am I to take first pew? Fuck worrying…if vanilla is what's on the table here, I'd gladly dine for the rest of my life and return for more. But I sense I'm not worthy.

I kiss her so hungrily she mewls at the back of her throat. I'm inside her and I'm grinding into the delectable, soft, hot, wet heat that is Kate, again. Her pussy makes me shudder, weak with the desire to screw her senseless, and before I know it, I'm pumping hard, bam, slap, grind. It's so incredible, she's calling out in the heat of passion, wanting as much hard vanilla as I can give.

Missionary, for fuck's sake.

I thunder into her, and know she's on the cusp of shattering beneath me, so I drill harder and force her thighs wider as I slam my dick at a heady pace to her deepest spot with frenetic repetition. Moving her to raise her legs high.

She's coming for me and I love every panted cry.

"Come, baby. I'm nothing you need—givin' you all I have."

She's coming. Loving the ride and saying my name over and over, breathing gasped entreaties and gyrating her pleasure so wantonly that I slam in once more, and come. My cum filling the condom at DEFCON One, and taking me to that sexual nirvana place in my head where no thoughts or remorse or recrimination are possible—for a few sweet seconds of time. Only this time they don't go.

The black smoke of grief and shame remain.

You're a beast.

Why should a woman this sweet and potent, with such deep past scars, ever settle for a messed-up wreck like me? She's no idea of my night terrors. Or that I have to play these kink games to settle the demons. Or that my last girlfriend was a hooker who was shot dead as a hostage in a drugs raid on a liquor store. Caught in the crossfire. First I knew was when I saw her photo on TV.

What kind of guy am I? How can I kid myself I've anything to offer?

My dad was right. I'm a drop-out embarrassment to the family name. I should have left her alone. Shoulda known better.

I pull out and I'm doing that thing. The one women disparage where the man retreats to stare at the ceiling and wish he'd thought it through. Wondering how to evade the look I know will be in her eyes when I dare to watch—disa-ruddypointment.

At max-carnage voltage.

Chapter Sixteen

Kate

I gawp in horror at Rich Redman. He's watching me over his steepled fingers, with news less welcome than the mayor at a brothel orgy. And here I'd thought earlier with Dan was a showstopper carnival of heinous. We parted not talking, then he walked me to my room in silence and shut me in.

I'm guessing our paths won't cross much if Dan can help it. I feel like I've tested a glass bridge with my little toe, only to have a mile of murderous shards crash under me. I'm hanging in there clutching the rope rail, but only just.

What we shared has turned us into limping casualties of kink turned caustic.

"We will take you from here tonight. You'll meet Donaldson in a carefully choreographed exercise," says Rich. "You're briefed, and the plan is set."

"I'm meeting him after all?"

He nods. "At the Santos Hotel—you'll have a suite there. While we lure your father there tomorrow night, the mansion will be under siege."

My stomach bottom's disappeared in a 'hey presto' moment—like Houdini down an escape hatch. He's taken my ability to breathe with him.

"Dangerous." I'm struggling to keep the jitters from my voice.

"You'll have cover. A carefully executed entrapment plan. The synchronized swoop on his mansion ensures all bases are covered and will allow us to rescue the trafficked women as planned. It's all comes down to this — the eleventh hour at hand."

Given the choice, I'd rather not have had him use the words 'execute' or 'strike'. But it's done and out there, and I'm hoping it'll be my only brush with these verbs in the foreseeable.

"Who's covering me? Draven?

"Him or Gonzalez."

The way we've left it I'm not sure Dan'll fancy playing Kevin Costner to my Whitney. Or Clark Kent to my poop scoop of peril. Right now, I've a yearning for Ben and Jerry's followed by tequila and it won't be pretty. I'm hoping Warbie has stock.

"I'd hoped that course of action had changed. Guess I'd banked on that more than I'd admitted," I tell him.

"We were anxious after recent field attacks that there's been too much threat. Flexibility is key and we've leaked information to Donaldson that you're staying at the hotel now. There's a big art sale there tomorrow night and you're exhibiting."

Me? I couldn't even doodle a dot-todot disaster to save my skin.

"Oh. Won't Draven be better placed at the traffickers' lair?" I ask. As if I know the first damn thing about black ops cop operations. Yeppo. Do blame Daniel Craig for my flights of fancy. Do *not* blame me.

"Judgment call. We're always ready for changes. Whoever is in charge will have a remit to keep you out of any danger. We'll ensure your safety."

The five star swanky Santos Hotel seems a bizarre locale for a Dad meets Daughter showdown. I find myself watching the incongruous Minion nodding desk toy waggling beside us on Rich's desk. Throughout all this gritty shit it's just grinning like a plastic loon. I wonder if somebody bought it in the black ops Secret Santa. Can I envisage Dan or Havana shopping for Minion nodders in a store? The thought of Dan doing anything as mundane as that causes my heart to wobble.

"Who bought that?" I ask. Don't ask me why but it matters somehow.

"My wife. She's Minion mad. If I stuffed it in a drawer she'd find out and kill me. Especially since the pregnancy hormones make her crazy and irrational."

"When's she due?" I ask.

"Last week." Then his jaw clenches as if I've just confessed to three murders and being witchfinder general on the side.

"Oh."

"But I should really be the one investigating *your* private life." When his gaze meets mine it speaks a silent code for rumbled. "Whatever has gone on between you and Agent Draven will be set aside. The mission comes first—Draven knows this—so should you. We're counting on you both to complete this mission, and we'll all be going home. Whatever happens outside of here is your own business, but while you're here I need total focus."

"There's nothing to take out of here. I think we can put it behind us. Be reassured nothing further will occur."

And here's the craziest part of all. Something inside me quivers at the realization that, by next week, this could be a distant memory—this crazy place, my incarceration, this gang of heavy duty top cop nutjobs. Rich, Warbie, Dan. Havana. I'll be back to my real life—yet more changed than ever.

And there are some gripes I need to air to the big man while I have access. "I don't appreciate being a honey trap for my Dad. Why didn't you all explain this better to me first? It's all 'push Kate around like an old chest of drawers on casters', and I'm sick of being steamrollered by the might of M I bloody whatever number it is you work for."

"Interpol Sex Crimes Protection Division, Security Force Nine to be exact," he says softly, and the detachment of it all dings my nerves. But, suddenly, Rich looks like he's a man who really needs a drink. He whispers to me, "Whatever is going on with you two in private should go on hold from now. Put whatever stuff is in the air on pause. That's a direct order. Draven has been formally warned."

"I won't work with him until he apologizes to me anyway," I reply. Though a part of me can't believe I'm talking to Dan's superior and being this petty. Yet, a part of me senses they need me badly and I can ask for whatever silly sundae I choose to order from the mission's menu. I choose Pique Speared Hurts Chip on Shoulder Surprise.

Rich takes a deep breath. The kind I've seen Freddie Mercury do in video moments when he's about to slay everyone with his vocal range.

"I'm sorry," says Dan behind us. "She's right, she deserves that much. I owe it to her."

Where the hell did he come from? A trap door? Like in a pantomime?

"Where did you...?"

He motions with his head to a glass panel in the wall. It's a two way mirror and I hadn't twigged. He's been watching the chat. Nice.

And now I don't know what to say. I've got what I wanted. Yet it feels empty. Hell, it *is* empty. Meanwhile, Rich stares at his iPad as if formulating a very large shopping list, probably for Minion-print baby goods — anything but be stuck in the same room as a pair of lustlorn lunatic odd bods like us.

"It's not you, it's me — isn't that what you're about to say?" I say softly.

"I really like you. I've been straight with Rich and come clean on us. I'd like us to have a future — though I sense I've screwed up too bad. But the mission will always come first. I'm tasked with protecting you — and for now that's all I can focus on."

Shit. Like a camouflaged ninja prairie dog, his through the roof surprise about 'a future' leaves me speechless. "Oh."

"Do you mind having me guard you? I won't proceed if there are grudges."

I shrug. Then I sigh. Then I shrug again and say no.

Rich nods. Dan nods back.

It's like being invited to the nodding dog convention, only my spring's burst, and I feel car sick from too much distance travelled.

"Strictly professional. Job comes top billing or no dice," says Rich.

"Strictly professional," we answer.

Dan hands me a note. "Here's your itinerary to refresh you. You'll be moved out of here at dusk."

I scan the note. There's an itinerary. But in front of it is another scribbled note. I sense now may not be the time to read its details. They might be personal.

Holy conscience attacks — this man is so full of dark mystery and most likely bull. I scrunch and pocket the details.

Rich Redman rises behind his desk. I hope to God he's no clue Dan's sending me personal notes as mission prep.

If he suspects he doesn't show it. Instead, he holds out a hand for me to shake.

"It's a pleasure working with you. We'll meet when this mission's complete. Best of luck, Kate. I know you'll nail this."

I nod at Rich and rise to leave. My eyes clash with Dan's in silent accusation, but he doesn't miss a beat and just stays unruffled and silent. Once we're outside the office Dan watches me and reaches out his hand to take mine.

I evade his touch. But he tugs me close to the hard planes of his chest.

"Strictly professional?" I whisper. Then I deflect by removing the note from my pocket and scanning.

The sex was outstanding. We're really good at it. But I can't be what you want or need, even though I want you. You're worth much more than I can give. I wanna try — I'll accept it if it's already over. Where do we go from here? Your call.

He says softly, "All the things you're thinking. You don't

know how wrong you are. You're worth it. I'm worth bailing on. We could be something stunning. This shit is getting in the way."

His eyes school me to stay silent. I summon courage and calm and sniff back surprised tears. Then realize I'm shaking, and I know he can feel it because we're closer than close. So much for our in-office promises.

The tears slide down my cheek and I'm so mad at myself I could voodoo doll my own emotional weakness. I try to stem the flow with fingers, but Dan thrusts a napkin at me to gently dab them away.

"I know you're frightened. That's okay. I won't ever let him hurt you and I think you can do this. You'll smash it," said Dan. "He's going down for a very long time at your hands — you're the heroine here."

I blow out a sigh and go with it. I stare back into eyes that cause mini-electric shocks inside my veins. I let my head fall against his shoulder and let the whizzing thoughts go as I take in the magnitude of what he's just admitted. I can smell him. Citrus and spice. Feel Dan's strong heady warmth through his thin, black shirt. I can perceive the latent strength in his arms and the great proportions of his body — we fit so right it freaks me out and already my pussy is pooling with need for him, and my clit twitches. I'm so easy I should be arrested and cautioned.

"Instead of doubting you and doubting me," Dan whispers, softly pushing away a tendril of hair, "take a few moments to think that you're here now — you've overcome. You're the only woman who's stopped me in my tracks. I'm not going to mess up this chance to prove how good we could be together. Let me try."

Dan's breath grazes the side of my neck and gives me goosebumps.

The sentiment of what he just said does something warm and squishy and emotionally gratifying, but it raises my respect. The touch of his hands on me through my clothes makes me inwardly melt and heat. I find myself seeking out his mouth with mine for scorching kisses. His tongue dips inside and claims my mouth. Filling me with his strength and clamoring need.

"Don't fancy you, huh?" he says. His cock presses my abdomen like a weapon of intent. Dan sucks in a breath. "How can I regret a move that's got me this close to you? We all have scars, Katie. Me especially."

His lips meet mine. Hard, hot, unyielding, vital and free. Soaring to the high heavens. Desire pools inside me as I kiss him, wildly influenced by the man who is driving me on. Dan has the power to blitz my good sense with his sexy allure and his attention. He makes me aware of my attributes rather than deficiencies.

But seconds later the sound of a slam in Rich's office has us on auto-react.

We spring apart as the door opens.

"It's happening. Gotta leave, gotta get there," says Rich. His face an ashen mask of shock and preoccupation.

"The mansion? Has something happened to the hostages?" asks Dan.

Rich only stares, wide-eyed and worried.

Dan—man of steel—takes his superior's arms between his palms. "Tell me, Rich—what's happened?"

"Baby coming. Now. Got to leave. You're in command. I'm out of here."

Adrenaline is racing inside me as I stand staring at Rich, whose stress is now tempered with relief. But only for a few stalled seconds—because now we're another man down. I'm about to be thrown into the pit without Dan as backup. In a weird daze I help Rich make preps to go and get to his wife's side. Could this get any odder? Who'd have thought a senior agent would take off for personal reasons when a months-long mission was about to go down?

Dan flicks me a glance, and I clock it. His jaw is vice-clenched. He's in charge and the promotion becomes him. If looks could give passionate hugs, his one just has.

"Let's get Gonzalez. He'll be your bodyguard, and

nothing's going wrong on my watch, honey. Trust me."

Shit going down here or what?

* * * *

Dan

I have to let her go and that pains me, because she won't be on my direct watch. It has me so wired I could take her across my knee and spank her until her gorgeous globe cheeks redden with my hand's attentions.

Or alternatively go to town with her tied to my bed.

Until Kate, I've taken to paying women for those tricks. A moment of reprieve until the mental vision of Nathan's prostrate dead body bleeding from two bullet wounds comes flooding back. With the taunting voices — *you did that, you let him die.*

I've been atoning for past sins with boudoir bullets. Until a civilian in my charge changed the sexscape so I no longer know which way is up. I'm standing with a thundering pulse watching her walk away with another guy.

"Gonzalez. Keep me regularly briefed."

"Copy that, Sir." Gonzales is such a ringer for Robert De Niro he could be his younger brother.

"Low profile. Any changes of play come through me."

"Got it."

"Got that, *Sir*," he gruffly commands.

"Got that, Sir."

I can feel my heart ramping, and as a pro shooter who prides himself on focus, that's never good. "Katie. Do as this man says. I trust him with my life, and yours."

She bites her cheek but she nods and fakes brave. "See you when I see you?"

"Sure will."

She nods and I see her lip tremble, and it spears my gut. Why do I feel like I'm in a storm buffeted by her low key unexpected and goddamn felling charms?

I run back a few paces. Gonzales keeps going, but Kate

stops, and I reach out to stroke her face. Softly, gently and she smiles at me with tear-rimmed eyes.

"Don't cry."

"I'm not. It's a hologram." Kate stares at me, and I'm still stroking her cheek. Longing to trace her mouth with my thumb. Longing to swoop in to claim her mouth with mine. I have it bad. So bad.

"Warbie will take care of you today. Make sure you say your goodbyes to Havana too. Believe me — I care about keeping you safe."

She smiles, and my heart springs like crazy.

"I'll stay safe. Sir's orders." Kate's look pleads with me. Her beseeching gaze beneath those dark curling lashes could have me sign my own death warrant. "You must stay safe too. Just because you're the one in command suddenly doesn't mean you're bulletproof."

"Trust me, *chica*. Nothing's gonna take me down. Count on it."

* * * *

Kate

I hang out with Warbie long enough to eat a last meal with him. Then we visit Havana, who's looking amazing, considering what she went through the day before.

"I can't believe I'm missing all the action," she grumbles. She's about as happy as a dog booked into a cattery for a vacation stay.

Meanwhile Rocco is arranging flowers — where did he get them? Why is he on nurse and florist's duty?

"Rocco's on ops tonight — mission take Katsaros down. I'm here reading chick books. Me? Chick books? I mean it's so bad it kills me."

I shake my head at her. Once an action-ass, always an actionass.

"I'm sure if you ask Warbie he'll magic you up some warfare titles."

All Havana does is grunt. But there's life in her. I'd rather she was angry and grumping, than pale and lifeless as previously. Her eye makeup really is rockin' the now vibe.

"Katie. You helped save my life. Thanks."

"Didn't. I just dabbed his brow and handed him stuff. Sterile stuff. I didn't look at blood. There was a lot of it. I found whistling a tune in your head helps with that."

"You done good, girl."

"Hav, so did you, and Rocco is more in love with you than ever." I reach out and lay a hand on hers. "I'm sorry that you didn't like me and we got off to a bad start. I apologize for being a brat around you. Dan thinks you're an amazing agent, by the way, though he'd never tell you that himself. So I am. You rock it. I hope you recover well, and when you're back out there doing action stuff — stay safe."

"Thanks," she says. "I'll see you later. Don't go giving me last epic monologues like you're not comin' back — you so are. Gonzales is the best in the business — besides Rocco, Dan and me." She grins. Actually, properly grins.

I nod. That's as much of an emotional bloodletting as we'll ever do. So I'm surprised when she hunkers up in bed for a brief hug. Wow. Havana loves me and I think I dig her back. Life is getting strange.

"Get off me. People will talk. Rocco is already staring like he's had a stroke. Get off me," she says quickly. I'm smiling despite shitting myself to the moon and back about what's ahead.

* * * *

I have to put my arm up his back, but I force Warbie to give me a last request. He doesn't agree lightly.

I let my bewildered eyes adjust to the darkness of this subterranean command deck where Warbie's taken me. This one is real deal crisis checkpoint. Smaller than the first room I visited, when I met Rich, with its sea of screens and operators. This one is silent and there are ten screens, tops.

It's the gruesome gallery of spy cop edits. Pentagon hot desk lookalikey.

There are three people in headsets with monitors before them, and I know one is Dan. The man I've come to see. I spy Rocco too — all clad in black and I'm guessing he's prepping men in the field with instructions.

The lasting image is CCTV, via a hidden cam — and there is a room full of women. Several are crying. One looks sick. They're huddled together like cattle, all sitting on a mattress. They're talking a language I don't understand, but I can pick up the tone to know their fear, loathing and sorrow.

Shit. Maybe I shouldn't have come here after all. I'm an outsider who can bring little value and I'm overstepping.

Shoulda listened to Warbs.

But I just want to watch. I'd love to interview each one of them and find out exactly what they're doing. Dan's true crucial role zooms to ultra-impressive in my mental ranking and I stay silent.

I struggle to comprehend that scenes like these do happen in real world law enforcement. That the sinister underbelly of this idyllic island should reveal such menace.

"Okay?" Rocco asks, taking me by surprise.

Just then one of the women shouts in the filmed room and a strong male smacks her so hard she falls back.

Dan is on his feet. "What are you doing here?"

"Is this what my dad is doing?"

"Maybe now you get an idea of what we're dealing with. Sorry you had to see."

I nod solemnly. But don't have other words to say.

"You fully packed and ready to go under nightfall?" He steers me to the door. I'm not wanted. Overstepping. So naïve and unprepared for the hardcore coal face of this job. So much for seasoned reporter.

"I am."

"You need to go. Warbie, take Kate to her room. Try and get some rest if you can. It'll fortify you." Dan nods. Then lowers his voice to a whisper, "I want this over so I can get you where I can be sure you're safe."

"And I thought my working conditions were tough," I remark, gesturing to the pitch-black and cramped conditions, and immediately feel pathetic for joking. No idea. Given the women's faces on the screen ahead.

Dan pulls me into his arms and puts his lips to mine briefly. It's a short but a searing kiss that answers all my questions and promises desires untold. I feel him—I feel his need. "See you soon. We're all behind you."

He hands me a large file from on his desk. "You'll want info—being a journo. Work out all about the nasty guys we're up against. Then realize you're doing the right thing."

The file reads *Confidential–Operation Mountain Goat.* My heart sinks and tension cranks before the file is even browsed, before atrocities are even explored. I suspect it will change everything. Or maybe everything is already altered? I know the answer already in my heart. My life will never be the same again because it can't be.

Chapter Seventeen

"Hey, Kate, you look like a duchess," says Gonzales. He's pretty damn hot in his tux suit too. As arm candy I've a great date and this one's tooled-up for trouble. Standing here in finery, I feel so far removed from the dire facts I've seen laid bare in black and white, in the mission file. Women and girls shipped like products for pimps, kept on tight leashes and in abject poverty. Lured by promises of a better life, money and security for their families. They've fallen for the lies, and into sex slavery, with no benefits beyond bed and meagre board. Some young women have disappeared, suspected murdered without qualms. It's so appalling my stomach still churns with the horror.

Gonzales watches me, and I try to shake off the scattered dark thoughts that must show on my face.

"I may feel like a clanking bag of nerves, but looking hot is half the deal. You're not so bad yourself. Shall we head downstairs to our doom?"

"Don't say that, *Princesa*. Never bring negatives to the table you intend to dine at."

"Just not sure what's going to greet me," I answer softly. "Or should I say who."

Gonzales may outdo me on the philosopher quotes, but I find I'm delighted that I've made him blush scarlet at the compliments. "I'm by your side every step of the way."

I'm decked out pretty good, dressed in my cobalt silk finery, with my hair dry shampooed back into life. Considering I've been secretly transported through Santorini under a blanket, it's pretty impressive that I've salvaged any passable style. The suite here is five-star VIP finest. I'm not even sure I'll ever see it again.

If this goes to plan, Grey Donaldson will be cuffed, and I'll be out the door before you can say *boomshakalak*.

Gonzales takes my hand and places it on the top of his arm, like a true gent. It reassures nerves that jangle like windchimes in a spooky weirdo's garden.

The hubbub of the art show throng in the main hall off the lobby grows louder as we near. The clink of glasses accompanies soft music and the hum of a mingling art crowd.

"You like this stuff?" asks Gonzales.

"Prefer photo prints from the bargain store, then you can change them when you hate them," I say, and he winks at my answer, then leads me to the far side of the main hall. There's a display set up on boards of four large-scale paintings—landscapes, sea views mostly. A symphony of color created by a genius is graced by my name hanging ludicrously above. As if I ever could.

"Clever girl," says Gonzales.

"I wish," I add, then notice the price cards. Four figure sums apiece make my eyes widen.

"Goatherd spotted at twelve o'clock."

I say nothing. I don't even move.

Gonzales continues, "Charcoal suit, drinking champagne. Wearing steel-rimmed specs. Do not look over. Repeat, do not." Gonzales says the words so smoothly, and without seeming to do so, that a ventriloquist could go to him for smooth show tips.

Goatherd. Code word for Donaldson.

"He's seen me?"

Gonzales doesn't make eye contact with me, but I know by the slow way he blinks, it's a yes. Call me super-psychic but I discern that's the subtle cop's signal for heads up, he's coming this way. The bastard's in the building and seeking me out. Just hope I remember to continue breathing.

* * * *

The team are down in the speedboat bay, readying to leave. I almost can't believe I'm stuck in a swivel seat, eyes on monitor, plugged into every comms device possible, but with no gun.

This is so not me. But as project team head the buck puck landed in my responsibility zone so I have to defend it with all I have.

"Buddy," says a familiar voice behind me. If I didn't know better I'd think Redman was back at base. But he's gone. To witness his baby's birth. Maybe I'm delusional and that's so not a good sign.

"Draven—I'm back." It *is* Rich. I swivel on this damn squeaky chair—how does he bear sitting on this?—to take it in.

"What the hell are you doin' back here?"

"Baby's a healthy girl. Nine pounds fourteen ounces. Chloe Rose. Now I'm back doing my job. Didn't think I could miss out on this take down, did ya? Worked my butt off to get here."

I shake my head. "And how did Jenny take that decision? You'll be in serious trouble."

Rich is already claiming the chair and the desk, and yanking off my earpiece. "She bloody told me to go. I'm no use to her when I'm only half in the room. She and the baby are doin' just fine." He flips open his phone to show off an evidence pic. I see his radiating pride, even in the dim light.

"She's perfect."

"Course. With me for a Dad why wouldn't that be so?"

A quick debrief and he's back sitting in the chair—it doesn't squeak much under him, I notice. Great. Not only am I totally action-denied, now I'm a spare part to my superior.

"So what you waiting for?" he asks. "Get down there fast."

"Too late. They've just gone."

Redman faces me, his eyes bright. "You think I didn't think to call ahead to order they wait up? You've ten minutes to get tooled-up and down there."

It's like Christmas early. This is what I wanted. This is what counts.

Even though a tiny voice in my head wonders if I'd've picked Katie's assignment over the mansion siege. Too late to wonder.

"Keep an eye on the Kate sitch, won't you?" I mutter as I'm leaving to go, moving fast to catch my ops bus to business.

"You telling me how to do my job? I'm top dog, remember?"

"You're the daddy," I answer. "You definitely are tonight, bro."

Redman mimics my accent so badly it's winceworthy. "Go move yo ass, fella. Move yo ass."

* * * *

I'm in the action zone, ready for kick-off. Rich's voice in my ear sounds as hyped as I am.

The evening air is muggy, and deep night falls swiftly around us. The environs of the Mone Dunamis — the gang's hideout-cum-fortress is barren, isolated and has little ground cover for camouflage.

Its looks belie its purpose — a summer holiday home, but with the benefit of high security fences and regular ninja style patrollers. The pool at the rear and planters on the terrace are incongruous with the gun in the current guard's hands.

Behind this façade lies a labyrinth of criminal activity. Storerooms for weapons and a cellar layout of holding cells below ground. I guesstimate right now there are at least fourteen girls being held captive prior to moving — France, the UK, Germany, Spain. They'll be working hard — Katsaros' girls can end up having sex with ten to twelve men a day.

The thought sickens me to my stomach, and I spit on the dry, dusty earth to rid the taste of fucking outrage and injustice from my palette.

The mansion has a control room, we're reliably informed by Andreas will be key to taking the place down. By all accounts, almost as well equipped as Interpol's base. Mone Dunamis, however, has more sinister intent. Trafficking for big money—blackmailing petrified parents in some cases, and warning them if they go to police they'll never see their daughters again. Using poverty, in other cases, as carte blanche to wreck young lives.

I scan the wall high above me and glimpse Timo peering over the rim of the roof in signal. I'm itching to get physical in Spiderman-climb mode. Signal received, I begin the ascent. I'll make entry on the second floor, and speed and glitch-free are our watchwords here. I see the guard slump and be dragged off by Dockery.

My abs are superglued to the side of the house as my feet and fingers move swiftly. I ignore a fly buzzing close to my ear, and sanction not a single twitch. Nothing will blow this. I've memorized my moves until I'm position pristine like a pro dance routine.

Counting to three, I climb higher with silent care—three steps, my foot on the ledge below the window, and I'm ready for entry after three swift slides of a wire defeat the lock deftly. *Nice.*

Downstairs, the boys will be taking care of the cellar's weakened door.

One step, two and slide—through the glass door. All in less than ten seconds. Levelheaded and careful and thorough are my mantra. This isn't about bragging. Lives count. I pride myself on tight ops.

Barely taking breaths, I circle the empty room, my back peeling along the wall as if magnetized. The fun will blast off soon when I get to the door—I check my watch and—boom.

Our planted explosives go off in perfect sync. I'm through the door and covering mansion ground with sharp and clean speed. My pistol is ready for everything—earpiece instruction from Rich at precise periods.

Too easy, says a voice in my head.

Much too easy — no hitches. No bodies, no blocking. No opposition. No man with a gun or guards to take out on the way.

Quiet. Still.

Shit.

What do I want—a corral fight? Flamethrowers and tanks and bodies flying through the air? Instinct screams this is off—not right. But I school it to silence and stick to the plan. Convictions must be achieved tonight, come Hell or high water. The women must be safely evacuated, with absolutely no margin for error. On a smooth, silent sigh, I put my hand on the door handle across the hall, aim my gun at the ready and pull open…

Bang almighty. Bullets. Rapid fire exchange. I'm rolling across the floor like a well-armed and bulletproofed cannonball out for whirlkicks.

And tonight—Katsaros is going down.

On my watch.

* * * *

Kate

Sweat trickles down my back, and my hands and forehead are clammy, as every nerve ending inside me is the definition of antsy day on an anthill.

I'd never have been any good in the police. Nor a police call center. The pressure is beyond belief. I long to just turn and run.

It makes me realize that the talking part of my job helps me cope with the uncertainties and unfolding drama. But standing, waiting for him to reveal himself is torture. I'm staring at these paintings like a crazed art-obsessed psycho. I flick my gaze to Gonzales, and in only a glance I can tell he's urging me to stay calm. He can sense my fear.

It's like watching a bomb disposal expert at work in the room next to you—nerves are frayed to frustration's edge, and my stomach is in numerous Mensa puzzle knots. Worst of all, my underwear is sticking to every inch of where it covers me, in this cloying heat. Not in a good way.

This makes me more jittery and I yearn to breathe easy. I chastise my own pathetic petty complaints, given what's likely unfolding at Mone Dunamis, and what the team are being put through.

The Greek night is oppressively hot, despite the many ceiling fans and air con in the hotel. I sense him before I see him. He doesn't speak. He doesn't turn to look at me. He simply walks up and stares hard at my fake paintings display.

I'm side-glancing like crazy. Charcoal suit and champagne glass as warned, plus an even, deep tan and silver fox hair. Nothing like I'd expected. He's so much smaller in the flesh, now I'm fully grown.

"Your paintings?" he asks. That Cockney twang still evident in his accent.

"Yes."

"Impressive. Joseph—not a name I'm familiar with. I know quite a bit about art. I'm something of a collector."

And that comment stalls me.

Is it an innocent observation, or a stab at my changed name? The identity changed option we chose as a family when we disappeared. I also know he collects—the trouble is he collects things that really should never be taken in the first place.

I turn. I'm absolutely bricking it and every sense inside me screams to flee, but I force myself to be professional and detached.

Two can play at this double meaning comments game and blow it out of the water.

"And what are your usual tastes, Sir?" I ask him, and stare at the man who really is so very unlike the crime boss thug I was expecting. Or the father who sired me, but didn't take any of the other fatherly duties to heart.

I'm yearning to say, "Young, vulnerable girls to exploit and terrorize? Blood money as a pimp middle man lowlife?" But I don't. I just stare, refusing to look away first.

"I like portraiture. People," he answers. "Faces can tell you so much without a single word."

I'm telling him plenty right now.

Fuck off.

Raw hatred. That I know who he is. That I'm onto him. That I hate him beyond anything I've ever known in life. The devil incarnate. I shrivel inside in shame at being related to this monster of a man.

Only this staring game is real life with sky high stakes and no fun conclusion.

I lick my lips and watch Gonzales. "I think I've done enough small talk tonight already."

"And is the big one for sale?" Donaldson asks.

"No. None of them are."

"Then why display your work? Why come?"

I swallow hard. I feel a little strange and dizzy. It's the heat, the pressure, and not knowing what to say or what not to say.

"I think we both know the answer. Coercion. It's something you've built a career on, yourself."

He's staring. Eyes the very same color as my own stare hard back into mine. Then his lip curls slightly.

"Weren't you even just a little intrigued?"

"Not at all."

"You are a very beautiful woman. So much like your mother. In many ways also like me. I wanted to apologize — now, I'm not sure you deserve it."

I can't answer. There's too much anger boiling inside me at him even mentioning my mother to me. The woman he hurt and mistreated most and chose criminality over family life.

She's gone now and to a place he'll never reach her.

"I can't undo the past. But I can tell you that I do have regrets. A great many regrets," he says slowly, deliberately.

I don't want to stay here hearing this but, instead of supporting operations by being cool and in control, I'm an annoying AWOL emotions grenade about to blow.

Gonzales says the words, "The temperature is climbing steadily."

It's my sign to know that the team are inside the Mansion. That Katsaros has been taken down. I need put up with this farce no longer. We can clear out and go.

"Once a bad guy, always a bad guy in my book. It's time I left. Keep the paintings. They mean nothing to me – you share that much in common."

Gonzales is at my side in a moment, and we walk out of the room together. I'm shaking so much I feel my ankles wobble on my high stiletto heels.

"Over, well done," says Gonzales in a whisper.

In a few minutes time there will be a swoop to capture Donaldson and arrest him. A nice dash of public humiliation to add to the melee. But Gonzales is tasked with protecting me and getting me out safely, sole objective.

I work to contain the pressing urge to scream, I feel sick. I hide behind my hands as soon as we're in the lobby. I run for the back exit and Gonzales opens the doors for us to go and find our driver as prearranged.

Shots and screams fill the air in a terrifying cacophony of chaos that drills through me like tragedy unleashed. My shaking turns to terror.

"What's going on?"

"Sounds like Donaldson's fighting back. To be expected."

I'm craning away, body pressed to the wall, tears running fast. My heart goes crazy with dread. A sustained volley from the main hall restarts, and I cover my ears. Not before I hear a woman's screams.

Why doesn't the bastard just give up, why does he keep hurting the innocent?

Who is shooting? Is it him? A booby trap, explosions,

what? I need subtitles to decipher this action hero shit I have no smarts about.

Gonzales' gun is out, and he's backing up to get a view. Trained to intercept.

"Go back in there. Don't stay on my account, just make sure he's taken down," I tell him.

"Only when I get you safely in the car," he says. "That's as we arranged."

Another loud series of shots sounds from the hall. Some people are running outside but it's surprisingly quiet, suggesting many are trapped inside.

"I'm going back in there."

Gonzales opens the door and shoves me through, where the car waits, a driver already at the wheel. Ten seconds later I'm inside. "Zante—take her back to base. See you later, once this is handled."

"Copy that," says Zante.

"Stay safe, Gonzales," I say softly as he nods and leaves. I climb into the car—it's an overkill limo. Too big for the task, but it's only then as the car starts to move, and I hear the click of a gun trigger nearby, that I realize we've messed up. Through the darkened screen beside Zante I see that we have company.

Messed up at the final moment.

"Good to see you again."

I scream. I shut my eyes.

"Noooooo!"

* * * *

Dan

There's a harsh male voice shouting in Greek in the next room. I can see running bodies through a nearby window and hear shots. One man hides behind a wall in the grounds, and he fires his gun repeatedly, bullets scudding off the building.

Then an explosion shakes the building—it has to be

explosion because the noise is teethvibratingly loud. There's more blasts and thudding. Then nothing. Quiet.

And I stare hard at where the shooting man is, and I'm pretty sure he's now sprawled dead. But who is he — one of theirs? Ours? I can't tell.

It's like a seriously messed-up soap opera with no available clues.

"Get control center secured," says Redman in my ear. It's our route to capturing Katsaros — slamming the mansion's systems into kaput on the way. I'm tasked with taking the control personnel down, to aid Timo in going for the top guy. The other agents are tasked with the safety of the women hostages — no loss of lives, and minimal harm inflicted.

"Do you copy? Over?" says Redman.

"Copy that."

I kick down the door to the control room, then commence fire, managing to take out the two men on the desk.

Another guard has run in and now stands shocked and cornered. A couple of choice martial arts moves and he's unconscious. I train my pistol on him at close range as I cuff him to his chair while he's sprawled on the floor.

In seconds, another man's hands are on his head and cuffs are on him too. Two dead — two captured.

Andreas runs down the hall.

"Timo got Katsaros?"

"Gone," Andreas confirms. "Still searching."

"The girls? Gone too?"

"Still here. Being taken out safely."

Job done. So why the unease?

The instinct says loudly too easy. No Katsaros. What's ahead?

It plagues me that these guys aren't fighting hard. Like very confused calves in a too fast rodeo. No fight — like an exhibit at a petting zoo — and this gang are famed for brutality — 'the mad lions of the mountains'.

Tonight, not so much roar or bite.

"This is wrong," I say to Rich over the mic link.

"You're right."

I won't yet let out a breath of relief at the capture, until I know the girls are safe and out of there. But it pisses me off majorly that Katsaros has slipped the noose. It smacks of bodged aims. I'm wired and ready for more — willing an opportunity to appear. I watch the screens ahead of me, scanning every nook as if waiting for a trapdoor to burst Katsaros in front of me.

Click.

Trigger flex. Bang.

"We've been expecting you," someone says with a heavy Greek accent.

A shot rings — it causes seismic, searing pain to my shoulder seconds after it fells me. The pain makes me stagger and collide with the wall then I slip to the floor. I land heavily on my side. There I lie. I didn't see who'd delivered the reprisal — only saw the back view as Mr. Trigger-Happy shot his own cuffed guard through the chest.

I put my hand to my shoulder — scarlet, wet fluid coats my hand. It doesn't scare me — all I'm aware of is heat buzzing inside me. Like I'm on a low electric current.

I realize with sinking certainty that this mission is in dire jeopardy. Underlined balls-up. So why haven't they hung around to finish the job on me? But, that doesn't cause fear to grip me. This mission was beyond the individual.

I shout to Andreas — wherever he now is I'm not sure, "Don't come after me — just get the girls out."

And I know what Nathan felt — on the floor while I played 'no talk' with the bad guys, out to kick a confession from any part of me ready to bleed. He'd gone by the time I got back for him. Chest wounds — he hadn't stood a chance. I stare at the dead man lying opposite me. It's such a graphic tableau flagging up that I did not kill my partner. The job did.

Nathan would have done exactly the same.

"Save the girls. Do the job. That's all that matters," I say the words again. "And keep Katie safe."

To myself. To Rich and maybe to Nathan.

I'm either getting what I've had coming to me — or I'm finally realizing the truth via taking a bullet to knock the knowledge in my head.

And as consciousness begins to flicker in and out like a dodgy TV screen, I wonder — will I ever see her again? Is she back safe?

I may not know her as well as I hoped — but I wish I'd told her what bright, burning potential she has. Like a stunning star. A vision of her at a graveside flicks into my head, and I realize it's my burial.

At least she won't lurk like I did at Nathan's — feeling guilty that his family would figure the bad cop escaped — the great cop took the fall.

And I fall back on the floor, energy draining, as my own future draws to a steady, seeping close.

Chapter Eighteen

Dan

Somehow—through which means I'm not aware—I've been dragged bodily from the Mone Dunamis. I can't tell you what happened—some legend cop, not.

It's all a hazy and dark, confused labyrinthine journey—don't ask me what the people around me were saying. I lost my grip on facts. But I remember gunshots and shouting and chaos in the mix and feeling like a loser. Yep, I remember that part—like a leaden lump of shit waste of space.

Like waking up in the midst of a war movie become real, but I can't be certain what's true life and what was dream. I blacked out due to blood loss, and my memory plays tricks like a meddlesome Medusa with a sabotage grudge.

So somehow, I was pulled to safety, out of the mansion, then roughly pushed onto a car backseat. I barely recall—but can testify to the rough pains in my ass and back from manhandling by someone strong with a point to prove. Who's saved my life?

"You're an asswipe low fucker, you know that?" Rocco's face appears. Damn handsome bastard even when messed up in darkness.

"You like to go risking the whole mission because you're too slow on the uptake to let me take center stage?"

I'd swear back but my mouth's too dry. So, I grunt and that just makes him madder.

"Mother fucking asswipe dude."

He lectures with lots of curse words, interspersed with the flow of angry shouting. At last I find my voice, though it's low and gravelly as a coffin in a grave awaiting the holefiller's arrival. "You saved me."

He slaps me right in the face. WTF?

"Yeah. I saved you. While you resisted, giving up the ghost and telling everybody to leave you for dead."

"Thanks, Roc."

Apparently, I'm an idiot and a good for nothing something or other with no cares for anybody else, and the C word was thrown in. Man, that's bad — as bad as he ever goes. He should've killed me in the gym, apparently, as I wasn't meant to be on maneuvers anyhow — he's already told Rich this.

"Shoulda let you bleed out. You screwed up — not in there — in there you were great — took out three men, even as you lay with a chest wound. I'm talking about falling for the civilian and pitching us a curveball. She's been taken hostage, by the way. Shoulda upped the game on covering her meet with Donaldson."

His words spear me straight in the fresh wound with salt and acid, plus bleach afterthought. "WTF? Gonzales was to stick to her like glue. He dead?"

"All went off. Hostages taken. Shootout with five dead. Somebody took Kate and Zante, her driver, off grid, out of comms contact. GPS been blanked. Kate so does not deserve every sorry sad inch of you. Does she know you like the dark side? Sex in leathers with chains and flames? She got some kinda death wish with this?"

The very mention of Kate's name has me full-on protective at what we've let happen on our watch. If I thought I was shit with Nathan this takes the pina colada cocktail of crapola.

Do I deserve the amazing woman I've fallen for? Shit, no. I can't bear this.

"What's happening now?"

"Redman, Warbie and Deano are on the case. You're in no fit state to argue."

"Did you carry me? You saved my life, you know that."

Whoever it was needed a manual handling refresher course urgently given my bruises but I'm not gonna complain about still being alive. "Thanks for saving my sorry ass by dragging me out of hell's depths and preventing me from slowly bleeding to death."

"We ain't outta the woods on that one yet, bad boy. You're still pretty touch and go with the blood thing. Gotta get you back to base. Let Medic Lekkas loose an' he'll be delighted — second bullet in a week. You like pain stuff — so does he. Should get you both off — win, win."

"We got the girls out? Say we didn't fail on that?"

"All out, no question. Andreas took Katsaros down personally. Payback for all the crap he's had to take for months. He was hiding in a cellar hole. We got the girls out. You weren't top of the pile, Bullet Man. Had to wait in line, don't forget that. I did my job. Bullet holing you was just the extra bonus." He forces out a laugh.

I don't say more. Mostly because it's only now I notice the driver is ex NY Interpol, Nicos. The sight of him hits me as bad as the bullet. Nicos was a good friend of Nathan's. Just seeing Nicos makes the guilt surge, especially caught here in another mess.

Nicos turns to watch me. "Hey. Let's get you back to base and stitched up, bro. Mission's completed but you're the casualty of the day."

"And Kate."

"Crazy bastard, always blaming yourself for things out with your control. You made the right call. Tonight and with Nathan. Quit the torture," he says in a low tone.

"And you know this because, as well as a sharpshooter, a driver and a big mouth you also have a hotline to heaven?"

"I know this because Nathan was legend. But so are you. Give yourself a passport to get over it. He died doing what he loved — and you both do it by the book. Can you stop the chatter — you're bleedin' out and I'm not losing you because you couldn't keep your tongue still, moron."

I lie back. Back at the mansion I'd experienced exactly

what Nathan had. I hadn't blamed my team. I want to close my eyes and just sleep but Rock Man is shouting things to make me keep them open and I just want to throw him the bird. But it's too much.

All that's foremost in my mind as I lie on the back seat willing my eyes open is words for my ex-partner.

"Love you, bro. Would've swapped given the choice," I say to no one but my ex-partner's angel. "Keep Katie safe. One favor is all I need."

I see him beside me. Nathan's face with his fair eyebrows rising as a reprimand. He's handsome in a halo and wings.

"Cool wings, bud!"

Rocco says somewhere far off. "Hallucinating. Hey – gun the gas, man."

"I'm finished but I have an angel buddy to guide me now," I tell them all.

"Who says you'd get in, jackass? You really think you qualify?" Nathan's angel apparition answers then chuckles as the lights start to dim.

* * * *

Kate

I'd gulp down my fear, but my throat won't work, so instead I try to swallow without choking. Zante is driving, but doesn't say a word or move. From the dark corner of the unlit passenger side of the limo Ivan appears, no smile, no lines, just menace and a gun. He's been hiding too low to detect.

"We meet again, Kate Joseph. This time no cameras to complicate things." Ivan's gun is trained on Zante, and his shitty gaze on me. He has another pistol pointed straight at me. Ivan fake smiles, and it makes my spine crawl. It's a twitch of pure 'ha, I'm an evil bastard and I'm winning while you're screwed', thrown in.

"No cameras maybe. But you don't think Troika will let you get away. Despite what you think, you're not that clever, you missed half the cameras the last time."

"No reason to think they can stop me. Considering I know all their tactics. Already have the GPS disabled, so we're flying free of Troika dweebs already."

Inside, I'm on fire with injustice and hatred. Ivan's my dad recast in shoddy metal that deserves to be smelted down and made into an ugly ass spade to dig a grave to bury the thing in.

Bent cop. Evil cop. Worst kind of lowlife bastard.

"What's that smell?" I answer. Not very cleverly, but under this pressure it's the only insult I can summon. "Oh. It's rat cop stench. You've been mixing with the wrong people, so I'm guessing money means more than principles or catching bad guys. You stink of bad shit, Falco. Your family must be so proud."

His eyes screw up with menace. "Sweet. You'd break my heart if I cared. Bet Bullet Man will be gutspeared I've trumped him with his squeeze. Your dad and me go way back. Your dad would hand pick me as your future date."

"If you're allied with my dad, then I'd die before I'd ever listen to either of you. He'll screw you in the end. He does that, old habits die hard. He'll fuck you over and leave you bleeding. He's that kinda guy."

Ivan's smile returns and this one is smug central. "Your dad's just escaped Gonzales. Your cop bodyguard may look great in a suit, but outnumbered he sucked. You can maybe send flowers to his family and a note that you were the last one to see him alive and send him in there. Duff move, babe."

"Bastard. You and me—as likely as me volunteering for rabies."

Ivan turns in his seat, but I know damn well his gun is still pressed against Zante, ready to blow big holes in his body. Another weapon is glinting in the streetlight flicker as my prize of the day. Ivan growls, "You'll be breathing and we won't be on the wrong sides for much longer. Figure we might have time for some squeeze of our own before I deliver the package as agreed to your dad."

"Package?"

"You're my payday, honey. Hadn't you twigged I've been trying to get you out of Troika since you arrived? Dad is mighty pissed you've got yourself involved in all this. Katsaros would have his balls if he didn't agree to get you out and finish you off. He wants that particular treat for himself."

"Forgive me if I pass on giving a shit what he wants." I talk a good bluff, but inside I'm screaming. Fear, anger, panic, it's all there.

Ivan's smile widens before there's an impact, the car shudders and rolls. We're going so fast I can't see, and there's gunshot firing and shouting. Tires scream like crazy at the crescendo.

The car rattles from what must be full on impact with some other car or object, and I'm shaken to teeth-rattle point. The smell of smoke and blood taint the air, and the windscreen has rained glass, and how I've missed that slash fest I'll never know.

Somehow I'm hanging upside-down, but I'm still breathing. While Ivan and Zante aren't moving. Even in darkness, I can see that blood decorates the cream interior of the car.

* * * *

"We'll have you out of there soon, Miss."

Two agents cut me out of our car. That's crazy in itself. But it's also crazy I know they're agents—I've developed some agent detector instinct. I still can't believe I'm unharmed. I feel no pain.

"What the hell?" I'm shaking now. There's a burning smell and I'm not sure from where. "What happened?"

"Ran you off the road. We'll get you back to safety, ma'am. Under orders."

"What about Ivan?"

"I can't confirm that at this stage."

I think they're dead. I'm really sure they're dead. They're not moving. Damn, but there's so much blood.

"What about Gonzales? What about Donaldson and his men? Was it all for nothing?"

I know I'm gabbling and my teeth are castanet chattering despite the heat.

"Mission successful. Let's get you checked over."

Not knowing what's gone on anywhere on this whole affair fills me with a tension and angst like I've never known. Are they captured? Is Dan okay? Did Gonzales prevail, or was Ivan right? "What about Katsaros? How is Agent Draven?"

They stare me down. No clues beyond a flick of clenched jaw. Damn these bloody automaton agent types and their waxwork facial training.

"Just tell me it's gone okay? Tell me yes or no?"

"More info to follow, ma'am. We're not at liberty to discuss further at present."

Call it instinct but I just know that means the news isn't good and whether it's Katsaros or Dan I'm just not sure.

* * * *

'Not at liberty to say' equals shit's gone down, and you'll find out when you're calmer. I now know this is agent code for chill the fuck out. Not that any woman has ever calmed down just because some man told her to do so.

I watch Dan lying in Troika's clinic room. Too many hours spent pacing the floor before they let me in. Apparently, assisting in Havana's op doesn't qualify me to stand in on Dan's bullet removal surgery. Though I seem to remember Rocco was ousted from watching Havana's. It's probably best, given my blood aversion issues.

When I'm finally allowed in, he's on the bed in a white gown, so pale. Deathly white. I struggle to breathe and gather myself as he lies there as if in state. The machine beside him beeps. He's getting fluids through an IV, and being monitored with lots of wires. So many wires. There are almost too many medical trappings, including a nurse who discreetly left the room when I arrived.

I feel my breath come out in shuddery exhalations, such is my level of distress to see that Dan Draven is back, but in pretty bad shape.

His face is beaten. His chest is covered in bandaging. He's too still. Dan Draven—the guy who brought me here under such false pretenses. Only now I don't feel selfish ambivalence. He's risked his life and been shot. Nearly died.

And he's always vowed to take care of me.

Inside, I feel like I've undergone bombing and laceration. I want to take what ails him and make it stop—help him heal.

As if reading my thoughts, he turns his head and blinks. Bandages hang around his shoulder and blood smears and antiseptic stains are still visible on his flesh. It makes my heart wobble and words almost fail me. I opt for, "Hi."

He doesn't say a word. But his eyes say it all. Until he whispers, "You're safe."

"The things you'll do to get my attention," I say softly. "Don't speak. Keep your strength," I tell him.

Again, he stares. Gray eyes so solemn they keep me hostage, and he reaches out. He encircles my wrist with his cold hand.

"I'm not going anywhere," I tell him. The grip is surprisingly hard.

His eyes plead again, boring into mine. Before I know it, I'm totally letting the side down—tears fill my eyes and fall—drop after betraying drop.

"Now see what you've done, Sir?"

"Don't," he says so softly I struggle to hear. "Don't."

I sniff the tears back and still the sobs. "It's the blood stains—makes me itch to get to work on laundry. OCD in that way."

"Just kiss me," he orders.

"But I could hurt you."

"If you don't do it these monitors will go beep-crazy anyway. I'll rip off the tubes…"

So I obey my Sir. I gently kiss those lips I've missed and crave so much.

I give him a questioning stare then lean forward. "You only had to ask me nicely, Sir."

"I don't do nice, remember?"

"Oh yeah. That's what I like about you, and how. We were only beginning to get started with exploring that. Thing is—I think you think you're way worse than you are. I happen to know you have a secret soft side."

We kiss. Long and deep. For a man as pale as hotel sheets, he's hiding the latent passion, because the kiss explodes between us.

He caresses the back of my head. I groan in appreciation at the back of my throat. "You scared me. Thought he'd got you."

"Scared us both. But no chance—trained by the best and they got Donaldson, though Gonzales took the honors, I believe. He tried to take a hostage, but no dice. Team were stronger and his guards are in custody. He's back behind bars where he belongs."

Dan opens his gray eyes wide. "This thing that I feel. I thought I might never see you again."

I eyeball him, my heart so full to brimming I can't hide or evade or pretend. He matters. "Everything about all this has scared me. Except you. You're the part I just can't kick."

Dan smiles. "So you may just like me? You might let me stick around?"

"Don't get ahead of yourself." I reach forward and grab his fingers. "I like you plenty. More than like. But I can't prove it until you're way better."

"Heart monitor can go hang," he says and goes to pull his cables off, but I stop his haste with a firm restraining grab.

"There will be time soon enough, *Die Hard*."

"Patched up and ready for action in a few hours I'd say." He winks. "Doctor will bow to my orders. Take my word for it."

I laugh, then falter as tears run down my face all over again. Tears of relief mixed with frustration and anger at what has happened since all this began. But foremost, tears of joy and elation and, yes, fear, raw and primal and life-affirming — that I want this man so badly. Katsaros has finally been captured. Donaldson too. After too many years of heartache for too many people.

Yet, if it hadn't been for that treacherous bastard, Dan and I might never have met. Dan wants me, really wants me. Which makes me completely lucky.

I sit on the bed and link fingers into his. He is warm, and alive. Time to confide, "I think I might love you."

"When a man has a near miss with death — he kinda wants to prove he's alive. Love you too, Katiepie. If the job scares you we'll work something out. Stay in Santorini for a while with me?"

I answer. "You'll have to clear it with my boss — to quote Havana's lingo — Mel can be a Mother. Think it's a boss thing."

Dan raises his eyes. "Holy hell. What has she started?"

I carefully kiss him and show him gently how much he really means to me.

* * * *

Only two days later, Dan is so much improved that he's moved from the clinic to his room. It's a move that he's been crankily nagging for.

I lock the door and return to his side on the bed. He pulls me to him with fierce hunger. His tongue slides inside my mouth and heat bolts spark through my veins. I feel them crackle and zip a lightning track around my body that leads directly to the places that matter. My nipples specifically, which are peaking immediately. Another achy destination that needs his touch is my groin, which is most insistent of all. My juices flow quickly from the impact of this man.

"I want you," I tell him.

"Me too."

"Early days. You're still in recovery."

"I'm more than recovered for what I have in mind."

"But we can't."

"Can't or won't?"

I sigh. Letting his tongue explore my mouth and tempt me afresh. "Won't."

I curl my hand roughly in his hair and around his neck to pull him close, and he revels in it. This is what it means to be alive. Dan nibbles my neck and slowly traces his tongue up to my earlobe, where he lingers.

But I know he's trying to change my mind and lure me. I pull back. "Wounded man—excitement isn't a good idea. You're in no fit condition."

"Fit enough to kiss you and make you come if you'll let me."

"But how about we make this show about you?"

I slide my hand beneath the utility medical gown he wears and find his hard shaft standing proud. He's as long and wide as I remember him to be, and a droplet of cum makes me salivate to claim him.

"Wish I could tie you—see your tattoo, baby. Do the things we never got the chance to try."

"We'll have time."

I flick my fingers up and over the length of him, concentrating on working the tip and I revel in the sharp gasps he makes in response, then his hips grind with the impact of my hand.

"You temptress."

"You hero," I tell him. Then claim his mouth with mine. Still letting my hand flick and work, and show him I mean business. It may only be a hand job, but right now all I care about is making him come.

My pace turns fast, and I can tell from his strained face

and thrusting hips and low growls he's near to closure.

"Come for me, baby," I tell him. Feeling like a horny saucepot and wanting to be one. I wish so much we could be alone — uninterrupted, naked and full of wild, wanton adventure, inhibitions thrown to the winds.

"Promise me you'll show me the stuff you enjoy when we get out of here. I like the sound of leather...and whips. I want to use them all over you, and do you as hard as you can let me."

"Christ..."

He comes in my hand. His dick weeping his desire all across his abdomen. Glistening on my fingers like magic juice. Vital and alive.

"Any way you want me, honey," he answers in a croaky whisper, and we both stare into one another's eyes. "I'm hoping you'll say yes to me taking you Stateside?"

I don't know what to say. Or think. Me and a cop? In America? Seriously?

Can I do this? Or am I kidding myself and dreaming? More to the point, is he?

"We'll see," I answer.

And blow me if he isn't ready for more of my intimate attentions.

* * * *

Next morning, after a long, long sleep worthy of the dead I go to Dan's side, then I kiss him, parting his lips so deliciously it sends a ripple of thrill through my entire body.

"Good morning, handsome."

"Well, hi there, Katie."

He quickly resurrects the raw, hot need of yesterday. His hand roams to cup the curve of my breast, and he finger-strokes my nipple. I discern his steely arousal beneath the sheets, and the impact I have on him sends excitement levels to incendiary. Even though I know making out on the bed after injury is not a prudent action — it feels all the more enticing, because it's off limits.

He dips his finger inside my robe, and he smiles when I quiver at his touch. Squeezing my nipple causes it to pucker and makes me suck in a breath. White hot need thrums inside me. He mutters when I moan my appreciation and let out a curse. He bends his head to kiss me from collarbone to breast. Sensing his discomfort and limited range I move towards him, allowing him full breast access. I'm wearing no bra — a turn on in itself even just for me — and I let him uncover me fully, so my breasts swing free when he widens the robe. I move so that Dan can taste my nipple, and I let him suck, and I gasp at the pleasure it incites.

There is only one act that can placate the need now. He wants me and I'm crazy with lust for him. I want him full inside me, thrusting to my sacred spot. Taking me higher as he widens and fills me. I've never been more certain of anything. I arch to him and let my own hands explore the hard planes of his body. I want to kiss and be kissed so thoroughly I will never want another man again. We're both so close to abandoning all constraints I can almost taste it.

I straddle him, glad that I locked the door myself as a precaution. I give a tiny moan that betrays my need and love that his eyes widen when he realizes I'm commando in readiness for this. I deal with a condom with urgency and straddle him then let his dick play against my pussy. I'm hot and creaming for him, and when I splay wide for him he curses as I pulse onto his cock. Then I bear down, slow, steady and sure. All the time, my eyes are on his as I take him deep and fill my own need for his cock inside me. I run a fingernail up his throat and watch the way his Adam's apple bobs in response.

"I like to think I have good bedside manners."

"Shit, honey."

"My honey is sweet and ripe for you, don't you agree?"

"Knew you were an upfront kind of girl when we met —

just didn't realize how much."

"All I ever needed was a live for the moment man ready to give me what I need, and this really is dangerous."

I'm turning Dan on—the rigid evidence is there, and I glide up and down on him with steady thrusts. Soon, I'm grinding hard, my tits jutting in my efforts to make him come. I'm getting off wildly. I love the feel of him beneath me and that he likes it when I touch him at the base of his cock with my fingers and his breathing becomes raspy. His hand skims the side of my body in one deft sensual move.

"If we ever get out of here I won't take no for an answer. We so won't surface for days," he tells me with raw lust in his voice. "This is some reward for being injured in the line of duty though."

"I'm...cutting you...a...little slack," I say. Then I shatter, coming again and again as I pump up and down his hard length, that's taking me prisoner with its fulfilling prowess. "The thing about us OCD particular types is—we love taking charge," I whisper to him once we're both resurfacing. "Maybe just let me care for you like you deserve, huh?"

With a smile he nods and doesn't say a word. Then produces his retro handcuffs from under the bed.

With an inviting smile, Dan draws me down and 'mmms' into my kiss.

I click the cuffs shut on him. So glad that at last we are properly reconciled and alone.

* * * *

Dan

Placing my hands at either side of her face, I draw Kate to me to kiss her.

She causes me an instant semierection in the way she kisses me back like a parched woman in the desert finding her first lake. I can't get enough of her fervor.

I tongue her mouth with naked hunger. Deft, raw strokes, but gentle. She's breathless in seconds and her mouth claims mine—out to prove it can shimmy, and makes me want to buckle with need.

She arches to me, pushing her curves against me. Her breasts are flush with me. I'm a goner. No hope of reprieve.

She gasps when I lick and nibble her lips. She bites my earlobe and runs the tip of her nose along my lower lip, before diving back into my mouth with her tongue. If this is a kiss, what will Princess Vanilla be like if given full freedom?

"Kate?" I tell her between kisses. "There's more about me you should know."

As much as I want to ignore it, my conscience is drumming its fingers on my dick's good time.

I fix her with a hard stare. "My crops and cuffs and whips thing came from a place that isn't good."

She shakes her head. "You don't have to tell me. I'm here—I want you. I want you again and again until we can't see straight. I want it every which way you can give me it. But most importantly I want you inside me now." As if to prove it she takes my hand and pushes it to cup her pussy. She's hot and ready. Man, her wet heat fries my brain cells in an instant insanity barbeque.

"Jeez," I hiss. My erection is straining like a wild beast in heat. "I so need to explain."

"Stop talking."

Quickly, my hands are in her hair and my mouth is doing sinful things to the skin around her collarbone, and she isn't complaining a bit. Her strident style is highly erotic. Because she's sweet, professional, uptight Katie and yet she's been sinful, commanding me like I usually prefer with the women who treat me bad. Only there's no leather, or whips. Or masks or implements here. So much for the theories about not getting it up without it.

I'm needy as hell to be inside her. It has escalated out of the bounds of my control in much too vanilla a fashion, but who cares—when it's working.

With my free hand I travel lightly up the length of her

torso, sending my own senses into a spiral of need. I already know from her moans she is ready and she's naked and game for more. I'm shaking with my need for her. She unfoils a condom and rolls it on me. I hold her, jamming my dick inside her, spearing into her hottest spot.

Will this be a two minute wonder? Is my vanilla-opposed dick about to fail now?

I prepare for the humiliation of feeling my erection wane, but it doesn't. Especially when Katie hitches herself higher to push herself onto my shaft, with a long satisfied moan that leaves me shuddering for release. *Please don't be a five second lay*, I school myself.

I'm telling myself this isn't a dream. It is really me doing fantastic vanilla as I move my cock into her and thrust it deep, with sensuous moves that make her breathe desperate entreaties for more.

"You're so good..."

If only she knew. Surely this will sound the death knell of my dick's prowess.

Because I'm not good. I have scars—most specifically a guilty conscience.

"Dan—I need you. So much," she whispers. "Fuck me harder, please."

Something inside me erupts and I thunder into this woman. Who doesn't see the black heart or the failed hopes and the letdowns I have about myself. I can feel her shuddering around me in a volcanic orgasm that thrills me beyond stunned.

"You are incredible," I tell her.

"Ditto, Dan boy."

Her actions, her reactions tonight have been so real, they rock my world. And it's also so incredible I just want more.

"Come to me," says Kate breathing hard as she whispers. Her eyes are like deep pools of dark heat. I can't read from her face the intentions beneath. "Whatever you had to say I'll listen. But it alters nothing—whatever you have to tell me, it really makes no difference about this chemistry we share. I'm guessing stuff's happened. But that's your past. This is now. Have you got that? We both deserve the now, don't we?"

And that's when it dawns. I'll never be the light-hearted lover she deserves.

She doesn't know that most nights I can't sleep, and sometimes I fight shadows. Or that the night sweats drive me crazy and the mood swings are a bitch. That I've only recently quit meds for anxiety. That, at one time, there were voices — psychiatric assessments.

That even a couple of girls back home told me they were worried about the things I shout at night.

"If it were that simple," I say on a ragged sigh, and realize that the dreams of futures are just that, dreams.

Chapter Nineteen

Kate

I let my gaze stray over the room, taking in the fact that Dan stormed out like a wild hurricane, and left me in the quaking aftermath of orgasm. My mind is in mayhem.

Why didn't I let him talk?

Why must I push for the story headline soundbite instead of listening to detail?

Who could blame the guy for storming out? Together — the sex was stellar, but I take too much for granted. He's trying to say we have no future. This was work with benefits.

It reminds me of Seb. His shallow promises — fears about the real reason he'd pushed me aside. There wasn't enough spark in bed.

"You okay?" comes a husky whisper from the doorway. "I hear that brain ticking away in the darkness."

I sigh. "I should have listened."

"Sorry for walking out, this talk makes pretty grim listening." He comes to me and holds out a hand. "Come sit." Before I know it I'm on his knee listening patiently for God knows what he's about to confide. He makes me look at him levelly with a finger on my chin.

"Before you start," I tell him. "I had a guy in my life who left me feeling like I'd never want to get involved again. He traded me in for a better model — it's left me feeling like I'm under par. I felt raw for a while. Then I found my new sexy side — but the guy I chose specialized in short-term turnons. Being dumped is a personal habit I can't seem to kick."

Dan stares. "This has nothing to do with you and

everything to do with me."

"Isn't that just a nice way of letting a girl down gently?"

Dan glares at me. "Never for a single instant think that this is because of you." He breathes deeply and shakes his head. "The guys had no clue how lucky they were. We just had the best sexplay of my life. Don't question it for a moment—or give them a minute's sorrow." He kisses my shoulder and kisses my skin, dipping to that tender spot at my neck. I know he can feel me tremble like jelly on a trestle table during a mini earthquake. "You are so sensual...we fit. We *really* fit—and, believe me, it's against all the odds that we do."

For a moment I'm abashed by his words.

"I don't usually like vanilla girls," he says. "Despite your tatt, you're way less dark than my usual kink partners. You're rich, decadent, royal vanilla pods and clotted cream. So sweet and refined, and deserving of the finest things. I'm a rough guy at heart."

"Meaning?"

"I haven't had straight vanilla sex in a long time. There are marks on my skin—they were sexual-adventure inflicted—I guess you could say I like to play hard. I'm scared I'd hurt you more than you're ready for. But before you go thinking I'm out to hurt you—the only person I want to feel the pain is me."

"I don't understand."

"I lost my police partner—my best friend, confidante. Shot on a job with me because of my inattention. Caught us both—drugs cartel. I mighta died too but I got free. Mexican drugs cartel—as hard as it comes."

"You do a dangerous job—he'd know the risks."

"I took risks I shouldn't have and it put us both in danger."

"Dan...I don't know what to say."

"Don't say anything. I don't have long-term women, Kate. I have call girls who come by to hurt me. They whip me, they cuff me. Sometimes they burn me. Sometimes they belt my throat. Because it stops the creeping guilt DTs. For a long time I've yearned for punishment."

"Dan—"

"Hear me out. You're so much better than what I can offer you. I tried to keep you at arm's length. I don't want to dim your pure glow. You're a princess. I'm a beast. So there can't be a future beyond short term. Not with my dark side."

I stare hard at him. He's Slash. All over again.

Screwing me over with his I'm not able to give you what you need line.

He wants to carve me into his perfect kink sculpture, then move on to fresh clay. Not likely—however high end the thrills.

My insides react with a mega-cotton cycle of anger and frustration at his words. Dan dips his head down and kisses the line of skin above my nipple.

I push his head harshly away.

"How dare you presume to know what's best for me?"

Dan asks huskily. "I'm madly in lust with you. You've knocked this dark knight straight off his horse. I want you to get out now while you can. I can't rescue you, and after those dickwads, you deserve better to show you they were wrong."

I gulp. Then I push myself away.

"I get it. You're selfish, and you're scared. Just like Seb was. You put yourself first rather than actually try to aim for better. That's fine and you're right—I don't need that in my life. I'm worth better. You keep telling yourself you're doing it to avenge the past—you're a coward. A selfish coward and a using prick who only thinks of himself. *Hasta la* freakin' *vista*."

* * * *

I didn't get my Operation Mountain Goat story scoop in the end. Interpol forces decreed an embargo, and as it happens, I don't want a byline on this story. I just want to forget it and start again anew.

The local Santorini police department's swoop to catch a heinous gang of international sex trafficking criminals will be the order of the day. There will be no mention of Interpol. Or agents. Or Dan, Rich, Havana — or any of the heroes beneath their spy-style rock.

The real heroes are happy to hide away in the shadows as true heroes are wont to do.

Except Dan. He's no hero in my eyes anymore.

Him and his crazy guilt complex and self-preservation rules.

Because no amount of persuading or cajoling or encouraging sex would ever make him see he may have this all wrong. He's damning his future. I know it — at heart he probably does too. But he's so far gone with self-loathing, he's ordered the whole enchilada meal on a daily lunchtime special subscription.

And it's going to either sicken him or kill him in the end.

Dan Draven is a lost cause. The quicker I can get out of here the better.

I pack and go to Warbie, because I know he is a mover and shaker when the chips are down and he'll listen to my pleas.

"About getting home?" I say. "Surely you could pull a few strings and get me out on express track channel? Being a man who knows people and gets the job done. When you're next in the Highgate area of London, I do a mean veggie lasagna that will have you changing your recipe and forsaking it forever after. I also know a great tapas bar for some appreciation payback meals on me."

"Fighting talk," says Warbie, then slips his big, cuddly arms around me. "You wanna go — even though we both know you're avoiding the big, angry black ops cop cloud?"

"Damn straight. I've had enough."

"How does tonight sound, Princess?"

I smile and have to keep the tears back. "Perfecto, Big Hunk of Wonderful Warbs. That Copacabana beach plan thing — they're so gonna love you all the way."

Dan

"You realize she's gone?"

I know the voice. It's Warbie's. Unmistakable, as is the sarcastic accusatory tone that tells me he'd like to punch me in the throat. He can try.

"Who?"

"Lady Katie."

"When?" I say the words without looking up. Mostly because there's a big cloud inside my chest that's filling it up with jet-black crapola karma, and it's making breathing hard. A cloud of guilt, but it has a lining that says push through, this is how it hasta be. It just hasta.

"Half hour ago. I took her to the airport."

"She get away safe?"

Warbs is mad, fit to burst. "Course she did. I waited. Somebody had to put her first."

I'm chest to chest with the big guy in an instant. "If you have something to say, big man — why not just spit it out?"

"You're a putz! A total self-flagellating putz. You're so full of bull you can't see it. You hurt her and yourself."

I pack my weapons in the case and clip it tight. Then move onto packing away my ops clothes. "I can see she deserves better. Even a big, fat oaf like you can't get the memo."

"She's way out of your league."

"How many black marks are you working for tonight, Warb?"

"The one that finally gets through your bone head that you're wrong. But since you won't listen to me — there's somebody else here who might just stand a chance of making a difference.

I glance up and I can't believe my eyes.

"Dan," said a rusty New York accent beside me. "Long time no see — might've guessed I'd find you blending into the background. Just like my brother would."

My mouth is dry and I don't know what to say. I've largely avoided Claire, Nathan's sister, since the funeral. Though I send cards and flowers and stuff. The easy stuff, I can do, that no probs. Credit card order, check, move on. It's eyeballing her that's the hard part.

"How did you get here?"

"Nicos told me about the mission. That they nearly lost you. Figured I'd drop by—I run a villa holiday art school deal on the mainland. Married a Greek husband. Can't keep him away from the place in summer. You can leave us now, Warbie," she tells the big guy. "I'll holler if he needs restraining."

I clear my throat. There's so much I should say, want to say but can't.

"Why are you here, Claire?"

"Like I just said, we have a vacation place—I'm an artist. Me and Stalli run a small art school. Warbie is my old friend. Nicos keeps in touch. We gonna talk? Do I have to hit you on the head to make you think straight? You can't crawl in the casket with my brother. When are you finally gonna see that?"

"I'm guessin' you think I'm a lost cause."

"So listen and listen good," she says, and I realize she's the vanilla I've hidden from. Not as in sex, or attraction—as in purity, family, justice, kindness.

She's the one I should have been facing and saying sorry to. But I couldn't, and so for years, I've totally wussed out.

Now's my chance. To vent the guilt. Guilt for Nathan and her family.

Now ain't that just something to think about.

She comes to me and hugs me. "So. Let's sit for a while and talk about why you really were not to blame about Nathan."

Chapter Twenty

Kate

"What's up?" Mel asks down the line from the newsroom, with a tone in her voice that says she is in news-editordragon mode. I can almost hear the flap of dragon wings, the flamethrower of her ire.

"I'm sick."

"You're not ill, you're hiding. First you get yourself involved in the biggest international crime story we've had in years, out of nowhere. Now you announce you'll just decide your own working hours and pull a sickie. Trying hard here to keep making excuses not to sack you."

I can hear the chatter and clatter of the newsroom in the background. I'm glad I'm not there. Since I've got back from Santorini work has really been a chore — am I losing my edge? My mind? My clues of how to proceed?

I snuggle deeper into the eiderdown blanket on my butter-soft sofa and turn the remote on the twenty-four hour news show to mute. Okay, maybe Mel is on the button and my tummy bug has more to do with 'willed nausea' than actual cramps — but I'm not admitting that to anyone. I have been feeling sick since Greece — sick to my stomach and sick to the heart.

"You want me to spread it to all the staff?"

Mel sighs. I can hear her pencil drumming. "I suspect you're not okay. That's quite an adventure you both had in Greece! Dan's retired from Interpol — unofficial sources and strictly off the record, but it's true. Yes, I know the real story — been privy to the info. Special clearance, apparently.

Anyway I asked him outright today — his retirement that is. Says it's true."

"Today? You saw him today? Why the hell is he back at the channel?" Suddenly the sofa seems to sway — even though I know it isn't moving. It is just my mind that is doing big dipper.

"He's in London tying stuff up. Though he's busy again now and probably won't be around for much of tomorrow. He took me to lunch and gave me the low down on what all happened."

My cheeks heat. Please don't tell me he's told her the full low down as in the red, scarlet, censored version.

"Hostages, shot cops, hiding out in caves. Nearly being involved in a terrible car crash — I hear that cop driver Zante is making a good recovery now. That guy that died, Ivan, sounded horrendous. Cop turned criminal — as low as it gets."

She's right. But the words still resonate with meaning for me.

Mel holds the phone from her ear so her words became muffled but just discernible. She's searing a staff member about some news story that's pissed her off and how she wants it handled with immediate effect. Blimey, she's tough. Interpol could sign her up without a need for training.

Mel says, "Go and cover that now because I say so or I'll fry your liver with kidney beans and kick your arse like a Five Nations rugby ball!" Mel then has an aside conversation with some faceless colleague. Does she really think she is the Hannibal of the Headlines? Is any job worth this kinda crap treatment and attitude?

I was once the most motivated reporter on the team. Diligent, I'd put in more hours then double them. Never one to shirk — yet now I don't care if they sack me with immediate effect. I'll live.

"Kate? Sorry no, I wasn't talking to you. He's asked to visit you. The attack and the kidnapping must have had a huge effect. As a company we feel a responsibility for your mental health. PTSD counselling and such."

And just there I fall flat at the concern.

Dan worrying about me and wanting to see me is one thing. What the station cares about is that I could sue the company. Nice touch.

"I don't want him anywhere near me. Got that?"

"He could pull rank and ask for your files. I have no authority to stop him."

"Interpol has no damn right to wade into HR demanding anything. Don't you start fudging the truth for your own ends." I fiddle with my hair as I sit with my knees pulled in on the couch. "As a friend I'm begging you—you owe this to me—do whatever it takes. But keep him away."

"Then let me run through some of the news highlights on this one in return for my cooperation—you and he had a rip roaring fling that did a bad somersault landing. It didn't recover from Santorini—am I right?"

I make an affirmative noise that wasn't quite a yes.

"And you're avoiding work—ringing in sick. Kate, you've never had a day off in years—not even when you had gastric flu and threw up in your handbag. Like a peekaboo negligee I can see straight through. He's due to go back to New York soon—just to be clear—coming back to work tomorrow is compulsory—dry your tears and I expect to see you back at the helm tomorrow." Mel stops what she was saying to yell at someone like a banshee. "Sorry, the intern just set the photocopier on fire again."

"Mel—"

"See you tomorrow, eight-thirty sharp. My leaving party." The phone slams down, and my excuses feel like the pyramid of crumpled tissues I knock to the floor—insubstantial and much too flimsy. She's leaving?

Hell, I'm considering resigning, and Dan is looking for me before he quits my life for good.

Trouble is—this uptight, frustrated, afraid feeling that's whirling inside me right now tells me exactly what the problem is here and it's me. It's not any of them at all.

I know what this is about. It's about me being too afraid to speak out. To say what I want and need. I've shut those things out since my family walked out of one life and invented another — shut it out for so very long in life it's become second nature.

And I grew afraid to hope for better. Do I risk asking for what I want? Do I push through the fear?

And reach out and give it a try — for the first time in my life since all the secrets started.

* * * *

I've pulled my ethical socks up and patched together my esteem enough to put Santorini behind me and go into work.

And pretty soon — within a few hours — my day feels back to normal. Had Dan really caused such a huge dent in my heart at all?

And as it turns out by the end of the morning I'm in for a surprise.

"Kate, visitor waiting for you," says Nancy on reception.

My pulse hammers and nerves kick off like an Olympian doing a kickboxing star turn in my stomach.

"Who is it?" I say into the line, but Nancy's already gone. I speed down there with emotions in a tight ball of trepidation. Is it Dan? What is he going to say when we lock gazes?

The realization that I now want the doors to open and it be Dan hits me like a cricket ball from a top world class batsman with a grudge to settle. I'm almost spitting out teeth. The doors slide apart and I hear them before I see them.

"Kate — it's us."

I try to mask my disappointment with the genuinely pleased reaction of seeing Havana and Rocco in normal 'human' clothes and no guns. They're holding hands and both wear matching leathers that are so past cool and sexy it hurts. They'll make beautiful badass babies together. I honestly hope they do.

"Great to see you, but what are you doing here?" I ask, hugging each in turn.

"London seemed as good a place as any for buying jewelry and exploring," Havana tells me, raising their joined hands to show off her brilliant, sizeable diamond, shining with a thudding zonk. "Just engaged and we wanted to see you. Heard from Dan lately? Happen to know he's in London."

I shake my head. "No. Not seen him."

Havana's disappointment shows on her face. "Shame. Look, I never got a chance to properly thank you so much for saving my life with the bullet op. I so wanted to repay your kindness." Havana removes an envelope from her bag.

I open it and inside is a travel voucher for a great deal of money.

"I can't. It's way too much."

"It's from Interpol and all of us. After what we put you through, you need a holiday. You deserve one. Redman says you did not pick up your dues—said I'd deliver in person."

I really try my best not to let go of the tears that are now, much against my better judgment, clouding my eyes.

"We're planning to get married. We want to invite you to the wedding. Not sure if you'll wanna come. Dan's best man. Three months' time in NYC. How about it? Use your voucher for the flight if you fancy, too? Figured we'd preempt your excuses."

I feel my heart shudder and quake, but do my best to keep control. It's at the thought of meeting the gang again under happy circumstances. The thought of trying to break through this ice face with Dan would finish me.

"By the way, expect to get a visit from Warbie soon. He's not letting you escape his fag hag clutches that easily. He's coming to London in a month or two."

Why are Interpol flocking to London all of a sudden?

"I can teach him how to cook better."

Hav laughs. "Maybe he should teach you better self-defense moves. Don't cry, Katie. We love you. Only question now is, do you love yourself enough to take action?"

I blot the tears that are flowing. I don't say a word. I can't. The ability to talk is hampered by the emotion that holds my throat captive. I simply hug Havana, then Rocco and let the tears fall.

"Your dad was a bastard. But those days are over, and it can have a happy ending without anybody having a guilty conscience. Maybe you and Dan both need a lesson in that. As in a big lesson—with guns to your head. Maybe a lot of knocking sense into you both with force too. You feel me?"

Chapter Twenty-One

Kate

The whole place has done nothing but talk about my life-threatening experience and mega story since my return — none have mentioned Dan's role and hero status. His presence at *Your News Today* has been more of a whimper than a fanfare.

Okay, his time with the company has been brief as well as fake. Now I'm back, Mel has had a meteoric rise to Channel Exec Director. Tonight there is a brief tribute party from the *Your News Today* guys, scheduled at a local inn. Free drinks, a buffet and goodbyes meets new pastures congrats.

At least Archie's bedroom extension financials will no longer be a concern and future female reporters won't be sent on faked jobs against their will.

"Coming for a quickie?" says Mel, grabbing her bag. "C'mon — you could do with a breather."

"I just want to finish making these arrangements for these jobs," I lie. It's seven o'clock at night. Chances are, most of the people I need to contact on my list won't be around at seven on a Friday.

But, I just feel weird knowing that any minute the man I had a big fling with will be arriving at the favorite journos pub two streets away. Mel told me she's invited him and he agreed to come. Dan's on my turf — due to walk into the pub where I've popped in once a week, every week for a baked potato and salad, or sometimes extreme loaded nachos.

"Well — make sure you don't disappear. I'll call you on your mobile if you don't show," says Mel. "If you've not turned up in half an hour. Boxing gloves."

Seeing Dan is a no-no because I just can't face it. My heart would be too squeezed — my conscience would smart too, but he really does have an effect on me and we've said enough already.

I'm an experienced TV news journalist. I rarely make big gaffes. I've done assorted jobs, many places in most conditions. I know the unwritten codes, the pitfalls, the things to avoid. Yet, in the last few days, I've made more balls-ups than ever. I am losing touch. Since Santorini I've lost my edge. Perhaps the time has come to call it a day?

I rise to leave and go home, when the office lights go out. Pitch black surrounds me, and if it weren't for the streetlights through the windows, I'd be seriously stuck to walk out.

I'm feeling freaked at suddenly being in darkness. It transports me to Santorini — the surveillance room. The only lights were from monitors...

"Anybody there?" The Friday crowd have fled. I scan the office, craning to see round the pillar by my desk. A lamp light flicks on, from the desk nearby. I know exactly who's in here with me.

Black ops. His favorite brand.

"I'm here. Taking direct action."

Dan's not in action gear. He's in a black cashmere coat. Black shiny shoes. Black expression too.

"You scared me," I say on a long breath. "You always do."

"You willfully ignored me. Though I might have guessed you'd be the only one here while everyone else is in the pub having a life. Hope you weren't expecting to stand me up at the Mel gathering. Not when I only arranged it to see you again. I happened to give a glowing reference to all of the team on their conduct with this operation. Might've encouraged strings to be pulled."

Of course. It's Dan. Of course he'd do that. Even for Mel. Why didn't I guess? He walks over and tugs me out of the seat.

His lips are on mine. Ravishing them, tasting them. Biting them, punishing me for being out of his life for this long, and I find that everything inside me melts and pleads for forgiveness.

"Apologize."

"Sorry," I breathe.

"Sorry who?"

"Sorry, Sir."

"Good girl. Some things never change."

This man, this is what counts. This is what matters.

And I've been a fool not to see, and admit to wanting everything I know he has and will give to me willingly, if I only have the guts to ask and make myself vulnerable. Can I do that?

"All this time I've been lying to myself, like I did with Dad. He doesn't matter. Said it so long I believed it," I say. My head falls against his chin. "But you count and no matter how much I tell myself that I can't make it stick."

There I've said it.

And suddenly I feel weak with relief.

"I love you like nothing else on earth, and there's no way we're screwing up this chance, honey," he whispers.

* * * *

Dan

I'm carrying her abandoned beauty bag. Such was her haste she left it, Cinders-leaving-the-ball-style. I lay it down like the Crown Jewels come home.

"A great agent always finishes the job."

She smiles at me. Coquettish to the core. "Thought taking out bad guys and sending them to jail for a long time was your remit. Not cosmetics logistics."

"I multitask very well. Try me."

She grins. "I've been privy to your bedroom skills. I can attest it's true."

I smile at her dirty thoughts track. "Ditto, babe. In fact

I'm here because it's been rather too long without those particular talents in my life."

"But I thought you had a harem of 'hard therapy' girls that keep you right."

"Not quite the same after you've had a Joseph epiphany. Once tasted never forgotten. Pretty hard to recover from. I'm a goner."

"I find that hard to believe," she says softly. So I tug her to me, with fingers on her hip bones. I stare deep into eyes that have had me bewitched since she glared at me at Manic Mambo and dared me to contradict her bravado.

Full of fight.

My favorite kind.

"My dad is putting whatever luxury hotel we wish for at our exclusive disposal. That's a lot of five-star bedrooms to try."

This girl deserves it. She's way more special than she knows. I intend to make it my mission to prove that to her so she'll never forget. Ever.

"You're something."

"I know I am. I have a bad addiction to your provocative ways. I always deliver on promises, and now my mission is complete." I say then turn as if to go. It's just for effect. I don't intend to leave her, ever. But I'm unsure about what's going on. "Coming to the party? Hav and Rocco are doing martial arts demos to rap music. Quite a sight."

Kate watches me walk toward the door. "Maybe I'm not in the party mood...you come in here and flirt and kiss me and walk away?"

"The only person who can do something about that is you. You reckon you have me all worked out. So what does Kate need?"

She lets out a long breath with her head tipped back, then pauses. "The trouble with me is rejection preys on old wounds. Being rejected by men is just a pattern I can't shake. I'm scared we'll be just the same. When you tire of me."

"You're really getting this one mixed up, and anyway, lots of us have rejection issues. You didn't do anything wrong, Katie. Ever. In fact you put the Dad thing right in a way nobody else could."

"I wasn't enough. I'm never enough."

"You're perfect and perfectly imperfect. I adore you and if it means saying goodbye to the job and taking time out for us—I'm there. Mission started."

She's crying. So I tug her close and let her get it out. I make Katie sit on my knee as I rub her back to comfort her.

"Donaldson was a very clever man. He's evaded multiple attempts to trap him. You can't go around blaming yourself for things that didn't happen the way you think. I also need to tell you something about misplaced guilt…it's a topic I'm somewhat experienced in myself."

She stares at me with those big pool deep eyes that get me in the gut.

"I spoke to Nat's sister. Nat was my partner—killed in action. I've spent way too long wishing I'd taken the bullet, not him. I blamed myself, I blamed everybody. It even got me to believing I wasn't worth shit. You showed me otherwise—I let a part of me die with him. But I'm alive—and I want to enjoy all that life brings. It's brought me you."

Kate's eyes lift to mine and hold for a brief, searing second before she looks away, my own wounded and shattered heart is racing butterfly circuits around my chest.

"We have us and that's pretty huge. If we learned nothing more in Santorini, it's that. You have to take your chance and just stop with the buts." The proximity of this warm, vital, eager woman who loves me, and who after all these weeks still admits she feels something is a massive realization. "What else is there to think or panic about, Katie?"

The lights flicker back on eerily. Somewhere a cleaning lady whistles Bruce Springsteen's *Dancing in the Dark* and we laugh. "Somebody's tampering with my plans," I say, then I reach out to trace her face, from temple to jaw line. "If it takes a boring desk job to prove I'm serious, so be it.

The memories of you kept haunting me and I couldn't stay away." I fix her gaze steady. "Most importantly, have you missed me?"

Kate blows out a long, ragged breath. "I guess."

So I push it further yet. "I'm glad you missed me — I plan on being around all the time."

She kisses me, and this time it a proper kiss. The kind I've missed. The type that makes my cock spring to attention and feel like warm liquid is being poured into me from the toes up.

"Future? Yes or a no?"

"Give a girl a New York minute."

A face Kate recognizes appears around the door of her office.

"Warbie! Wherever have you been hiding?"

She leaves me to hug him like a long lost brother. Which kinda makes me pissed — I'm the hero, right?

"Been at the party. C'mon, guys, you need to get there before all my appetizers are gone. I've so gone to town — satays, wontons and my own invention, the bruschetta bonanza." He catches my eye. "Wanted to know what she said's why I'm here?"

"She hasn't said yes yet," I say.

Kate smiles at us both. "It's a yes. Of course it's a yes, you guys."

I grin at her then at Warbie. "Why would she resist this much awesome?"

Warbie adds, "Awesome. Erotically matched and set to drive one another crazy from dawn 'til dusk."

She loops her hand around me and kisses my pride better. "Maybe I like his kinda crazy dawn 'til dusk."

"Counting down already, honey," I growl cupping her rear with a very happy, claiming hand. "You've so got it coming, d'you feel me?"

She grins. Then nods. "Every which way, then some."

Scoring With Sir

Excerpt

Chapter One

"Dis me and you're roadkill."

"You and whose skankwad army, loserboy?"

It's a gray Monday morning and I can't miss the yelled swearing across the school car park. My iPhone's Bruno Mars megamix can't sweeten the F-bomb napalm by the third years at the tennis courts. I long to flee but I still have hours of teaching torture ahead.

Today will herald a watershed in my life. Because I—Izzy Tennant, English teacher at Netherfield Secondary School in Barnet, North London—have a secret. Over the years, I've hidden the real me behind the mask of an oh-so-nice and proper English teacher. But at heart I have dark, private appetites. I may teach the classics of literature to kids that don't give a stuff by day, but at night I'm an insatiable erotica-holic.

Little do I realize that my fantasies are about to ignite with a man who can liberate these passions.

This is the story of my journey.

With *he who must be called Sir*.

* * * *

If David Attenborough studied chavvy North London school kids, instead of mating penguins ice-bonking for hours, he'd explain the brawling teenager ritual. I've consumed insufficient coffee to try. I beeline for the school's back door but the yelling mob turns and charges straight toward me.

"Is it true, Miss Tennant?" asks Darren Blackwater. He has the name and look of a repugnantly splendid extra in *Game of Thrones*. One you hope will get impaled before the ad break. From what his mother said at open day he's no stranger to sticky ends — he gets a little too much solo bedroom exercise and I don't mean kickboxing his punch-bag.

"Tell us," Eddie Childs butts in. "They're sayin' 'es comin' 'ere? We're askin' you cos, for a woman and a teacher, you know most about football."

I yank out my iPhone earbuds, succeeding in thwacking myself in the teeth. I remember not to swear but shouldn't bother — none of the pupils pay me such regard.

"I've nothing to impart. And no time at present, boys."

But Darren, Small Lord of the Blackwater and perpetrator of much school evil, is not mollified. "Ethan's brother said we're gettin' a new PE teacher and 'e's famous. Tell us if it's true, miss."

My tooth's throbbing. I'm more interested in calculating if I've brought painkillers or my dentist's number.

"I don't know anything about a new teacher."

"Ethan's bruvver said, miss," says Darren, "'E 'erd it from Matt Riley. 'Is mum's a cleaner an' she reads stuff on the desks. An ex-premier league player as head of phys ed, she says."

"If Matt's mum's so good at surveillance, who is he?"

Always answer a challenge with a question. This is my 'teacher's gold' tactic. "Tell Matt Riley he should employ his mother's reading habits himself if he wants to pass English."

I walk away, feeling like Khaleesi in *Game of Thrones* and pretending I look like her. Then I hear words uttered from behind a hand.

"Told ya she don't effin' know. Told ya not ta bovver!"

It's Mickey Peters. The boy who dented my car bonnet with a cricket ball. I pounce like a cougar.

"Peters!" I yell and his rigor mortis response gives me a delicious trickle of thrill. "Another word and it'll be detention and Mr. Rogerson's office. If I hear another curse, I'll be mentioning Matt Riley's mother. Then you'll have Knuckles Riley at your door and he's only weeks out of detention center."

They pout at me but I'm already high-fiving myself from atop my high horse.

"If I knew about the school's latest staff member, do you think I'd tell a car smasher? Disperse now."

I'm only through the door when Jack Carson, school janitor, corners me breathlessly. Creosote Carson, as he's affectionately nicknamed, is out of puff.

"Are you still seeing the doctor about your emphysema, Jack? If not, you need to go and get checked out."

Jack stops me with a hand. "Izzy, love, we're getting a new teacher."

I'm more worried about his dicky ticker and the wheeze like my nana's busted accordion than school staffing. "I know. Apparently he's a premier league footballer. As if." I roll eyes.

Jack stares with squished?up eyebrows. "How in feck's name did you know that, girl?"

Jack has fingered more gossip pies than Betty Crocker — he's a loveable Columbo with a wood preserver and chutney-stained coat. I hate to see him thus disappointed.

"Heard it from the future prison inmate reserves in the car park."

"Then you'll already know the worst."

"I know the bare minimum, Jack. It's best with Viagra Rogerson in charge."

Jack's jowls wobble at me. "The new sports head—he only used to play for feckin' Spurs, Izzy. Sacrilege! And us Gunners lifers—a viper in our midst."

I take this as my cue—Mother of Dragons, Daenerys Targaryen, could play this no better. I throw down my bags and breathe deeply, closing my eyes. Then I stare at Jack with the iced fire of Boadicea.

"Oh fuck. Bollocks. Crap. Piss. No!"

In the religion that is Arsenal Football Club, at the cathedral that is the Emirates, I am bishop in training to Carson's cardinal of fan worship.

Being a loyal season ticket holder for two decades solid does not come without fortitude and sacrifice. Nor does it allow for a high?caliber Tottenham Hotspur ex-striker to come waltzing into our school staffroom without comment.

We're reeling—and I don't mean doing *Riverdance*—as we head past phys ed toward the English corridor.

"Who is it?"

"You don't wanna know, girl."

"I do. You can't not tell me." Much as I'm dreading the answer, there's no avoiding it.

"Brilliant finisher—two hundred and five goals in two hundred and fifty games. He joined Spurs juniors in 1994…"

"Naff off, Carson! Don't play *Question of Sport* with me at eight?forty?two on a Monday morning or I'm liable to kick you hard. My shoes are killing me, I set fire to the toaster this morning and my key broke in the back door again. Spit it out in the name of Arsene Wenger."

He pouts but his stare goes soul deep, so intense I see the name before he speaks.

"Darby. Will bloody Darby!" we say in unison.

I take a step backward to hold on to the wall for support and my ankles feel wobbly.

More books from
Totally Bound Publishing

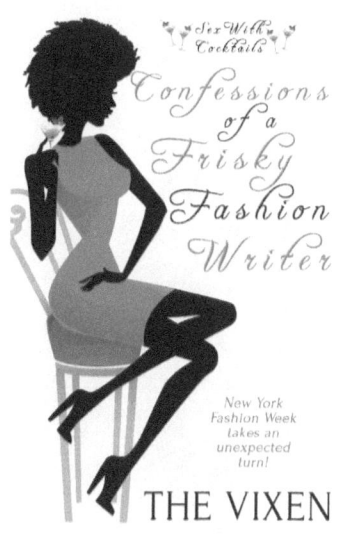

A girls' night out during New York Fashion Week takes an unexpected turn when a dashing gentleman enters the scene.

JILL STEEPLES

She knows everything
there is to know
about love...
Doesn't she?

Molly Matthews
MEDDLES IN
Marriage

Matchmaker extraordinaire Molly Matthews is an expert
in love, but her skills are put to the ultimate test when
Rory Campbell waltzes into her office.

667 WAYS TO F*CK UP MY *Life*

Lucy Woodhull

Sometimes, there's nowhere to go but f*ck up

*Sometimes, there's nowhere to go but f*ck up…*

Chasing dreams is never easy but when you have great friends and gorgeous Hollywood actors to hang out with, the journey is a whole lot smoother.

About the Author

Judy Jarvie

After winning a lovely boxed pen for writing a poem about the beach in a school competition aged eight, Judy Jarvie decided the writing game promised untold exciting treasures. It took her a while to turn that poem into any full length work that anybody would want to read so in the meantime she worked in Press and PR in London until she moved back to Scotland and realised she'd been spurning her one burning love of writing love stories. So she gave in to the call to do it and has kept going ever since. Now the writing keeps her sane and happy and dreaming up new heroes on a regular basis. She lives in a village in Scotland with her husband, two very special daughters and a crazy black cat who all keep her out of trouble and cause a fair bit in return.

Judy Jarvie loves to hear from readers. You can find contact information, website details and an author profile page at https://www.totallybound.com/

TOTALLY
BOUND

Home of Erotic Romance

www.ingramcontent.com/pod-product-compliance
Lightning Source LLC
Chambersburg PA
CBHW021517240626
47154CB00002B/671